THE SUMMERS

THE SUMMERS

IVA-MARIE PALMER

SKYSCAPE

SKYSCAPE

Published by Skyscape, New York

www.apub.com

Amazon, the Amazon logo, and Skyscape are trademarks of Amazon.com, Inc., or its affiliates.

ISBN-13: 9781477827307
ISBN-10: 1477827307

Cover photograph by Colin Anderson/Blend Images/Getty Images
Cover design by Liz Dresner
Book design by Liz Dresner

Library of Congress Cataloging-in-Publication Data available upon request.

Printed in the United States of America

For my mom, who would have read this on the beach

PROLOGUE

THE END OF summer was supposed to be a letdown, but I never believed that was true. If you'd spent it right, it just meant you could look forward to the next one.

My family always spent it right.

Mom was locking the door to our beach house. It was two stories, with blue paint and a white porch, just two blocks from the beach in Harborville, Massachusetts, a little town at the "elbow" of Cape Cod. Even though I spent most of the year in New Jersey, when I thought of home, this house was what I saw.

She gave the door three quick taps, with the same soft touch she used to scratch behind the ears of our ancient calico, Merlin.

Becca rolled her eyes. "Mom, you're such a dork."

"I know." Mom's grin was a living thing. She could never quite get it right in her self-portraits.

"She's *my* dork," Dad said, pulling Mom to stand with us. He kissed her forehead.

"Now what do we say?" Mom asked.

1

"Thank you, house. 'Til next time," my parents, three sisters, and I chimed in unison.

The car was loaded up. Driving out of Harborville, we'd go to our secret spot on Cockle Cove Road just off the highway to pick blueberries from bushes that told you it was September by the way they were weighted down with berry clusters. Mom would pack them in our lunches on the first day of school, so we'd feel like we had one more day of summer. And halfway home, we'd stop on Interstate 95 to go to our favorite diner, where we'd order all kinds of breakfast foods for dinner. It was a family tradition.

Before we left, though, Mom always had one last thing to do.

She put a painting on the white wood steps. This one was of Dale's Dream Cone, the ice cream shop on the boardwalk. The CLOSED sign was up and a girl sat on the counter, clearly at the end of her shift, licking a strawberry cone and looking at peace with the world. The girl was my sister Eliza, and her stint at Dale's had been her first real summer job.

FREE PAINTING TO GOOD HOME, read the handwritten sign Mom placed in front of her work. Sometimes she sold pieces—the whole town hall of Harborville was filled with Mom's work, and she even had shows in New York galleries from time to time—but Mom believed that art should be free, too. I liked that idea. Someday, when I was a published author, I wanted to leave copies of my books on park benches for people to discover.

"Okay, let's get a move on." Dad knew if we waited too long, our hunger pangs would begin well before we reached the diner. He claimed a man's worst fate was driving a car full of hungry women.

So we piled into the car. Mom and Dad in front. Teagan, my

littlest sister, who was twelve, sat in the way back of the minivan. Eliza usually sat next to her, preparing her day planner for the new school year. (She was proud to be the only Coolidge High student with a day planner.) Becca and I took the row behind my parents.

"Wait one second," Eliza said, even though we were all in the car, ready to go. She slid open the minivan door and stepped on my foot as she hopped out.

I watched her jog to the driveway next door. Ryan Landry had just come outside.

Even though Ryan was out here for Eliza, my gut seized up. He must have thrown on his blue hoodie to come outside, but he had no shirt on underneath. He was eighteen to my fifteen, so I knew my daydreams were crazy. But I was jealous anyway. I watched her throw her arms around him, my cheek resting on the cool glass of the car window.

Every year, Ryan and Eliza were together all summer long. Every year, I was just one of Eliza's kid sisters.

And every year, Eliza was perfectly content to basically shrug him good-bye. She went back to school and always found a new boyfriend just in time for the first dance of the year. She had businesslike precision with boys and she'd always been big on advising all of us not to get our hearts set on just one guy.

But I'd always had my heart set on Ryan. Someday, he'd notice me back.

Maybe even next summer.

Three summers later

CHAPTER ONE

"COUNT OF THREE?" My sisters and I stood on the porch of our summer home. The door was unlocked but we hadn't yet gone inside. Going inside was never a problem before. But then, our problems weren't problems before.

"Count of three," Eliza said, popping her gum so her words came out a spearmint cloud.

"One, two . . ." Becca said in her husky voice. My dad joked that she'd sounded like a sixty-year-old smoking barmaid when she'd said her first words. Or, he used to joke, anyway.

"Three," we said in unison.

None of us moved.

I guessed it was because no one goes running into a haunted house.

"How about deep breath, then in?" Tea, at fifteen, loved deep breaths and yoga and adopting mantras, especially since Mom died.

"We are doing this," Eliza said definitively. She looked more like Mom than any of us—they shared the same ashy blond hair and that olive skin that never sunburns—but where Mom quietly coaxed you into doing something so in the end, you thought it was actually your idea, Eliza liked you to *know* she was making you do something. "Besides, I haven't been a bridezilla yet, so you *have* to. For me."

"You're some kind of 'zilla," Becca said. "Maybe a bitchzilla?"

"Oh yeah, bitchzilla," Tea squealed. Her mantras only went so far.

"How about this?" I proposed. "We close our eyes, count to three, step inside, deep breath, open eyes."

"Works for me," Becca said.

"Fine, good plan," Eliza added, with a grateful look to me.

My sister was only twenty-one and had just gotten engaged to her boyfriend, Devin, in March. They'd been together for almost all of college, so I was used to having him around, but the sudden big Cape wedding took me by surprise. Eliza had practically scripted the proposal, right down to giving him my mom's engagement ring for him to propose to her with. The day after they broke their news, Eliza had announced they'd be getting married on Morning Beach at the end of the summer, which was why we'd all come back to Harborville.

We hadn't been here since Mom died, but we couldn't avoid the beach house forever. The last few summers had felt bleak and gray. I'd driven with friends for the day to the Jersey Shore a few times but it was rhinestones to the Cape's diamonds.

Now Tea grabbed my hand. Becca took my other one. Eliza stood behind us, her arms stretched across our shoulders. We closed our eyes and counted to three together.

Eyes still closed, we stepped inside, moving as a gawky unit, like we were trapped together in some kind of sixteen-limbed Halloween costume.

"Deep breath."

The air was déjà vu. Every year, our first day in the house, the air was always this way. Last time we were here, three years ago, it tasted the same way. Like salt water, winter dust, and something else that I only tasted here.

The air was summer.

I hadn't breathed summer in three years.

"Open your eyes," I said.

My mother had made a nice home for us in New Jersey but this beach house was where she'd made her mark. Her charcoal drawings of beach scenes were still hanging in their frames. My eye went right to the one of a golden retriever running crazily over a sand castle. Over the bookcase in the living room was a mosaic of a turtle that she'd made from pieces of sea glass we'd collected for her.

I watched my sisters' faces, to see how they saw things. Eliza, imperturbable as ever, looked around coolly. "Looks good. Like we left it." Even after Mom's funeral, when the days were gray, even when they were sunny and I felt the ache for my mom like the fly, like a sickness that washed over me in waves, Eliza never cried in front of us. But I knew she did. She had to.

Becca went right to the sea-glass turtle. "One of the pieces is missing," she said, zeroing in on an almost imperceptible square from the turtle's front foot. Becca could ignore her room when the mess got beyond reason, but could spot a small imperfection like the missing glass from a mile away.

Tea started to cry then, her breaths coming in ragged gasps, her feet planted to the driftwood floor. She was the littlest of us, in age and size, but her tears were always the biggest. And they had the instant effect of making you go to her to calm her down.

So we did. We hugged her.

"It will get easier," Eliza said. "We needed to do this."

"She would have wanted this," I added. I knew it was true, even if I hadn't believed it until now.

"Maybe, if we go to our rooms?" Becca suggested.

Before, we'd have run to our rooms, our feet pounding on the stairs, the wooden banisters trembling. Four girls who'd just found summer. We'd root in the drawers, check the closets, unearthing any stray oddities left behind by winter renters. Always, inevitably, some waterlogged paperback, maybe a scarf, candies secreted in the back of drawers. Eliza once found a super-old copy of *Playboy* crammed beneath her mattress and spent the rest of the day disinfecting her room.

We broke apart, and headed in our different directions. Eliza went to the ground-floor room next to my parents' master bedroom. Dad wasn't here yet; without Mom by his side, he'd only reluctantly agreed to come at all. He wouldn't drive out until a few days from now.

The rest of us had rooms on the second floor. Instead of running, we took the steps somberly. The stairs stilled creaked in all the same spots. The door to my room still had the little ding in the brass knob where Becca had accidentally smashed it with her softball bat. Inside, the bedspread was new but still a pale periwinkle, like before. Over the dresser was still my mom's drawing of ten-year-old me, my teeth seeming too big for my face, my eyes happy and almost dancing.

It was nice to be in my room, alone. The drive here had been an exercise in distractions. Becca complained that Tea, who'd earned control of the stereo, was playing a Deepak Chopra audio book, while Eliza, in the driver's seat, talked about wedding cakes. I filled the empty spots by blathering on about UC Berkeley, where I'd be going in the fall.

I pulled aside the curtain and looked down on the narrow street in front of our house. It was still early in the season. Though we were in the part of Harborville where more year-round residents lived, in a month the streets would be crammed with parked cars and people dragging coolers the few blocks to the beach, teenagers riding bikes barefoot and screaming kids.

A dark blue pickup truck pulled up and stopped in front of the house next door. Without even seeing the driver's side, I knew who it was. I'd watched Ryan Landry pull his car in front of the house next door a million times before. There was a way to it. Even when the street was at its most packed, Ryan could glide right in. It was the thing about Ryan: He just knew how to get where he was going, and how to be where he was.

As I stood by the window, a memory washed over me. Three years ago, sitting in this very room.

"Do you like the blue, or the green?" Eliza had asked, holding two sundresses, one in each hand. She was getting ready to go to a party in Ryan Landry's carriage house above the Landrys' garage. I'd never seen the inside.

She came toward me with the dresses, holding them up to her chest. She smelled like the ocean and coconut suntan lotion. I lifted my arm to my nose, sniffing and only smelling sand and sunburn.

11

"Are you smelling yourself again?" she asked. "Don't be weird."

I brought my arm down. "I like the blue," I said. She knew I'd say blue. Blue was my favorite color, but it looked better on Eliza. Everything looked better on Eliza.

I peered out my window, watching the street for Ryan's car. "Do you think I can go to the party?" I was going to be bored out of my mind at a barbeque with my parents, their friends, and my little sisters. We'd have to sit there, playing Uno, while the adults shrieked with laughter about stuff they'd done before they'd had kids.

Eliza patted me on the head. I hated when she did that. "You need to keep Becca and Tea company. And besides, you'd be the youngest one there. Maybe you can have Jessica over. Ask Mom." Jessica Ambrose was my age and we'd hung out on the boardwalk a few times while Ryan and Eliza were doing whatever they did when they were alone. But Jessica would just want to talk about what they were doing at Ryan's party. I couldn't think of a better way to feel less invited.

Ryan pulled his truck into the open spot in front of the Landrys'. He hopped out of the cab and opened the tailgate, pulling out cases of beer.

He looked up and saw me and, with a big smile, waved at me. Eliza shoved me out of the way, heaving the window open. "Did you get the strawberry wine coolers this time?"

"Morrison's bringing them," Ryan called up.

"He'd better not forget this time," Eliza said, and slammed my window shut.

She tossed the green dress onto the bed and slid the blue on over her bikini. The Landrys had a hot tub out back.

"Okay, the blue," she said. "And make sure you're not hogging the bed when I get back tonight. I'll be tired."

As I reached the end of the memory, I snapped to attention, shaking my head as if to physically shake it off. I realized I'd been standing here for a few minutes, and I felt like a weirdo, standing at the window, watching Ryan.

I hadn't seen him in three years, not since the Landry boys had come to my mom's funeral, all three of them looking strange in their dark suits. Up until then, we had only seen them in summer clothes. The most dressed-up our two families had ever got was putting on nice jeans and sundresses to go to brunch at the Chatham Bars Inn, a few towns over.

We had all kept in touch, sort of, if you counted showing up in someone's Facebook feed as keeping in touch. Ryan wasn't on Facebook, but if I was lucky, I could find glimpses of him in the background of his brothers' photos. I still remembered his birthday—March 19—every single year. He was twenty-one now to my eighteen.

And if it was possible, he was even better-looking. He hopped out of the truck's cab and unlatched the tailgate, pulling a box of paint cans out of the back. The box must have weighed at least fifty pounds, but he didn't even flinch. His jeans were paint-splattered and his navy shirt was just tight enough, not like the practically Spandex things guys at my school wore to show off their abs.

I hated myself, because I couldn't look away. It was the same as when I was fourteen and saw Eliza and Ryan kissing on the beach. I'd just stood there awkwardly, looking at them. Not for the kiss, but for Ryan. He was magnetic. Or at least he was to me. Like now—why couldn't I stop staring?

Then he looked up.

He didn't look surprised exactly, but he stopped what he was doing. I was tempted to drop the curtain and run, like I really was some apparition that he imagined. But he had seen me.

I knew because he smiled. I watched his lips as they formed the words, *Hi, Katie.* I was Kate now, but he didn't know that.

I waved, bending all my fingers like a little kid in a parade, and nervously brushed some of my dark hair away from my face. And Ryan smiled again, bigger this time, nodded, and took his paint cans wherever he was going with them.

It took a few seconds for it to happen, but then came the special, delicious kind of agony that only Ryan Landry could bring. He was like signing for a delivery of your favorite cake for a birthday party you weren't invited to. He didn't cause a warm sensation, or tingles. That was kid stuff, for bad novels that didn't understand his powers.

He brought on a rattling. My body vibrated. Muscles shimmied against bone. My skin jumped. It was unstoppable. It was wrong, wasn't it, to come here and be flooded with emotions about my mom only to have them replaced almost instantly by *this*?

Ryan Landry. I had always wanted him. I wanted him when Eliza had him and I couldn't have him. For three years, I'd thought of him, but only a little, like I could outgrow him. But now, here I was, and after two seconds of eye contact, I was a mess.

I was already in my running shoes. I clattered down the stairs and out the front door, running past Ryan's truck, head down in case he could see me from the house. Exertion was the only thing that would still me.

I'd probably see Ryan every day.

It was going to be a long summer.

CHAPTER TWO

FIVE MILES LATER. I felt like a normal person again. A dripping-with-sweat person, but a normal one. After a shower, I would even be capable of carrying on a conversation with my new employer.

This summer, I'd be working for one of my favorite writers, Grace Campbell. The whole thing had happened totally at random. I tweeted to her one night that I loved her latest book and how it had made me look forward to my Harborville summer. She must have read my profile line, in which I described myself as a writer (even though I hadn't published anything of course, I just wrote stories for fun). She'd messaged me to ask where I stayed in Harborville. I told her, and mentioned that I'd be looking for a summer job. In my craziest dreams, I hoped that she'd offer something, but I was still shocked when she asked if I wanted to assist her with a few projects over the next few months. I'd really thought it was a joke or a prank, but we'd messaged back and forth, and it had all proven real.

I was supposed to meet her at Clark's Coffee, a local spot in the bottom story of a house about a mile from Morning Beach. Even though our car was in the driveway, I decided to take a bike. The little garage next to the house held a handful of beach cruisers. My turquoise one must have been kept in shape by renters over the years because the tires had plenty of air and it wasn't covered in cobwebs like some of the stuff in the garage. My mom and dad's bikes, a yellow and a red, leaned against one another in a far corner. The bright, cheery spot of yellow brought a pain to my chest.

Clark's Coffee wasn't somewhere I'd gone often when I was younger, but it was a favorite of my mom's. Some of her paintings and charcoals were even framed behind the diner's counter. She'd always claimed Clark's blueberry scone replenished the artistic brain. Then she'd chide herself for saying something so pretentious.

The corner booth where Grace Campbell told me to meet her was empty, just like she promised it would be. I let the waitress fill my mug with coffee, even though I was too nervous to drink it, and I ordered a fruit plate even though I had butterflies in my stomach. Then I pulled my Moleskine out of my purse, flipping through the notes and story ideas I'd recorded there, hoping to look like a real writer. There were a lot of ideas but nothing I was in love with. I'd heard the advice to write what I knew, but I didn't want to write about a girl whose mom had died and, beyond that, not much had happened to me yet. I went to a suburban high school, ran cross-country, and made the honor roll, hardly the stuff of great stories. So my ideas were always about things that didn't happen to anyone, at least that I knew of. I'd jotted notes for a short story about a cartographer who learned there was nothing left to map. I had another idea for a novel about a world where people were literally born without a reckless bone in their bodies. But everything I thought to do seemed so crazily different from the idea before it that I never could quite commit to any of them, often starting them but unable to finish. I thought maybe working for Grace would help me figure out what kind of writer I'd be. Or at least inspire me to be all the different ones I was.

A minute later, Clark himself came over to the table, setting down a fruit plate. "Are you Kate Sommers?"

"Yup, that's me." I was surprised he knew me, since I'd only come here a few times with my mom. But he had those eyes that softened at the corners when he looked at you, like he was a man who remembered every last customer forever and ever. There might have been a story in that.

"Grace left you this," he said, handing me a napkin, folded and with my name scrawled across it. "Was your mom Lanie Sommers?"

"Yeah?"

"Great lady. We've missed her here. Your food's on the house." He nodded at the napkin with a small apologetic smile.

I unfolded the napkin. On it, in nearly indecipherable scribble, were the words, "Headed to NYC. Job off. So sorry. Have lovely summer. XO, GR."

Clark shook his head. "She breezed in here this morning on her way out of town and told me you'd be coming. I know it probably seems harsh, but that she remembered to tell you at all is something for Grace. She's brilliant but she's, well, spacey."

I nodded at him, but felt the heavy weight of disappointment settle in my stomach. No job would mean . . . what? A summer spent at Eliza's beck and call? Endless hours to eye-loiter all over Ryan Landry?

"Thanks for the heads-up," I said as I got up from the booth. "Hope to see you around!"

I walked out onto the sidewalk and stared at the street signs, my eyes not really registering anything. The summer spread out before me, completely empty, and I felt aimless.

I dragged my bike from the rack and got on. I sped away from Clark's toward the beach, picking up speed as I let my irritation and anger sink in. I knew I probably looked like a maniac, but I didn't care. All I could think was, *who does that?* Sure, Grace Campbell wasn't a bank or some other corporation, but a little professionalism should have been warranted, right? It was times like this when I missed my mom the most. She always calmed me down whenever I got unsettled. I thought about what she might say now if she were here: *"Take a deep breath and try to reset; think about what you really want; remember all the great things you still have going for you,"* but it wasn't the same. I let the wind tangle my hair as I turned my bike onto a side street.

My mind scrolled through job possibilities. I knew I could always see if the Landrys needed a hostess but that would mean seeing Ryan every day. Or more. While the idea had appeal, I'd probably look like a dumb kid with a crush if that was the first job I ever took on the Cape. Eliza had never worked there, even when they'd dated. She'd been at Dale's Dream Cone, which might be okay as a last resort. There were cute shops up and down Main Street—even a bookstore, the Perch—but if I wasn't working for Grace, I didn't really want to be stuck inside and away from the ocean. I pedaled toward Morning Beach, the biggest in Harborville. If I wanted to work this summer, I needed to find something right away before everyone else arrived for the season. Luckily, I knew a place that probably hadn't been actively advertising for employees.

Joe's Surf and Bike Rental looked closed as I marched across the sand, but I knew better. At the back door, I knocked three times. When the door opened, plumes of sweet marijuana smoke rolled over me.

Smokey Joe coughed. He had to be at least fifty by now, but he had the worry-free expression of a sixteen-year-old who'd just passed his driver's test.

"Hey, were you expecting me?" he asked.

"Um, do you mean were you expecting *me*?" I replied.

"No, I meant the first thing. What's shakin', Katie Sommers?"

I was amazed that he remembered my name, but I took it as a good sign. "It's Kate now," I said, smiling so it didn't sound curt. "And I was wondering . . . are you hiring for the summer?"

He paused. He looked behind him at the rows of things for rent. Boogie boards and bikes haphazardly leaned against the wall of the shed.

"Yes. The summer is a hard job, but it's the only one you'll ever love." He nodded at this, like he'd said something very wise.

"So, does that mean I have the job?"

"Sure thing, milady. You get early shift, nine a.m. to four p.m. I'll pay you twelve dollars an hour, but I like to give bonuses. You know I don't need the money." Joe was all business as he said this. I hadn't realized he didn't need the money, but I nodded like this was an irrefutable fact.

"Smokey, you're the best. This is just what I was looking for." It was half a lie, but I was still grateful.

"The things we're looking for have a way of finding us," Smokey said cryptically.

I was certain that Smokey didn't know what he was saying, and yet I could have spent the evening trying to parse meaning from his comment. So what if the Grace Campbell job had fallen through? This would be an interesting place for a writer, I told myself, people watching all day. Plus, I wouldn't be inside a store, or serving food, and it was just a couple minutes from our house.

"Well, I'll come find you tomorrow," I told him. But Smokey was already back on his perpetual break. I wondered if he ever closed up the store.

I went to retrieve my bike from where I'd leaned it against the shack and, with a sinking in my stomach, saw it had a flat. A big nail was stuck through the back tire. I hadn't noticed it with all my furious peddling from Clark's Coffee. A breeze rolled past me, carrying the sugary smells of taffy and cotton candy being made on the boardwalk. Normally, I would have breathed them in, but right now the aromas mocked me. Today was not all that sweet so far.

I examined the tire, realizing that I'd have to get a new one. The rubber was torn where the nail had made its impact. When we were kids, Ryan had always known how to fix things. Once my bike chain had fallen off when we'd all been riding on the beach and Eliza had told me I'd have to walk back, but Ryan had fixed it in two quick motions. "Don't listen to your sister. This kind of stuff is easy, if you just look at it the right way," he'd said.

I remembered staring at the faint stubble on his chin; it was the end of August, and the hair on his face was darker than on his head. His hair always lightened in the sun over the course of the summer. He was fourteen, and it was the first time I'd noticed facial hair on someone who wasn't my dad. It was also probably the first time it occurred to me that Ryan Landry was good-looking. I was a late bloomer, and the only sixth-grade girl without a crush. But suddenly, I had one.

"Wait," I'd said, prying my eyes away from his face and pointing at the chain. "Show me how to do it, in case it happens again."

He'd grinned, making him even more beautiful. "Eliza would never think of that," he'd said. I'd stored that precious moment away for years now, pulling aside its wrappings every now and then to relive the memory.

"This summer is not about Ryan Landry," I told myself aloud. This would be my mantra; Tea would be proud. "He was a crush and just a crush. You are beyond crushes."

"Katie, Katie, Katie, bike troubles again?" The voice was deep with a hint of a smile in it. It was a voice I hadn't heard in years, except in my head.

You've got to be kidding me.

I looked up from my tire toward his voice. The sun was starting to sink in the sky and I had to squint. He was in shadow, the sun behind him, framing his silhouette. He was somehow larger than life and just the right size.

Why had I picked right now to start talking to myself about Ryan Landry?

"Just a flat," I told him. I laughed, trying for light, tinkling *now-be-on-your-way-Man-of-My-Dreams* giggle, but the sound that emerged was a long wheeze. "Oh, and it's Kate now."

Instead of leaving, Ryan crouched down to examine the tire,

half kneeling over me. He looked, for a long time, at my face. Heat rose to my cheeks. I wished I already had a tan to hide my blushing.

"Oh, is it? Interesting." He smirked but not in a cruel way. It was more like he wanted to tease me a little, the same way he used to when we were kids. I could tell that he'd heard me chanting mantras about him.

"So, should I walk you home? Or do you want to see if Smokey can fix that?"

Ryan Landry wanted to walk me home? "Smokey just gave me a job. I'm not going to press my luck today."

He stood up and extended a hand to help me back onto my feet. I took it. His palm was cool and callused and muscular. The hand of a man. It almost made me laugh to think of it that way. The last time we'd been here, I'd still thought of Ryan as a boy.

"Working for Smokey. That should be an adventure." He grinned, but only halfway. He had eyes the same color and clearness as green sea glass, darkening as they grew more serious. He was looking down at me intently again, in a way I wasn't used to. I liked it, a lot, even though I didn't know if I was supposed to.

He took my bike by the handlebars and hefted up the back end, so he could roll it home on the front wheel. We started walking along the boardwalk, winding our way back to our street. His shoulder, solid and lean beneath his shirt, was barely a millimeter from mine. It had taken me five miles of running to get rid of the rattling, and now it returned with force.

"Are you still at the restaurant?" I asked him, referring to his family's place on the pier.

"Yup," he said. "I've been taking over more of the management so my parents can slow down a bit."

"That's good," I said, trailing into small talk about his brothers, Pete and Garrett, and what my little sisters were up to.

Then we found ourselves in a sort of half-comfortable, half-awkward silence. Ryan peered at me again, his eyes settling onto my face. "So, I don't really know how to ask this but, are you okay being back?" His voice was low and softer and his words fell close to my ear.

I looked up into his face. My lips came up to the hollow under his Adam's apple, and if I tilted my head, I could kiss my way up to his chin. I blushed and turned my gaze to my feet, clad in my nicest sandals for the meeting with Grace. My second right toe was permanently bent from a soccer injury; I wished I could hide it from Ryan. His toes were straight and long in his flip-flops. Could someone have sexy toes? He did.

"I'm okay," I said, finally answering the question, not knowing if my answer were true. "I mean, maybe I'm not okay, but I know it's good we're back. Eliza's getting married, you know."

Why had I said it like that? Like, "Eliza's getting married, ready for me and my bent toe?" I hated the way I sounded.

"Yeah, I heard," Ryan said. I wanted some hint of what he thought about this, but the way he said it was the same as if I'd said, "The first day of summer is in ten days."

We'd reached our houses. Even though we were on Pleasant Street and near the smaller beach it connected to, it was a quick walk to and from Morning Beach.

He leaned toward me, knocking his shoulder into mine. It was not a big gesture, coming from someone who'd thrown me into the water, high-fived me, tickled me, and chased me during games of tag. But this time, we were all alone. If I leaned back toward him, we'd kiss. Or we *could* kiss. It felt like the start of every daydream I'd ever had about him but I was stuck under a total emotional paralysis. This wasn't *real*.

"It'll be a good summer," he said, putting the handlebars of my busted bike gently in my hands. The side of his hand brushed the side of mine and I had to bite my tongue so I wouldn't gasp. His hand was warm, and I knew if he took my hand, his grip would be strong but not overbearing. Without the bike between us, there'd be no space between our bodies. I looked up at him, realizing how close my lips were to his chin. A slight trace of dark stubble grew there, almost asking to be touched.

Finally, he backed up, toward his house, deflating and relieving me at the same time. My jaw hurt from clamping my teeth so tightly. He smiled at me, and for a second, I caught him looking at my legs.

"Keep running, *Kate*. You look good."

As he turned and walked to his house, I felt the bike start to slip from my hands, like his words had made me completely lose control.

In a way, they had.

CHAPTER THREE

I'D BEEN IN my room since my failed meeting with Grace Campbell and my walk back with Ryan. I heard my sisters downstairs in the kitchen, getting dinner ready. I hated the thought of going down there and having to tell them that my big summer job had fallen through. I wished I'd never even mentioned it.

I slouched deeper into the blue-and-green throw pillows on my bed, rereading the exchange with Grace to see if I'd missed something, or said anything to make her change her mind. But, no, aside from her job description being "doing assistant-y things," everything was very straightforward.

I closed the laptop and wrote a quick note to myself, a plan, really:

1. Get up with the sun
2. Ocean swim or run
3. Write until 8:30
4. Smokey's

I thought about the room above the garage, where my mother used to paint. Even though we'd rented the house out for the last three summers, that room had remained off-limits to tenants, a fact that irritated the leasing company—they liked to remind us about the added value of its separate plumbing and entry, "*should we choose to make the space available.*"

I looked around my small room, and thought of Eliza's much bigger one on the ground floor. I needed more space now, too, didn't I?

I thought of how my mom sometimes said, "Art can be self-ish." Creating something new forces you to claim time and distance from other parts of your life, but I wasn't sure if being selfish also entitled me to the studio. Especially when I didn't know what I was working on.

I finally forced myself to head downstairs to the kitchen. The smell of garlic hit my nostrils and my stomach growled.

My sisters were gathered around the counter, with Becca at the stove. The Blueberry Man, a foot-high round man whose hat opened up to hold all our spoons and cooking instruments, gave a jolly smile from his usual spot. He'd been a tacky gag gift from my dad to my mom. She'd kept him and named him Alonzo.

"Check this out." Becca was moving a skillet over the flame, shrimp skittering across butter. With a flick of her wrist, she got the shrimp to hop out of the pan, the pieces leapfrogging over one another.

"Mr. Landry's shrimp jump!" Tea exclaimed, practically jumping up and down herself.

Becca put the shrimp on the sunny yellow plates Mom had found at a flea market her last summer here. We helped ourselves to homemade coleslaw, corn on the cob, and grilled chicken from the grocer's.

"How'd your first day at the Landrys' restaurant go?" I asked Becca. She'd already taken over most of the cooking at home, and I knew she was looking forward to learning some new skills in the kitchen.

"Mr. Landry said he'll teach me all his tricks. And Mrs. Landry said no one else is getting the lobster roll recipe." Becca smiled proudly. "Ryan didn't mention it?"

Eliza cocked her head at me. "Ryan? When did you see him?"

I can't seem to NOT see him, I wanted to say, but I swallowed my food instead. "My bike got a flat, at Smokey's. Ryan was on his way home and we walked together." I tried to sound as blasé as possible.

Eliza arched an eyebrow. "Okay, as long as we're not breaking the sisters-before-misters clause," she said with a laugh.

I rolled my eyes. "Like I want your sloppy seconds, anyway." The very idea of Ryan as second-grade *anything* made me feel terrible, even as my temper flared toward Eliza. She was getting married. Why would it matter if something did happen between me and Ryan?

"What were you doing at Smokey's?" Becca teased. "Smoking with Smokey?" She made a gesture like she was inhaling, half closing her eyes in a blissed-out state.

"Actually, I'll be working there this summer." I tried to sound upbeat. "Grace Campbell got called to New York suddenly, so that job won't work out."

Eliza made a sad cooing sound and rubbed my shoulder. "Well, it'll be better for you to have a low-key summer before Berkeley."

Why? I wanted to ask. Eliza, who'd finished college ahead of schedule—even after mom's death—who got engaged and decided to plan her wedding over the course of a few short months, who already had an offer from a great PR firm to start in the fall—definitely did *not* think it was good enough to do something low-key the summer before college, or ever. Coming from her, it felt more like an insult.

I turned back to my food, and the conversation wound down. Dinner was much quieter than the laughing, boisterous nights we used to have with Mom. In a way I was glad Dad wasn't here to see it. I didn't want him to feel he'd made the wrong decision, giving in to Eliza and bringing us all back here. I didn't want this summer to be a mistake.

"Let's finish eating and go to the attic," Tea said finally, and I was grateful for the suggestion. "There's a bunch of Mom's stuff up there. I think you guys should see it."

The attic was Mom's museum. My dad had never been a big saver of things—he trusted Mom to maintain the archives. And she did, in a scattered way that made sense only to her. Walking into the attic was like stepping inside a living treasure chest.

"Oh my God, look at this," Becca said, pulling piles of photos of our parents from an old shoebox. They were all from the early '90s. Mom had poufy hair and Dad's shirts glowed. In one, Mom was pregnant with what must have been Eliza, and even though she was peering out from a thick layer of hair-sprayed bangs, she still looked pretty and timeless in a loose, fairylike lace dress.

I opened another box, which contained birthday and Fourth of July party invitations from other Cape families who'd invited my sisters and me to their gatherings over the years. "Look at this, guys."

"The reason you girls are invited to everything is because we are part of this town. This is our home. We're not just *summer people*," Eliza said, in a near-perfect imitation of Mom.

We all laughed—Mom always wanted us to be part of the town, not just the tourists that filled it up each summer—and Eliza's dead-on impression made it feel like, just for a moment, she was back with us again.

And then there were her paintings, everywhere. When I thought about how much of her work she gave away, like what was hanging in Clark's Coffee and at the Landrys' restaurant, it hit me just how much my mom painted. I hadn't reached a place like that with my writing, where I felt constantly inspired. I wanted to be that way, but it hadn't happened yet. I wondered if the words would ever pour out of me like the colors spun out of her.

"Can you believe these?" Tea said as she blew dust off an oil painting of swirling octopuses. It was an ethereal underwater scene, and I remembered my mom working on it a few summers before her last one.

"And her clothes," Eliza said, from a far corner of the attic. "Come here, guys. This still smells like her."

Mom left her summer wardrobe at the beach house. Eliza had pulled out a rolling rack of sundresses and the oversized button-downs she wore while she painted.

Eliza was right—everything still smelled like her. There was a hint of her lilies-of-the-valley perfume, and the scent of her that was always beneath the perfume, like some delicious baked good from a recipe you'd never find in real life.

"God, there's so much stuff we'll have to pack up," Eliza said.

Tea pulled a crisp J. Crew shirt away from her face and asked, wide-eyed, "Why would we pack it up?"

Eliza shook her head, waving off the question. "I just mean, we should have some of this stuff at home, instead of letting it sit here forever."

I pulled one of my mom's old sundresses on over my clothes, and Becca helped me tie the halter at the back. I looked in the mirror and laughed. My mom was curvier, like Eliza. I was more athletically built. "I will never have Mom's boobs," I said to my reflection. I looked for hints of my mom's face in my own, but I had fairer skin, from my dad's side, and dark brown hair that really did nothing in the sun. Eliza's locks always grew blond in the sun. At five seven, I was taller than all my sisters, though Tea probably would come close in a couple years. What I did have were my eyes. They were a faint blue, like my father's, but flecked and rimmed with my mother's dark brown. I'd hated their odd-ness when I was younger, but now they felt special, and like the perfect hybrid of my parents.

"Well, you got the artistic talent," Eliza said, picking up a clothespin and pinning the dress so it would stay up on me.

"Becca got her laugh," I continued, and saw Becca beam from under one of my mom's old sunhats.

"And Tea got her spirit," Becca added, wrapping a starfish-print scarf around Tea's neck.

"But you got her boobs," I reminded Eliza with a laugh. "And Mom had nice boobs."

"And feet," Eliza said, pulling a pair of sandals off a shelf. I immediately recognized, with a pang, the mermaid shoes—as

I always called them. Their t-straps were embellished with tiny white shells and pieces of blue sea glass. In the sun, they sparkled like the water.

Seeing them immediately brought me back to the memory of the first time I'd seen them, years ago at the Harborville Arts Fair. It was always one of my favorite parts of the summer. The town would close off Main Street and vendors from all over the Cape would rent little tents and tables to showcase and sell their work. But what I liked most about it was that it was something my mom and I did together. My other sisters always said it was boring, but I loved to go. My mom would talk to other artists about what they were working on and sometimes they'd trade tips.

That year, though, Eliza wanted to go, too. A model in the back-to-school issue of *Seventeen* was wearing a pressed-heart pendant and when she'd shown it to us, Mom had told her they might have something like it at the fair.

"Bleh, more shell necklaces. I'm never going to find a pendant," Eliza complained. She grew more impatient each time Mom stopped to talk to someone she knew. "And I'm starving."

"We might not find one here," Mom said. "But give it a chance."

I offered her a bite of my Dutch soft pretzel. It was better than anything you could find on the boardwalk and I got one every time we came to the fair.

"No way," she said. "That's kids' food."

Something in a stall down the way caught Mom's eye and she dashed ahead, gesturing for us to follow.

When we caught up with her, she was holding a pressed-heart

pendant out to Eliza, who smiled enough to show all her braces—something she never did. "This is perfect," she said.

"We need something for Katie, too." My mom petted my hair quickly, something she did all the time without thinking.

Right away, my eyes landed on a pair of sandals that twinkled in the sun. They looked like the ocean, with tiny shells and sea glass woven onto the straps. I looked down at my beat-up gray Keds. I didn't normally like things that were so feminine, but there was something magical about the sandals. They made me think of mermaids.

"Those are beautiful, Katie," Mom said. She asked the woman if they had the sandals in my size.

"I'm sorry, those are the last pair."

My mom slipped them on her feet. "What if we share them?" she said, looking at me. "I'll wear them for a while and I bet a few summers from now, they'll be just the right size for you. I'll take good care of them, promise."

Eliza looked at them and rolled her eyes. "Those are the fashion equivalent of a shell necklace."

But Mom squeezed my hand as we waited to pay. "Nope. They're special, just like Katie." As the clerk put the shoes in a bag, my mom smiled at me. "Ours?"

"Ours."

Now, I couldn't take my eyes off the shoes. I'd forgotten about them until this moment.

Eliza slipped the sandals on. "These are perfect for the wedding. Something old *and* something blue," she sighed as she admired them on each of her pedicured, perfect feet. No bent toes there.

I felt the words, "They're mine," on the tip of my tongue, but I knew Eliza wouldn't even remember the day we bought them, or that they were supposed to be mine. She had already appropriated mom's engagement ring, and now she was taking my sandals. Why did she assume she got first dibs at everything?

Almost instinctually, my eyes drifted out the attic window, alighting first on the roof of my mom's studio and next on the roof of the carriage house in the Landrys' yard.

Just once, I wanted something that was all mine.

CHAPTER FOUR

SUNLIGHT FELL OVER me as I forced my eyes open. I pulled on my swimsuit and my hoodie and slipped on my Vans as I jogged down the stairs of Mom's studio.

Over the last few days, I'd staked my claim on the garage room without a word. Little by little, I'd been moving things from my old bedroom there, where I slept on a surprisingly comfortable futon Mom had kept beneath the window. I'd justified it all by forcing myself to get up earlier than my sisters; this way, I wouldn't wake them up as I got ready in the mornings. No one said anything, but none of them had come up here to see the room, either.

I made my way to Pleasant Street Beach, loving the quiet. The "summer people" were starting to move in, and the streets were packed with cars, but hardly anyone was up and moving yet. Here and there, neighbors sipped coffee on their porches and smiled as I passed.

In the cool dawn air, the smells of the Cape enveloped me. I caught bursts of hydrangea and damp grass and, as I got closer to the beach, the briny air. The ice-cream shops and stands devoted to games weren't open yet and the quiet was its own presence. Across the beach, the pier looked silent, the only motion coming from birds flying overhead and a few fishermen at the very end. Later in the day it would be filled with people watching taffy-making demonstrations, riding the old wooden carousel or visiting the Harborville Maritime Museum.

Without stopping to think, I dove into the water and began to swim. The cold, salt, and current woke me up in a way coffee never could. People on the Cape called the water "invigorating," but that was just a way of saying that it chilled you to the bone.

I swam just far enough to warm my muscles up, then turned back and swam to shore, body-gliding through the wave break. After this, I'd write for an hour before starting my shift at Smokey's. He didn't get in until noon most days, so I handled the morning rush by myself.

The swimming and my new job were going better than the writing. I'd thought maybe being surrounded by Mom's work and canvases and her little collections of sea glass and shells and vintage postcards would inspire me, but I still didn't know what I wanted to say. I was working on the story about the cartographer who'd mapped everything there was to map, and it was lonely to think about. What did you do when you had reached the very end?

The morning shift at Smokey's was a tidal wave of rentals from beachgoers who were visiting the Cape but staying in motels or at bed-and-breakfasts. People who didn't have summer houses stocked with gear always wanted to make the most of their beach

days and needed to rent bikes, boogie boards, and kayaks, sometimes all at once. Today was no exception.

"Can you put this on my back?" A hairy dad handed me a
tube of sunscreen, turning around and leaning into the counter.
I winced.

"I'm sorry, it's really busy right now." I handed him back his
SPF 30.

"If I get burned, it's on you," he said flatly as he turned to leave.

A woman in a wide-brimmed hat held up a pair of water
wings. "Will these help my son swim?"

"The lifeguards don't like kids wearing those in the ocean,
actually," I explained. "You could get pulled by the current." The
lifeguards were in a constant battle over floatation devices that
could do more harm than good.

"Someone could have told me that."

I just did, I thought, but smiled instead. Customer service
had its low points, to be sure. My phone buzzed with a text and I
looked down, eager for a distraction, but it was just from my ex,
Matt Garrity. We had dated for two years of high school, and he
was also headed to California, to Stanford, in the fall. We were
still friends and had broken up in a friendly way. We'd even talked
about him being my date for Eliza's wedding, if I decided to bring
anyone.

He was hinting at coming out to visit for a day or so. I knew
he wanted to get back together with me, and I'd even occasionally
thought about it—what it might be like to be with him out in
California, starting our new lives together. But now that I had a
little distance, I wasn't so sure. Part of me liked the idea of starting
college with a totally blank slate.

I wrote back to him, trying to avoid flirtation, and slipped my phone back into my pocket. I turned on the radio that Smokey kept behind the counter, and a Justin Timberlake song poured out.

"Oh, I love this song."

I turned to see Eliza, leaning against the rental counter in her turquoise two-piece. She was already tan. Every summer, she was always the one with the deepest tan, and she never burned. "How's work?"

"Busy," I said, even though the rush seemed to have died down just as Eliza showed up. "What's up?"

"Remember Jessica Ambrose?"

"Of course." Jessica was more my friend than Eliza's. She was my age, and we'd known each other since elementary school. Though Jessica had reached out when Mom died, after my family stopped coming to Harborville for the summer, she and I had lost touch. As time went on, we e-mailed less and less and now we really only wished each other a happy birthday on Facebook. I realized guiltily that I hadn't even let her know we were going to be back this summer.

"She's having her clambake tonight." The party was usually thrown by Jessica's older brother, Todd, but he was living in Oregon now I'd heard. Jessica must have taken over the tradition. It wasn't really summer until the Ambrose clambake.

"Oh, really?" I tried to smile but it didn't reach my eyes. It was my fault for not calling Jessica since I'd gotten to town, but the idea that she'd spoken to Eliza before me hurt.

"Yes, and we're going," Eliza said firmly. "Devin is coming in from the city and I want to introduce him to everyone."

"Are we even invited?"

"Ryan told me about it," Eliza said, and I felt worse. When had Ryan talked to her? Did they run into each other, like we had, or did he call or text? I suddenly felt foolish for thinking that one walk with him might have *meant* something. "We can't stay hidden away forever," Eliza continued. "Becca and Tea are going; it will be weird if you don't. Jessica's really *your* friend." She said this like she was gifting me a particularly rare gem.

I gave in with a shrug. She had a point, and it would be nice to see Jessica. "A party is a party, I suppose."

You could smell the party before you could see it.

My sisters and I had tried and failed to replicate a clambake in our backyard the last few summers, but nothing came close to actually having one on the beach. When it was time to cook, you layered in seaweed over the hot coals, then added corn on the cob and lobsters, clams in their shells and foil packets of potatoes and onions. The savory aroma of the seafood and veggies washed over me familiarly.

"Oh, I've missed this," Becca said as we approached the designated section of beach. Now party noise mingled with the tantalizing smells. "I wish Dad had come." It was a Friday, and he wasn't arriving until Sunday. He needed to finish the workweek and get some things squared away at our house in New Jersey before he headed up.

"I don't think there are going to be that many parents here, anyway," Eliza said. "Ryan told me his parents aren't coming this year, because it's mostly kids now." The fact that the party had changed since we'd been gone felt strange, but I was more caught up in wondering just how many things Eliza and Ryan had discussed, and how long they'd talked for. Our walk home suddenly seemed brief and obligatory by comparison.

As my sisters and I made our way across the beach toward the cluster of people who'd gathered around the clambake, heads turned to look. It felt like the moment in a movie when the music screeches to a halt and the whole party gets quiet.

Jessica came over first, followed by some other Harborville kids, most of whom I recognized. She immediately wrapped me in a big hug. "Oh, hon, it's so good to see you. This must be so *hard* for you." She squeezed me so tight, I could barely breathe. I knew she was being sincere, but the last thing I wanted to do right now was talk about my mom.

"You, too, Jessica. Thanks. I'm doing okay," I said, stepping back from her death grip. "I've missed this party," I said, and I meant it.

A girl named Allie, who'd gone out with Ryan's best friend, Morrison, stepped forward next. She squeezed my hands and said, "I'm so, so sorry."

Eric Houser, a brash jock who always cheated at sand volleyball, awkwardly patted my shoulder with his meaty hand. "It must be so hard to be back here without your mom."

I nodded, and said nothing in return. I got it, of course: People simply didn't know how to act around someone who had lost their mom. They felt badly if they didn't say something; *you* felt badly if they did. But no one really understood that.

Next to me, Becca looked trapped in a hug with a girl her age who'd slept over at our house a few times. I could tell Becca didn't want to cry, and I was having a hard time holding in tears, too. It felt like being at my mom's wake all over again, but now, with a speaker pouring out Macklemore's latest song, it felt all wrong.

This was the one part of coming back to Harborville that I'd been dreading: being the girls who'd lost their mom. When I got to Berkeley, I'd decided, I wasn't even going to tell people about it. It would be mine to share if I wanted to, but I could finally avoid being defined by what had happened. My mom would always be a part of me, but for now, I wanted to try as hard as I could to just be Kate.

"This sucks," Becca mumbled next to me. She pulled on one of the elastic hair ties she always seemed to have on her wrist, snapping it back with a painful zing.

"Just be polite. We'll get through this," Eliza said. She was the only one of us who didn't seem rattled.

After accepting a hug from a girl named Renee, whose family owned a boat-tour company, I pulled away from the crowd and told Eliza I was going to get a drink.

"Okay, but come back," she instructed, checking her phone. "Devin will be here soon."

"I'll make sure to see him," I said, making my way toward the coolers of drinks on the fringes of the party. Jessica's uncle Tom was a Harborville cop, which was how they always got away with serving alcohol at their clambake.

I smiled at some of the people waiting to fill red Solo cups at the keg. I knew some of them better than others. Everyone gave me watery half smiles, like it would be wrong to seem more than half happy in my presence. The whole thing was awkward and I decided to just head home. I could text Eliza that I wasn't feeling well, and call Jessica tomorrow to see if she wanted to do something alone.

I started heading away from the crowd, drawing my phone from my pocket, when I crashed into someone.

"Whoa, Katie." I looked up to find Morrison Davies, Ryan's best friend, looking down at me.

"It's Kate now," came Ryan's voice, just a few steps behind Morrison. He was freshly shaved and carrying a six-pack of beer in each hand, displaying every sinew of his arms. Flanking him were his younger brothers, Pete and Garrett. Garrett had always had a touch of a baby face with blond curls that only served to make him more angelic, but now his hair was cropped close to his head, military-style. I wondered if he was trying to make himself look more manly. The youngest, Pete, had Ryan's darker hair but a stocky build. He was a talented baseball player, and had always dreamed of someday playing for the Cape Cod baseball league, a feeder for the majors. But you'd never realize what a tough competitor he was thanks to his ever-present, affable smile.

"Kate," Morrison said, and—as if remembering something—his smile faded. "I'm so sorry. You know, about your mom."

"I know," I said, suddenly remembering, "You were at the funeral." The Landrys, because they were old family friends, had been the only Harborville people invited, but Morrison had come with Ryan. He was practically a fourth Landry brother. "Thank you for being there."

"Hey, man, Kate is here for the party," Ryan interjected. "Let's get her a drink, and get her sisters drinks while we're at it. Pete, Gar, aren't you gonna say hi to Kate?"

His brothers seemed relieved to be given the prompt and said hello with easy smiles. I smiled right back, and for the first all night, it didn't feel forced. "Did Becca come?" Garrett asked.

"Yeah, she'll be glad to see you," I said. He and Becca were the same age and had always been really close.

As they headed toward the party, I allowed myself to be swept up into their group. In the center of this group of boys I'd known for so much of my life, I felt more protected than I had all night. I knew they'd take care of me.

We made our way to my sisters, still clustered together. Eliza saw us first. She beamed widely, eyes locked on Ryan.

"Sommers sisters in the *house*," Ryan said, high-fiving Becca, Tea, and finally Eliza, who looked a little shocked to be given the same greeting as the other girls. . . . His brothers and Morrison followed suit, and I could see Becca and Tea smiling.

Eliza looked at my hands. "Where's your drink?"

"It's, um—" I began, fumbling for an excuse, but Ryan cut in.

"She saw us and figured why wait in the keg line? She knows we've got the good stuff." He opened the case of beer and winked at me, and I wondered if he realized that they'd caught me in the middle of an escape attempt. "A clambake is not a clambake without Sam Summer."

He handed a Sam Adams to me and one to Eliza. Morrison passed some out to other older guests. Eliza allowed Becca a beer, but shook her head no at Tea.

"As if I'd drink that crud anyway," Tea said, holding up her palm in refusal.

Ryan grinned at Morrison. "You like making toasts, Mor. What can you say to this?"

Morrison held his bottle aloft, as did a few dozen partygoers. He raised his voice and addressed the crowd in mock-formality. "The Sommers girls are back, which is momentous in its own right. But tonight, we have many things to celebrate. I officially declare this *the start of the summer!*" With that, he let out a loud cheer that was picked up by the rest of the revelers.

We held our bottles and cans aloft and clinked them together festively. Across the circle from me, Ryan raised his eyebrows, as if we were in on the same private joke. He mouthed, "Aren't you glad you stayed?" and I tipped my beer toward him in salute. "Aren't *you* glad I stayed?" I mouthed right back.

There was a solemnity in his gaze as he nodded at me, sending shivers down my spine.

CHAPTER FIVE

"GREAT PARTY, RIGHT, bee-yatch?" Jessica and I were sprawled out in the sand, both of us a little tipsy.

"Wasn't it only cool to say 'bee-yatch' for four seconds like four years ago?" I tried to kick some sand at her, but instead sent my flip-flop sailing toward the tide. I pushed myself off the ground to retrieve it, being careful not to tip my beer.

"What do you want me to call you instead? Ho-bag?"

"That's *Miss* Ho-bag to you," I said, laughing.

"I'm glad you're back, Miss Ho-bag," she said. "I've missed hanging out."

I bumped shoulders with Jessica. "I've missed this, too."

The party was starting to get fun. Either that or I had finally had enough to drink to feel warm and fuzzy inside.

Devin had finally arrived, and he and Eliza were now cuddling near the bonfire. Tea, Becca, Pete, and Garrett were playing some game that only they seemed to know the rules to. Jessica and I had hung out with Ryan and Morrison for a while and then I'd made some small talk with people about what schools we were going to in the fall.

In New Jersey, I was invited and went to some gatherings, but I wasn't what anyone at my high school would call a party girl. I was the kind of person to whom well-meaning aunts gave copies of books about introversion. But I didn't think that label fit, either. It was just that I was most comfortable when in the company of the right people. And right now, I was there.

"Should we get another?" I asked Jessica. She was looking down the beach at a group of guys getting out of the water.

"Aaron Gray is single again," she said, ignoring my question, her gaze distant. She didn't need to say any more. Jessica had had a crush on Aaron Gray for just about forever, but he was kind of a player, dating around during the school year and then finding a different summer girl as soon as June rolled around every year. "This is *my* summer," she declared. "No more of these stuck-up summer bitches. He's dating my townie ass whether he likes it or not." She turned to me. "No offense."

I laughed. "None taken."

She stood up determinedly. "I'm going to talk to him."

"Well, okay," I said, clapping for her. "This summer bee-yatch isn't going to stop you."

She strutted across the sand, bolstered by the night's drinks. Aaron definitely wasn't ignoring her, judging by the way his gaze took her in.

On my own, I made my way over to the keg—Ryan's beer supply long gone at this point—and poured myself a cup.

"Hey, Kate." I turned to see Devin, Eliza's fiancé. He smiled, his deep dimples showing.

"Hey, Devin, having a good time?" I hoped he couldn't smell just how much beer was on my breath. Though he was only a few years older than Eliza, Devin felt somehow parental to me, probably because he had a job in the city and said things like, "I need to check my calendar." But he was nice, and he was a good match for Eliza.

"I love it here. It's a lot more low-key than the Hamptons." He looked out over the expanse of beach, where the waves were quietly lapping the shore.

I nodded, even though I'd never actually been to the Hamptons before. Devin was from Connecticut, from a family that was definitely wealthier than mine. He never came off as snobby or above us, which I appreciated. Still, he was an investment banker, or hedge fund guy, or something, and it was always hard to know what to talk to him about. "Are you going to do anything fun tomorrow?"

"I think we're in wedding-planning lockdown," he said, with a look of faux-horror. "I'm hoping to work in some beach time, but as you may have noticed, your sister's a bit of a taskmaster."

"That's Eliza," I said. I leaned in and gave him a quick hug. Though he'd been around plenty over the last few years, I wanted to get to know Devin better now that he would be family.

"Yeah, I'd better get back with these. The taskmaster awaits. But we'll talk more later," he said, giving me a quick kiss on the cheek. "Have fun, Kate."

He headed back to the bonfire with the rest of the couples. I did notice that Ryan wasn't paired with anyone around the fire. I decided to look for Becca and Tea. It felt good to be on the beach at night, and sleep could wait.

Sipping my beer and trying not to spill as I flip-flopped over the uneven sand, I saw Morrison coming toward me.

"So, Sommers, been dreaming about me?" Morrison asked. He had a red cup in each hand. Some beer sloshed over the side of one and he lifted the cup to his mouth, slurping the overage.

Morrison was cute and goofy, and I knew that he'd had his fair share of girlfriends. Even now, I could see his ex Allie watching us, despite the fact that she was sitting by the bonfire with another guy.

"You wish," I laughed. Morrison and Ryan were opposites. Morrison tended to run at the mouth, where Ryan was quieter, but could deliver a sly remark better than anyone. Morrison was reedy and thin where Ryan was solidly lean, and he loped where Ryan glided. But they were the kind of friends who stuck by each other for everything.

"Is that a fresh cup?" Morrison nodded toward my beer and looped an arm over my shoulder. A bit of his beer dribbled onto my shirt but I ignored it; it was just an old blue tank top. "So, let's do this: You'll be my beer pong partner."

"You guys play beer pong at this party now? Man, the times they are a changin'."

Morrison grinned around his solo cup. "Gotta get some of you kids ready for college life."

"How'd you know I was declaring a minor in beer pong?" I said, scrunching up my eyebrows in mock confusion. "My major is a toss-up, though. Do I do foosball or quarters?"

"More money in quarters," Morrison quipped, steering me toward a folding table where a crowd was watching a fierce beer pong match.

"Kate and I got dibs on winners," he said.

The game was nearly over, he told me, and had me watch how it was played.

I'd never played before, but it didn't seem all that difficult. Like a liquid version of shuffleboard. We played a few sets, and I had to drink several times, but we were holding our own thanks to Morrison. Despite his crazy limbs, he was ultra-focused whenever it was his turn.

By my fourth turn, I could feel my competitive streak start to force its way to the surface. I leaned over and whispered to Morrison, "I've totally got this."

"Don't I know it? That's why I picked you," he said, rubbing my shoulders like I was a boxer gearing up for my next round. He stood back, giving me space to concentrate. I arced the Ping-Pong ball across the table and it splashed perfectly into my opponent's cup.

"Nice!" Morrison whooped. Then he surprised me by lifting me into the air and spinning me around.

As he put me back on the sand, I saw Ryan standing in a circle with some other guys, watching us. He gave me a small smile that didn't reach his eyes. I smiled back, wondering why he looked so disapproving. I knew he could be protective of Morrison, but I also knew that nothing was going to happen between us.

Morrison and I had won three more games of beer pong, but still celebrated each victory with ample quantities of beer. It was just hitting midnight, but it felt like it was three in the morning. Any party that started before sundown and went late into the night always hit a point where it felt much later than it was. Or, so Morrison had declared. His party wisdom reminded me a little bit of Smokey's.

With a yawn that sealed it for me, I said my good-byes and started to head up the sand.

"You're not going home yet, are you?"

I paused where I was standing. How was it that his voice was like its own physical presence? Was this a phenomenon unique to Ryan Landry or unique to Ryan Landry when he was talking to me? His words at my back were enough to make warmth spread across my shoulder blades. His voice made me want to be touched.

"I was thinking about it." I turned around to see Ryan smiling. The moonlight added shadows to his jaw. He looked as good in the dark as he did in the light. Maybe better.

"Walk with me," he said. He didn't seem like he'd had much to drink, but I could smell a faint whiff of beer on his breath.

I fell into step beside him, watching our feet as they hit the sand, leaving footprints that would be washed away when the tide came up. The celebratory sounds faded and it started to feel like we had the beach to ourselves, save for the odd slivers of laughter or beer pong cheers in the background. We were headed away from our houses, not toward them.

We moved up the beach, into the dunes, and every star was apparent. I inhaled the smell of the water, briny but clean. The ocean sounded like it was sighing contentedly, again and again.

"So, how's working for Smokey?" Ryan asked.

"He's not really someone you work *for*, now is he? I think you just coexist."

Ryan's laugh welled up from somewhere deep within him. It was a generous, warm laugh and had been one of the very first things I liked about him before I even knew how to like boys.

"And you're still writing?"

I looked up at him, surprised, in the dark. I'd never told Ryan about my writing. "What do you mean, 'still'?"

"You were always writing things down in your journals in the summer. You seemed to bring a notebook everywhere." He shrugged and peered at me. "Do you still do that?"

I didn't know what was the odder revelation: that Ryan Landry had noticed I carried around notebooks all the time or that, aside from the day I went to meet Grace Campbell, I hadn't really carried a notebook around with me since my mom had died.

"I'm trying," I said. "I've been a little stuck. Life feels weird, sometimes. Like earlier . . . I don't like being the person everyone feels bad for. I know they mean well, but still. Thanks for what you did back there." I didn't know why I was telling him all of this. The drinks probably had something to do with it, but I also got the sense that Ryan understood. He'd always been RYAN LANDRY, all capital letters, and someone I regarded as so out of my reach, but now I realized that there was a lot I still didn't know about him.

"Well, Morrison wasn't sorry for you," Ryan said, his voice slipping lower. "It looked like you guys were having fun."

Not knowing how to answer him, or if it was even a question, I waited for him to say something else.

"Are you, you know, into him?" Ryan had stopped walking and was looking away from me, anticipating my answer. Had he really led me on this walk down the beach to see if I liked his friend? Morrison was a big boy; he could ask me himself.

"I mean, you don't have to tell me," he added, suddenly

sounding shy. It dawned on me in a rush. Was Ryan . . . *jealous*? Of me and Morrison? Was he asking for himself?

I suddenly couldn't make sense of anything. The air felt hot and the stars felt too close. Ryan had been Eliza's, every summer, without fail. If Ryan *was* jealous, and even if I did want him . . . that wasn't something I could do to Eliza, was it? Her chant of "sisters before misters," ridiculous as it was, crossed my mind.

But did that apply? Didn't the game change now that she was getting married? I thought of the way she looked at me when Becca revealed she'd seen Ryan and me together. And the way she smiled at Ryan tonight, expecting that he'd only be interested in talking to her. What would she do right now, if she saw me and Ryan Landry, alone under the moonlight?

"No," I said, finally. "We're just friends." No, I wasn't into Morrison. And I was ready for whatever *not* being into Morrison meant for me and Ryan.

He looked at me then and however long it was, I could have lived in that moment forever. His gaze felt like when the sun comes out on an overcast day, warming you instantly.

"Your eyes are really pretty in this light. The blue and the brown . . . I've never seen anything like it," he said, studying me.

"Dahlias are like that. The flowers," I said, the words springing from me before I could stop them. "If you plant similar enough ones near each other, they hybridize the two colors. Or something like that. I've always liked that it's science that seems like magic." Why had I chosen this moment to give Ryan a genetics lesson? About a phenomenon I didn't even really understand, no less?

"Dahlias, huh?" he said with a sly grin, lowering his voice to barely above a whisper. He grabbed my wrist and pulled me into him slowly. I felt like we were learning how to dance. Tilting my face up to his, he leaned in and kissed me. It wasn't a drunken kiss. It was leisurely, and flawless. His fingers found my jaw and traced their way up the back of my neck. Our bodies pressed against one another, and everything strong in him made me want to be that much closer. I gave way to the kiss, letting it wash over me in waves.

Here it is, I thought. *Here we are.*

Ryan Landry was kissing me. Me, and not Eliza. I wanted him. He wanted *me*.

And then, I panicked.

"I have to go," I said. Somehow, I leaned away from him. Somehow, I turned around. Somehow, I got my feet to move and I didn't stop running until I was back in my room over the garage, listening to my heart race.

CHAPTER SIX

THE MORNING CAME too fast. For the past week, I'd loved the way sun filled the studio at dawn. Today, it felt like an assault. The day had not come in peace.

I had snoozed my alarm through my swim and writing time, but I didn't want to miss my shift at Smokey's. It was Saturday, which meant we'd be busy—the absolute last thing I needed in my hungover state. But I also didn't need to lie in bed all day, replaying that kiss—and my horrifying escape—over and over again.

I slunk into the house, which was still dark and quiet. A half pot of coffee was still warm on the kitchen counter. I found a travel cup and filled it, feeling slightly more human as the French roast aroma reached my nose.

The stairs creaked and I inched for the front door. But I was too slow. Eliza came down the stairs, a white bundle in her arms.

"Kate, wait . . . do you have a second?"

"Uh, sure." Guilt, I realized, had its own special way of rendering you speechless. I felt like anything I said might reveal that I'd kissed her ex-boyfriend.

"Can you hide this in the studio for me? But hang it?" She thrust the bundle toward me.

"What is it?"

"Remember that picture of Mom, from when she was pregnant with me, in that lace dress?" Eliza was beaming. "This is the dress. I'm going to use it to make my wedding dress."

Now I was speechless for a different reason. I must have looked dumbfounded, because Eliza peered into my face.

"Um, isn't that a great idea?" she said. "With the shoes and the dress, it's like making Mom part of the day."

"Yeah, definitely." I forced a smile. "So you need this up in the studio so Devin doesn't see it?"

"Yes ma'am! So smart, even hungover." She kissed me on the forehead and skipped up the stairs. I wished there was a way to transfer a hangover to someone more deserving.

I brought the dress carefully up the stairs to the studio, making sure not to spill coffee on it, and put it in a closet, holding the delicate lace between my fingers for an extra second. How did Eliza so casually appropriate Mom's things without even considering how it made the rest of us feel? I wanted to say something, but I knew that wasn't fair of me, either. Eliza had been through as much as the rest of us, and she was the one getting married. What was I really going to do with the dress, if I told Eliza she couldn't have it? Hang it up in my closet and write a story about it?

As I made my way back out of the studio I couldn't help but take a peek toward the Landrys' house. Of course Ryan wasn't there, waiting for me. I wasn't even sure if I wanted him to be.

I jogged toward Smokey's, hoping that even at half speed I could sweat out the toxins, and maybe my own confusion while

I was at it. Why did everything this summer—Ryan, my sister, my job—feel like it had to be *handled*? Why was nothing feeling simple, here in this place that had always been exactly that?

"Kate!" I'd just made it to the bike path when I heard Becca's voice. Of course, on the day when I felt most ill-equipped for even one early a.m. sister talk, I now was on number two. I half expected Tea to appear behind me.

Becca came toward me, trying to balance a donut and a cup of coffee from the Beach Ball, a diner that opened earlier than anything else on the boardwalk. I thought of the crane machine I used to play there as a kid. If only I could put in a quarter now and scoop up the answers to my problems. "Wasn't last night fun?"

Yes, and utterly mystifying and panic-inducing and pretty much what I'm going to obsess about until the end of time. My eyes are blue and brown, hybrids like a dahlia. Ryan kissed me. Eliza will kill me. Ryan kissed me.

"Yeah, it was great," I said nonchalantly. I needed to process things away from my sisters. Like, maybe back in New Jersey. "But I really have to get to work. Let's talk later, okay?"

I gave her a quick peck on the cheek and tried not to notice her disappointed expression. Then I ran the rest of the way to Smokey's.

"Miss, this boogie board doesn't work." A heavyset woman in a skirted bathing suit slid a blue board across the counter to me.

"Is it cracked?"

"No. It just hasn't caught any waves. My son is very upset." She blinked expectantly.

"Tell your son that you never truly catch a wave. You find a moment," Smokey said.

The woman grimaced. "That's not helpful."

"Okay, Kate, she needs her money back." Smokey drummed on the counter, humming. "If you don't get the waves, you shouldn't have to pay." I knew this was Smokey's version of an insult, but the woman seemed quite pleased with herself as I handed over a refund.

The day had started with irritable customers, mostly because I'd been ten minutes late opening the shop. It was continuing with more of the same. No one was happy, even though the sky was cloudless and the sun and breeze were working in perfect tandem, one warming you up and one cooling you down.

Smokey came to pat me on the shoulder. "The days Mother Nature brings it the most are always the ones when people can't deal with the teensy shit. Weird, right? It's like you're this close to perfection but you just can't handle it."

Smokey was uncanny with his random life philosophies. And he was right, the day was perfect. But I couldn't get past the kiss with Ryan to just enjoy it. Though, the kiss with Ryan hardly felt like "teensy shit."

He nodded away from the counter. "Go take your break. I got control of all this, because I know I don't have control of anything."

I put my hands up in defeat and retreated into the back. The shack had a surprisingly comfy break setup in a far back corner. Smokey kept the place stocked with munchies, of course, so I settled into an overstuffed armchair with a mini bag of barbeque chips, my favorite hangover food. I closed my eyes, picturing last night in my head.

Maybe I was overreacting to the kiss. Maybe it was just a weird, drunken thing that didn't really mean anything. Ryan could have even just wanted to talk because he felt sorry for me, and then the kiss had just happened. But there was all that stuff about Morrison. Ryan had seemed almost resentful of his best friend, hadn't he?

"Kate, know you're on break and all, but you have a visitor."

I trudged out to the counter, already weary. And then I saw . . . Ryan. He didn't look as hungover as I felt. He smiled, but not in the trademarked Ryan Landry way. His normal grin was assured, but now he looked almost sheepish.

"Hi . . ." I said, my voice barely making it over the counter. What was I supposed to say? *Can I offer you a boogie board?*

"Hi . . ." he said, seeming equally uncertain. He leaned across the counter, coming down to my height. Our faces were aligned, and I thought again of how our kiss had unfolded and deepened, like there'd been layers left to explore. I realized I was staring at him.

"So, I came to find you because . . ." Ryan stopped. "Can you come out here? It feels weird talking to you over the counter like this."

I looked behind me to where Smokey was doodling on the back of a rental agreement. "I'm going to take my break out there," I said.

"Cool" was my boss's one-word reply.

We walked outside and came around to the front. My legs were wobbly. I leaned against the side of the shack, facing Ryan.

We were tucked away from the beach, standing so no one could see. I managed to speak. "So you came to find me because . . ." *You think last night was a mistake. You were drunk and didn't mean to. You don't want things between us to be weird for the rest of the summer.*

I looked at him, steeling myself.

"Well, what happened last night?" he said, studying my face with real concern. "Why'd you run off?"

Oh. That was what was bothering him? And how did I answer that? "It, well, I . . ." I took a deep breath. I was so bad at this stuff. If only I could just write it down first. "You were Eliza's for so long. I guess I just panicked."

Ryan grinned. It was back to his typical grin again. "But I'm not Eliza's now, am I?" He looked down at himself, grabbing the hem of his shirt as if checking for a mark, or a tag. I wouldn't have been surprised.

I laughed, but then shook my head. "Well, no. She's getting married." It came out more matter-of-fact and guarded than I'd intended.

"But I mean, even before I knew that, I wasn't hers," he said. I liked the way he put it. "And, you're not anybody's, right?"

"I haven't heard anything to the contrary." There was Matt, of course, but it wasn't like we were together, and he felt very, very far away right now.

"Well, that's good for me." Next to me, Ryan leaned against the shack and tilted his head up to take in the sun. His sunglasses slipped off his head and smacked down onto his nose. With a smirk, he lifted them back into his curls. I didn't think that had turned into the suave move he had expected it to be. Nor was this the conversation I'd been expecting to have with him. If anything, I'd been expecting to avoid Ryan until I absolutely had to cross paths with him again. But now, here he was. This wasn't some hallucination, or fantasy. My neck was stiff from the weird position I'd fallen asleep. My eyes hurt. My head still throbbed; kids shrieking as they splashed in the ocean made me want to yell, "Keep it down!" So, if those sensations were all real, wasn't the warmth felt from Ryan's words—*I'm not Eliza's now, am I?*—just as real?

"You could look at it that way."

"I do. Look at it that way. And, one more thing, it's a little weird but . . ." I tried to think of something weirder than what was already happening. The sky turning green and a marching band of dolphins stomping out of the sea? ". . . But, I came here to maybe get your phone number?"

I smiled. I wasn't going to make this easy for him. "You've called our house before," I said.

"I know how to call the house. But maybe I want to call just you." He moved closer to me, his shadow falling over my body. The pangs in my head and my neck faded, replaced with the liquid heat of my blood moving more quickly through my veins.

I grabbed a crumpled rental agreement from my pocket and a pen from behind my ear, scrawling my number across it.

Ryan folded it and put it in his pocket. "Thanks. You know I'm going to ask you out, right?" He smiled and, gently pulling me to him with his hand on my upper arm, gave me a lips-only kiss that was short, but long enough to make me glad I was still leaning against the shack. Before I knew what was happening, he was jogging off with my phone number in his pocket.

Smokey poked his head out the side door. "You need to extend your break?"

I nodded, sliding down the wall of the shack and into the sand.

CHAPTER SEVEN

SUNDAY WAS MY day off. Smokey thought work-life balance was important. What he didn't get was that my routine kept me sane. My lack of anything to do left me lounging on the couch in front of the television, far too absorbed in an edited-for-TV version of *Pulp Fiction*. It made almost no sense, thanks to the alteration of all the questionable dialogue. Every time my phone buzzed or dinged with an alert, I first hoped it was Ryan, and then looked up in a panic to see if one of my sisters had entered the room. But all my dings were just Facebook notifications and a few funny reddits from Matt.

So when I got a text from Jessica asking if I wanted to lie out on the beach, I said yes immediately. I needed to get out of the house. I texted Matt back with a funny emoji in return, avoiding his mention of a visit.

"Did you see Alison Climes pass out right on Zach Taylor? That girl talks a big game but she's a lightweight. Cannot hold her liquor." Jessica examined her nails, which bore a striped print even more complex than the one on her bikini. My own nails were bare and my swimsuit was a faded blue one-piece. Maybe it was time for a new one.

I'd suggested the quiet of Pleasant Street Beach but Jessica had wanted a pineapple smoothie from one of the stands at Morning, so we'd lugged our stuff and staked out a place on the sand. On one side of us were two middle-aged women giggling over a book with a half-naked man on the cover, and on the other, a gaggle of skinny preteenage boys who kept ogling Jessica.

"I missed the Alison thing, but more importantly, what happened with you and Aaron Gray?"

Jessica smiled like a cat who'd eaten a canary. "I think I have him where I want him. At least for the summer," she said proudly. "He's a little full of himself, though, just because he's headed to Syracuse. You know, Mr. Bigshot getting out of Harborville. But it's cool. I'll represent for Cape Cod Community."

I couldn't tell if Jessica felt as blasé as she sounded. Mostly, people in Harborville stuck around after high school to get their associates at the community college, or went as far as UMass Dartmouth, then maybe finished up with a teaching or nursing degree at a nearby state school. Even Ryan had gone to CCC for two years before moving back home. The people who did leave, like Aaron, were rare. It made me question whether I should even talk about Berkeley, or if that would somehow be rubbing it in. I flipped onto my stomach, to try and get some color on my back, but also so my baseball cap shaded my face from Jessica.

"And, what did you guys talk about? I asked, changing the subject. "Or did you go mute again?" Despite her thick auburn hair, confident style, and pixieish face, Jessica had always been pretty shy, especially around Aaron. Her marching up to him the other night was at least partially a by-product of beer, though she definitely was gutsier now than when we were younger.

"What can I say? I finally found my voice." She grinned again and I could tell there was more she wanted to say.

"Did you find it behind his tonsils?" I raised an eyebrow.

"There may have been some aggressive making out," Jessica said, sitting up to reapply some sunblock. Her adolescent fan club did everything but take pictures. "PDA is so not hot when you get old, so I'm enjoying it while I can. And anyway, it's Aaron. You know better than anyone what this means."

I nodded, because I did know. I wanted to tell her about Ryan so badly it almost felt like needing to pee. Of everyone, Jessica would appreciate my news the most. She'd been there from the early stages of my crush all the way to when it consumed me like a disease. But Ryan hadn't even called yet, and I didn't want to jinx anything. More than that, I was worried Jessica might let it slip to someone, and the last thing I wanted was for Eliza to hear.

"Speaking of public displays, Morrison got pretty flirty with you," Jessica said. "He would not stop talking about you after you left."

I shrugged. "He doesn't stop talking, period."

"No, this was different. Are you interested?" Jessica peered at me over the rim of her oversized sunglasses as she lay back down.

I took a long sip of my iced coffee before I answered. "I mean, he's Morrison. He's great, and obviously he's really cute. But . . ." *I'm kind of obsessed with his best friend. And I'm kind of hoping he might feel the same way about me.* Instead I said, "I just got out of a long-term thing back home." I hated not telling Jessica the truth, but it wasn't technically a lie, and if anything did happen with Ryan, I would tell her eventually.

The fact was, Matt had been sweet and cute and we'd been a good fit when we were together, for part of junior and most of senior year. We'd been each other's firsts: first "I love yous" and first times. He was the type of boyfriend who would meet me after class to see how I did on a test, who always let me pick which movie to see on a Saturday night, who opened my car door for me without fail. But when I compared the way I'd felt with Matt to the way my body rattled, thrumming with energy, whenever I thought of Ryan, it struck me that we'd always been more like good friends—and that that was why it had been so easy to break up. "I'm not really ready for a relationship," I said with a finality that I hoped read as me not wanting to talk about my ex, though not for the reasons Jessica probably thought.

She patted my arm gently. "Poor baby. We can talk about it when you're ready," she said. "But summer flings aren't relationships. Just ask Aaron."

I thought of Ryan and his smile as he took my phone number. I'd settle for a summer fling.

I was a little sunburnt, a lot parched, and completely starving when I stepped onto the patio of the beach house, hoping someone had gone to the store to pick up food for dinner. My towel was around my neck and a fine layer of sand and salt coated my legs, despite the fact that I had taken one last dip in the ocean to rinse it off. I glanced over at the Landrys' house, hoping for a Ryan sighting, even though I had already noticed his truck wasn't parked out front when I walked up the street.

Before I even got my key in the door, it swung open and Eliza yanked me inside. "You're here," she said urgently. "Come in."

"Okay," I managed, feeling my neck get warmer. Did she know about Ryan already? What did she, have spies everywhere?

I was between her and the front hall closet, feeling trapped and looking at a framed family picture from before Eliza had her braces off. She was going to be so mad at me. I looked her in the eye, trying to get my bearings. But she just said, "Dad's here."

I released a breath I didn't know I'd been holding. "Oh, that's great," I said.

"Yes and no," she said, reaching out to brush some sand off my shoulder.

Becca made her way into the hall. "Did you tell her?"

"Yeah, Dad's here, so?"

"Well, we're going to Landrys' tonight," Becca said, looking at me like I'd understand.

"Oh." I did. Every summer, we used to make a point to have a Sunday meal at Landrys' Restaurant. Even though they would often cook for us in their own kitchen, it was always a treat to eat hot buttered bread as we overlooked the ocean. The restaurant occupied a prime spot at the end of the pier, and the views were magnificent. But I understood why Eliza and Becca were worried. At our first dinner of the summer, Mr. Landry used to arrange for us each to get a piece of their famous molten chocolate birthday cake, and have the staff sing to our whole family, to make up for the fact that all the Sommers' family birthdays occurred in the winter.

But keeping up the traditions we'd had with Mom had been especially tough for Dad. Harder than for any of us, it seemed. Where Eliza, my sisters, and I clung to doing things Mom's way,

Dad just seemed more acutely pained by her absence when we did the things she loved.

In other words, a dinner like this was going to be really hard for him.

"Well, it's still a big step that he's here," I said, not convinced. "I'll go say hi."

My dad was in the kitchen, standing at the counter with a glass of water. He smiled as I came in, but he had a faraway look in his eyes. I gave him my brightest smile in return.

"Just got back from the beach," I said, kissing him hello. "Today was beautiful."

"Yeah," he said. "And Becca's going to show off at Landrys'. She's quite the cook, she said. I'm glad you're all having a good time." His voice was even as he spoke, but there was a hollowness to it—and to him. He'd lost twenty pounds after our mother died, and he still hadn't gained it back.

"You should get to the beach for some R and R," I said. "You've been working too much."

Then I excused myself to get ready, dodging the look in his eyes that made me unsure of what to say next.

We'd made it to Landrys' before the dinner rush, and Becca had proudly given us a tour of the kitchen and shown us her regular station in the kitchen. Unsurprisingly, she was a star at the stove, managing two burners at once while making a hollandaise sauce under Ryan's instruction.

I'd been nervous to see Ryan when I was with my whole family, wondering how he'd act. Getting ready had been nearly impossible, and walking into Landrys' had been one of the hardest things I'd ever done in my life. He'd said hi to me in the same warm but casual tone he'd used for the rest of my sisters, and it was making me paranoid. What did it mean? Were we back to just being friends? What had I screwed up?

Now, I tried to act normal, and quietly sipped my Diet Coke as we waited for our food. We were on the deck, occupying our usual spot and watching the sun sink below the horizon. The sunset, as always, was stunning. Strong magentas and orange clouds—colors that I knew my mom would have wanted to bottle in a jar. From this vantage point, the ocean looked like it went on forever, but somehow my dad seemed like he was actually able to stare beyond it, to something no one else could see. I could tell my sisters were noticing his mood, too, and our table was oddly silent. I thought of the lively meals we'd had here in the past, and the memory pinched at the edges of my heart.

Two waiters delivered a massive seafood platter, setting it in the center of our table. The aromas—of grilled shrimp, oysters, and seared scallops, my favorite—took hold of my nostrils and my stomach rumbled. Worrying why a guy hadn't called certainly burned some extra calories.

"That takes three cooks to prepare in order to get the timing just right so everything comes out together," Becca said, grabbing an oyster. "I helped with one the other day." I was relieved that our food had given us something to talk about. Becca swallowed her oyster with gusto, and I waited for my dad to seize one, too. He loved oysters.

"That's nice," my dad said. His hands stayed folded in his lap.

Eliza looked at me across the table. "Speaking of the other day, did you even get to see Devin when he was here, Kate?"

I nodded. "Yeah, we bumped into each other at the party. He was having a great time. It sucks that he already had to head back to the city." I didn't add, *I saw him right before Ryan Landry got jealous of me and Morrison, which was just before Ryan walked me down the beach, and I said weird things about science and he kissed me better than I've ever been kissed.*

Becca grinned. "It was a fun party. I had to keep Tea out of trouble."

"Whatever, I keep myself out of trouble," Tea said. "You were the one flirting with Garrett Landry. Is that why you wanted to come here? You don't see him enough at work?" Tea knocked her skinny arm into Becca's. She was also working at Landrys' as a part-time hostess, but had been complaining about not having enough hours.

I didn't hear Becca's response because I was distracted by my dad as he quietly tucked into his broiled sole. Usually, he and Mom would share a surf-and-turf platter along with the oysters. Today, he'd barely looked at the menu before ordering the plainest thing on it.

I squeezed a lemon over my oyster as I looked inside the restaurant. Through the big glass windows, I could see past the dining room into the kitchen. Every so often, I caught a quick glimpse of Ryan. He was in constant motion, chopping vegetables one second and checking a cook's sauce another. He didn't seem to register me at all.

"So, next time, it would be nice if you could at least spend a little time with Devin. Becca and Tea went to breakfast with us today." Eliza looked at me expectantly, as if waiting for me to apologize. But it wasn't even like I'd been invited to go with her and Devin—they'd left while I was out for my morning swim, and I'd missed them. I enjoyed seeing Devin, but I was doing my best to get to know him on my own time. "He might fly in again if he can get Wednesday off work."

"Well, the two of us will braid each other's hair and talk about boys, I promise." I stuck my tongue out at Eliza, trying to lighten the mood.

"Good," she said, even though I could tell she was still annoyed with me.

I heard my phone ding with a text message and unzipped my purse to peer at it, expecting another set of gifs from Matt.

But no. It was a text from Ryan: "I'm trying not to get distracted by how pretty you look."

I glanced up and saw that he was now just inside the window in the main dining room, showing a few first-day busboys where the place-setting supplies were kept. He was looking right at me and gave me a wink. If I couldn't eat before, I definitely couldn't now.

"Thanks," I covertly texted back. Across the table, Eliza rolled her eyes. "Can't it wait?"

"Sorry," I muttered, though I wasn't sorry at all.

Another text from Ryan followed. "Free Wednesday? Before sunset?"

Taking my chances with Eliza, I texted back: "Definitely."

I pressed send and looked up again, trying to keep my smile in check. I felt like my face would reveal everything. Ryan was looking back at me with a grin of his own. "Can't wait," he mouthed.

Neither could I.

CHAPTER EIGHT

RYAN PICKED ME up at Smokey's at four-thirty on the dot. He had a picnic basket on his arm and he looked both cute and ridiculous at the same time, like a macho version of Little Red Riding Hood.

"So, do you think it's okay if we use some bikes? I know yours is busted and I came right from work."

I nodded. "One of the many perks of working for Smokey," I said. "The contact high is optional."

Ryan laughed as I signed out two beach cruisers and told Smokey I was headed out for the day.

"Be good," he said. Even though it was a typical Smokey good-bye, I felt the slightest twinge of guilt, like he somehow knew I was doing, getting involved with my sister's ex.

But then I saw Ryan waiting patiently at the counter and as his sea glass–green eyes looked me up and down, I felt warm inside, and suddenly not worried about being good at all.

We rode down the beach slowly, Ryan insisting he was fine carrying the picnic basket in one hand. He ably steered the bike with the other. "How are you doing that?" I asked.

"A lot of practice maneuvering with Sommers girls on my handlebars," he grinned. "You could probably hop on right now and I could manage. Though I might be thrown off by the spectacular view."

Was I the spectacular view?

"No need to show off," I teased him instead.

"Oh please," he responded. "If I recall, you were the queen of no-hands steering, daredevil."

It was true—I had always been the most stunt-attempting of my sisters. I loved that Ryan knew that about me.

We rode to the bikeway that went through town, only pedaling back toward the shore when we reached our spot. This far out some of the coast was rockier, and only locals and lifers knew where to find comfy places to sit. The privacy was part of the appeal.

We stopped at a tiny enclave with big boulders and lots of pebbles. It was low tide, and up toward the top of the shoreline, you could find small sandy spots clear of rocks. The houses along this beach were much farther apart than in Harborville proper. Most days, you could have an entire stretch of beach to yourself.

"Here," Ryan said, laying out a blanket and handing me a bottle of chilled white wine. "You can sit down, and open this." He handed me a corkscrew and two plastic cups.

"Wow, you come prepared." I got to work on the wine, impressed and maybe intimidated by how adult the date suddenly felt. Eliza would expect this kind of thing, but it was new to me. Matt and I had been regulars at the movie theater and the mini golf course, but our most adult date had been going to Bacino's before prom—the same Italian restaurant I'd gone to after eighth-grade graduation.

"Well, I started planning this the day I got to walk you home from Smokey's, so I've had some time." I didn't know how to respond to his admission. What could I say? "I've been planning our first date since I used to spy on you and Eliza"? Creepy.

He started to pull items from the picnic basket. "This is a goat-cheese-and-arugula tart, with a lemon–olive oil aioli." He opened the container to reveal a delicious-smelling pastry. "And this one is a chicken cordon bleu wrap." The wraps looked like something he must have picked up at a gourmet shop. Main Street had several new places since we'd last been here, each one with a wooden sign or a chalkboard advertising farm-to-table ingredients. I wondered where Ryan had picked all this up and couldn't believe all the trouble he'd gone to. "And this is heirloom tomato salad with seared scallops." My mouth watered at the perfectly cooked scallops. "And for dessert, I made flourless chocolate cake with raspberries."

"You made dessert?"

"I made everything. I know how much you love scallops." He gave me a plate and utensils and urged me to take what I wanted.

I made myself a heaping portion, looking at the food—and Ryan—afresh. I'd always thought Ryan's work at his family restaurant was out of a sense of duty, or tradition. I had never realized his interest in cooking was more of a skill than a job he'd been handed down.

As I ate, Ryan watched my reactions to the food. Fortunately, every bite of it was delicious. I think I even hummed appreciatively when I bit into the first scallop.

"So, is your family having a good time being back, or is it weird without your mom?" Ryan asked, as I dabbed my face with a napkin. As if there was anything dainty about me, after I'd just eaten two helpings of everything.

"Sorry if you don't want to talk about that," he added, holding up his hands. "Just tell me and I'll ask you something else."

"No, it's fine," I said, setting my napkin on my plate. "It's different when it's with someone I know—someone who knew her. You know, the whole thing is weird because we don't actually talk about it. It's like my mom's presence is looming, but no one ever wants to bring it up, including me. It's too daunting to talk about the big stuff. I guess, sometimes I just wish we were really and truly dysfunctional, so feeling weird like this would just be normal. Like *The Royal Tenenbaums* or something."

"I love that movie," he said, surprising me. "But I have to say, I'm glad you're not in a weird relationship with your adoptive sister."

I laughed, knowing he was talking about the Gwyneth Paltrow–Luke Wilson roles, and tried to hide my surprise that he had seen a Wes Anderson movie. I'd just always thought of Ryan as more of an outdoorsy type, who preferred to spend his time playing sports instead of watching movies, but it occurred to me how little I really knew about him.

"If I was, I supposed I wouldn't be out on a date with you," I said, wondering if it was okay to call this a date. It was, wasn't it? "So what about you? What's new with the Landrys?"

He shrugged. "We're kind of the same, kind of not. My parents are little more checked-out about the restaurant, that's for sure. So they leave stuff up to me, but then when I do things my way, they comment on it," he said.

"Like what?"

73

"I don't know, like, to get business in the winter months, our slow time, I did some advertising in Provincetown to get an artier crowd in and held these theme nights with special menus based on books. *The Great Gatsby* one was really cool," he said.

My mind went to an image of Ryan Gatsby-ed up in a tux and bow tie. "That's so cool," I said. "I would have loved to see that."

"Yeah?" He said, with obvious pride. "I'm glad you think so."

I looked at him, with his button-down shirt rolled up to the elbows and his muscular legs stretched out in front of him. He had the perfect balance of muscle and lean in his forearms and calves. With his windblown hair, he looked like a model in a men's fragrance ad. And he was worried what I thought? "I'm impressed," I said. "Really. So tell me . . . What else do you have up your sleeve?"

He smirked. "That's about it. I could show you all my Harborville High trophies if you come over."

I imagined going to Ryan's carriage house and being alone with him there. Even staring at the top few buttons of his shirt made me blush. "I hope they're dramatically lit."

"Yeah, music plays and they rotate on pedestals whenever someone comes to my room," he said.

"Do you still play baseball?" It had always been Ryan's best sport. He'd helped coach Pete's Little League teams.

"I was in a league for a while after graduation," he said. "But it's just too much, you know? I started to feel like I was still in high school, seeing so many of the same people all the time. So, now I mostly run or bike, or just work out. Sometimes I'll do a game of pickup basketball if Morrison wants to play."

It was another surprise to learn that as much as Ryan embod-ied Harborville to me, he was keeping part of himself separate from his town. He was in it, but growing beyond it. I admired that. "We should go running sometime," I said, hoping that I wasn't pushing it.

"I'd love that," he said. "If I can keep up with you. You got skills, Sommers." As he was saying this, he cut a piece of chocolate cake and offered it to me.

The first bite was enough to make me never want to eat any-thing else for as long as I lived. The man could kiss and he could cook. Stick a fork in me and call me done.

"I have skills? This, everything, was amazing," I told him, stealing another bite of chocolate cake. "And I don't toss around that word lightly."

"I know you take your words seriously," Ryan said, taking a slice for himself. We devoured it. After we emptied the rest of the wine bottle into our glasses, we sat side by side, watching the waves crash. With an arm around my waist, he pulled me closer. Then he kissed each of my cheeks, my jaw, and trailed his way down my neck. I heard myself gasp. Then his mouth was on mine, tasting like chocolate, and wine, and Ryan.

He kissed like someone who wanted me to forget who I was. And in a way, it was working. With him, I had the momentary sensation of just being Kate. I clutched his back, aware of every ridge of muscle, wanting to touch his skin but holding back.

We came up for air. Ryan's forehead was pressed against mine and I peered into his eyes. "I guess you did like the food." He smiled.

The beach was still ours, and dusk was settling over the ocean. Here, at the elbow of the Cape, we could see lighthouses and bluffs stretching out in both directions. Boat lights twinkled in the water.

Down the way, I heard voices, but couldn't make out what they were saying. I peered over Ryan's shoulder. Across the beach, coming down the path, were Eliza and Devin. Devin was carrying a bottle of wine. Apparently, he'd been able to get out of work. And unfortunately, the two of them had had the same idea as Ryan. A sudden thought made icy panic wash over me. Was this Ryan and Eliza's old place? Had he brought her here before me?

"We have to go," I said, pulling away and downing the last of my wine. "I just remembered, I, um, promised Tea I'd, um, help her with some PSAT prep tonight." I prayed Tea didn't have a shift at Landrys' tonight. Though if she did, I could pretend I'd mixed up the days.

Ryan's eyebrows lifted. "She's doing that already?"

"You don't know Tea. Well, you do. But she's borderline scary with her goals. Like a robot or something. I'm really sorry. This was great. Thank you." I fumbled with the picnic basket, and tried to fold the blanket while Ryan was still sitting on it. Devin and Eliza still hadn't seen us. "I mean it."

"You're welcome." His grin had faded.

"Let's go the long way, though, after all that food. I can't be a good quiz master with such a full stomach." I pointed my bike away from Eliza and Devin.

"Whatever you want," Ryan said, but his words made my chest ache.

I hated myself more than a little for cutting the date with Ryan short. The whole evening, which had started so wonderfully, had left me in a foul mood. I was resentful of Eliza—for showing up at the beach, for bossing me around since we'd arrived, for seeming so entitled to everything, not to mention for having Ryan first. And I was starting to resent the summer here. We could have stayed away and kept the house in our memories, instead of coming here and opening wounds that had only started to heal. The job I'd hoped for hadn't panned out and every day, I found myself seeking alone time in Mom's old studio, when I was supposed to be bonding with my sisters. Nothing was going as planned.

And now I'd probably destroyed things with Ryan when they'd just begun. The worst part was, maybe they shouldn't have started in the first place.

I took my computer downstairs, planning to at least spend some time in the main house with my sisters. It was late, and I needed sleep, but I was too worked up. Maybe Tea really was studying for the PSAT, at least making me less of a liar.

But the house was empty. I set up my computer on the kitchen counter and checked my e-mail. I had a Twitter notification for a direct message. It was from Grace Campbell: "NY a no-go. Back in Cape after all. Can you start in two days?"

I resisted the urge to roll my eyes. This *was* a nice development, even if it was a little late. I wrote back that I would and promptly began to daydream about what I might be working on. The characters in Grace Campbell's books always had interesting backstories and occupations, like war veterans, archaeologists, or astronauts, the kinds of things that required research. I wondered if she'd send me to interview people, or just send me to libraries and museums.

I was clicking around on some of my favorite writing sites,

telling myself not to worry about the Ryan thing right now, when Eliza and Devin stumbled into the kitchen, groping and making out. They didn't even see me at the counter.

From the way they were going at it, they'd clearly enjoyed *their* picnic and I was more annoyed than ever that I'd cut my time short with Ryan. Did Eliza's sisters-before-misters rule really apply when one of the sisters in question had so obviously moved on? Or did it only apply when one of the sisters was Eliza?

Eliza's cheeks were flushed and she had one arm tightly around Devin's neck. His hands were on her hips, pulling her into him. Eliza started to tug Devin's polo shirt off when I finally cleared my throat loudly.

Devin backed away from Eliza like he was spring-loaded, toppling a half bottle of water that had been left open on the counter. "Uh, hey, Kate," he said, his dimples the only parts of his face that weren't red. "We, uh, we were just . . ."

"She's eighteen. She knows what we were doing," Eliza said, waving him off. She came around to my side of the counter, her movements loose. She leaned her head on my shoulder. She was obviously a little tipsy. "Whatcha doing?"

"Just e-mail," I said. I couldn't look her in the face. I felt like she'd see right into me or would know by scent or something that I'd been with Ryan.

"How was your day?" Devin asked. "Anything interesting?"

I knew he was being sweet and brotherly, but today was the last day I wanted to tell Devin and my sister about.

"Eh, the usual. Smokey's. Took a bike ride," I said, hoping if a person could ooze nonchalance, I was oozing it. Plus, it was not entirely a lie. But Eliza's expression mimicked Ryan's from when

I'd abruptly ended our date. Like she wanted to believe me, but was having a hard time.

"Devin, I didn't know you were coming today," I said casually.

"Yeah, he flew in, but the poor thing got called back to work tomorrow when he thought he could take a day off." Eliza made an exaggerated sad face for Devin's benefit.

"That sucks," I said.

"It's newbie stuff, I guess," Devin said. He opened the fridge and pulled out a bottle of beer. "I thought newbie stuff ended after my first two years, but I guess they can abuse me until I get another promotion." Devin was a few years older than Eliza and had been working long hours since the day he graduated. Eliza had always been a little bit proud of his crazy schedule, even when she was still in college and humble-bragged that she felt like the widow of her sorority because Devin could never visit. But to Eliza's credit, she always seemed most proud of Devin's drive, not his paycheck. My sister liked nice things, but she resisted her boyfriend's attempts to spoil her with expensive gifts.

Eliza had been a business major, and had graduated early in January, always a step ahead of everyone else. With nothing standing in her way, she had gotten engaged in March and then rushed to plan and hold her wedding on the Cape. She had no qualms about being a young bride. And, true to everything Eliza did, she'd probably not suffer for it in the least.

Now, she lingered next to me, and it made me uncomfortable. "It's my last day at Smokey's tomorrow," I told her. It was something to say that wasn't about Ryan. I faked a yawn. "So I better get some rest, too. I actually get to start as Grace's assistant on Friday."

Eliza's eyes brightened as I pushed away from the counter. "Wow, so do you know what you'll be doing for her?"

"I'm sure research for her next book," I said, even though I really had no idea. It was a lie that was easier to tell than one about any of my other summer activities. "Maybe some publicity stuff."

"That's great," Devin said. "You'll have to tell me what she's like. My colleagues are reading *Bent Castle* for their book club."

"It *is* great!" Eliza came to my side of the counter and threw her arm around me, squeezing my shoulder. "See, aren't you glad we're spending the summer here? This is going to be so good for you!"

I squeezed her back, trying to be affectionate. Only Eliza would try to make my decent summer job seem like an outcome of her decision to come here. I wondered if she'd see the developments between me and Ryan the same way. Doubtful.

"Yeah, I'm super excited," I said, remembering Ryan's face as I'd rushed us from our picnic. With a closed-lip smile, I shut my computer and walked past her to the front door.

"I'm really happy for you," she called after me.

"Thanks, good night," were the safest words I could think to say as the door shut with a click.

CHAPTER NINE

I WOKE UP later than I wanted to for my first day at Grace's. I wasn't going to be late, but I also wasn't going to be able to make my swim. Instead, I took a long shower, trying to process everything. Was there a way to get things on track with Ryan again, but without him knowing I thought anything was wrong? I knew it had only been two nights, but the way we'd left things made me anxious.

Sitting on my futon, I toweled off and—though I'd resisted for days—opened my curtains just a few inches. Before, in the main house, I could see out to the street, to where Ryan parked his truck. Now, I had a direct sight line into his room.

His blinds were shut.

I ran a comb through my hair, telling myself things would either be fine or they wouldn't. My priority had to be putting in a good first day with Grace.

Something flickered in my peripheral vision and I instinctively looked left. Standing in his window, blinds up, and wearing only a towel around his waist, was Ryan. Or, what I assumed was

81

Ryan, since I couldn't tear my eyes away from his taut abdomen, with its narrow trail of hair leading south from his belly button. When I managed to pull my gaze up, raking my eyes greedily over his still-wet chest, we were looking right into each other's faces. The right corner of his mouth turned up in a smile.

Ryan scribbled something on a pad next to his bed. He held it up. "Have a good day, sexy."

I had a pink towel around my chest and he thought *I* was sexy? If that was the case, there were no words expressive enough for what *he* was. I picked up a legal pad and scrawled the words "You, too" and offered what I hoped what my sexiest smile. Reluctantly, I turned to get dressed and leave for work.

My new job, I thought, had better be interesting.

Grace Campbell's house was far down the beach, away from all the tourists and not far from where Ryan and I had picnicked a few days ago. I'd left on a bike from Smokey's at nine in the morning, hoping to be early for my ten o'clock start time.

Smokey had understood when I'd told him I had to quit. It probably had helped that I'd suggested Tea to work for him instead. Even though she had the hostess job, it wasn't that many hours. And at fifteen, Tea desperately wanted to work. Either hanging around the empty beach house was getting to her, or someday she'd run the world. Maybe both.

Grace's front porch was a collage of plants in various stages of life. Some were healthy and abloom while others looked like they'd been left in their pots to die. The front door was painted an iridescent blue that glittered in the sun.

I knocked.

I waited.

I knocked again. Looking down at my phone, I checked the address. It was right. But the house didn't even appear to be inhabited, let alone by a writer I assumed was very productive. Maybe someone had hacked her Twitter account, and Grace Campbell was still in New York.

"You're early." The voice came from behind the array of plants on the windowsill.

"Ms. Campbell?" I crouched to make eye contact with the face peering through the screen. "I'm Kate Sommers. You hired me? As your assistant?"

"Don't make statements sound like questions or you're fired." She cackled. "And don't get here early again. But since you're early today, come in. The door is unlocked."

I opened the front door and stepped into the small foyer. On my right was a large room that must have been Grace's office. A writing desk was just behind the window from which she'd spoken to me. The rest of the room was filled with bookcases brimming over with books. Some looked ancient and some brand-new. The room had the lovely smell of dusty pages.

To the left of the foyer must have been a dining room. Or, it would have been. All that was in it, besides a painting of a reclining nude woman that took up most of one wall, was a large rectangular table. On it were scraps of paper, plastic bags, takeout menus, and newspapers, all of which contained bits of scrawled text.

"I am blocked," Grace said. She swept over to the table. She wore a faded blue bathrobe over a completely normal and flattering outfit of a white button-down and black ankle pants. Her hair was swept up into a loose bun held by a bejeweled pin. Gray streaks through the dark brown hair made her look very regal, and her bathrobe almost seemed like a cape. "These are my notes. Some are scraps of dialogue, some are ideas, some are characters, some might be my grocery lists, for God's sake. Some, I've probably used in other books."

I was starting to feel an impending sense of doom but I kept a smile glued to my face. "And you need me to organize them?"

Grace smiled. "Organize them, type them into a readable document, unearth something genius I forgot about. Read it the wrong way so it sounds better than it is, whatever you want." She pushed a creaky laptop in front of me. "Here you go."

She handed me a small USB drive. "Oh and there's this," she said. "My e-mail mailing list. My publisher suggested you organize these and select a service provider, or something, so I can start sending newsletters in advance of my next book. I think it's their nice way of reminding me I don't *have* a next book. I hate technology."

I looked at her skeptically. "But you're on Twitter."

She shrugged. "That's me rattling off one-liners for easy attention," she said. "The rest, I don't get. But start the newsletter. See if one of my fans knows what I should write about next."

She left me with the laptop, which I was pretty sure wheezed when I pressed the power button.

"I'll go make some tea," she said.

So much for my big research aspirations. Looking at the sea of random notes, I was starting to miss the ocean view at Smokey's already.

"Oh, guess I'm out of tea," Grace called from the kitchen. "Before you start, can you run out and get some? And watch out for the neighbor's cat. She has it out for me."

CHAPTER TEN

RYAN TEXTED ME for another date. I was at Grace's when it came through, sifting through papers, and unsticking them from some Chinese hot sauce that had spilled. "Can we go out again? Make sure you don't have other plans."

And I, being of an eternal crush on him, said yes, despite my fear of how awkward and awful things could get if Eliza found out.

After our early morning towel sighting, we'd spent the next few nights texting one another. I'd jumped at every chime from my phone, unfolding myself from my hunched position over the laptop from Grace's. (I'd taken it home and was trying to catch up since she'd spent the first two days of my job just gossiping about her various neighbors' eccentricities, which seemed ironic.) Ryan's texts arrived during his breaks at the restaurant, where he sometimes worked well past midnight.

It was funny, because Matt, my ex, was sending texts at the same time. But the backlog of Matt texts grew steeper as I enjoyed the bounty of missives from Ryan.

Last night, he'd urged me to meet him outside, in the space between our yards, for a quick kiss goodnight. If it hadn't been for my fear of getting caught, the kiss would have been way more than quick. But still, Ryan needed only a few minutes to send me back up to my room understanding what cloud nine meant.

"So when can I see you?" he asked.

"How about tomorrow? This time, I'll plan everything," I told him over the phone. Grace had told me on day two that she hated texting. "It seems like the perfect way for two people to never really say anything to each other. Life should be lived with all five senses, not on screens." So, here I was, watering Grace's plants and listening to Ryan's voice on the line as he uttered a semisurprised, "Okay, if you insist. But I did ask *you* out."

So now I was waiting for him at the marina, where my family had a small motorboat. I saw that Dad had previously been here, because the boat was cleaned and fueled. He must have taken the boat out without us, even though we usually had the first day out as a family. Not that I could really complain, given that I was using it for a secret date with Ryan.

I'd arrived a bit before him and brought a cooler of beer and sandwiches onto the boat. It wasn't nearly as good as what he'd prepared, but I didn't have his years of experience in the kitchen and I couldn't exactly ask Becca.

"The S.S. *Merlin*, nice. I've missed the old girl," I heard Ryan say. We'd named the boat after our eleven-year-old cat, who could never join us on the Cape. Now the poor thing barely left his corner in the sun, and Tea had gotten a friend to watch him while we were gone. I turned from the cooler and couldn't help but stare. Ryan belonged to the water and the beach. He looked so perfect against the backdrop of the bay. The sun even did its part, reflecting off the water and dappling light across his hair. Already, the tousled tips were turning golden.

So when he pulled me up by my hand and kissed me, deep, and his sun-warmed skin touched mine, I wondered for a second if he was really here for me or if he'd made some mistake. If he had, I was going with it. I may have been the tallest of my sisters, but I felt small as I pressed myself against his body. I nestled into his shoulder as he kissed the top of my head. Even though I liked feeling strong, I didn't mind being in his arms.

"I missed you," he told me when we finally pulled away. "You look beautiful, Kate. You against the water is my favorite way to see you."

That he'd echoed my own thoughts about him was strange though nice, but I didn't reveal what I'd been thinking. "I'm sure it's just good light," I said. "You ready?"

"Sure, Captain," Ryan said, planting two soft kisses, one on my jaw and one just below it, as I stood at the helm.

I wasn't the best boat driver but I'd done it enough times to have half a clue. And I knew Ryan and his brothers were always out on the water, so I felt confident he could steer us out of trouble if we needed it. But I really had meant it when I'd said I would take care of everything. I could tell Ryan wasn't used to giving up control on a date, but he let me take the reins and I appreciated it.

We made our way out onto the water, heading away from Morning Beach and farther down the Cape, where the population thinned out. I steered us toward a calm spot in the middle of the water, the sun shining down on us. We were entirely alone.

"There's beer and sandwiches in the cooler," I told Ryan. The gentle current rocked the boat farther away from the shore. "I know it's not up to your gourmet standards, but we can make do, right?"

He fished out two cans of beer and the chicken salad sandwiches I'd painstakingly tried to make look pretty this morning. They now looked a little smushed. But Ryan gratefully took a bite. "This is pretty good," he said. "And I can't write worth a damn, so we're even."

"You don't know I can write, either."

"Eh, sometimes you just know." I tried not to add a layer of meaning to his words as he smiled at me. I sat down next to him. Again, the heat of his skin made me want to press in closer. I kept myself trained in my spot, trying to eat even though my hunger for food was nonexistent.

Taking a long sip of beer, Ryan leaned back, his face in the sun. "So, can I ask you something?" he said.

"Shoot."

He studied me for a second. "The other day, we left in a hurry. And today, we're out in the middle of nowhere." His eyes searched mine, and I couldn't look away from him. I knew what was coming next. "Do you not want people to know about us for some reason? I mean, if it's the thing with Morrison . . ."

"No, no, it's not Morrison." I laughed a little at the absurdity of that. Morrison was nice and cute, just like I'd told Jessica, but anyone who believed I'd choose him over Ryan was slightly nuts. I took a deep breath, trying to figure out how to say this without invoking Eliza. "I guess, I didn't want the world to know about us right away." *Especially when the world knows you and my sister were together summer after summer.*

He didn't reply right away, and I instantly felt like one of those girls who wanted to have a status check before the relationship had a status. And yet, I still blurted out: "Are we real? Like seeing each other?"

Ryan closed the gap between us and kissed me. His hand ran down my side, each of his fingertips making sensation burst beneath the thin cotton of my shirt. "I'm seeing you right now," he said.

"You know what I mean," I said, forcing myself to breathe as his hands traced the outline of my waist. "I just don't want to put this out there and have people interfere. I want to take it slow, to see what's there."

"I understand," Ryan said, planting a featherlight kiss against my jaw. "Slow."

CHAPTER ELEVEN

THERE SHOULD HAVE been a study of new couples in the hours after they decide to "take it slow."

Stage One, I'd think researchers would find, is awkward small talk. For the first hour after our "slowing down" decision, Ryan and I acted like people who'd just met, talking about how beautiful the water was, and how the *Harborville Herald* had reported less visitors were taking tours of the Cape's cranberry bogs this year and what a shame that was. We discussed every lighthouse along the horizon in detail. We probably could have started our own tour company.

Stage Two would be compulsive eating. Ryan and I made our way through everything in the cooler and most of a bag of pretzels. In the moments when the water was its most still and the breeze died down, the sound of us crunching seemed to echo across the ocean. I don't think either of us was that hungry, but eating gave us something to do with our mouths. Kissing when we were dangerously secluded felt like the opposite of slow.

Stage Three would be the realization that, out of food and topics to discuss, the date should end.

It wasn't a bad end, but it felt like we'd hit pause on the momentum we'd been building since the picnic. We both knew we liked each other, and that we were capable of good conversation and our chemistry was beyond obvious. So, this new rule had just served to put an unnatural layer over what came naturally to us. I wanted to kick myself for suggesting that we take the path less traveled, when I really wanted to keep going all the way.

I'd ridden a bike to the marina, but Ryan offered to take me home in his truck. I almost declined but remembered that Eliza had mentioned plans to meet with several caterers and bakeries and how it would take all day. I was tired from a day of sunshine and restraint and thought that a ride home would be nice. Tea and Becca were working, and I knew that even if my dad was home, he probably wouldn't notice me coming in. When he was around, he seldom left the living room couch.

Ryan pulled into his usual spot in front of his house and I smiled to myself, thinking of how many times I'd watched him arrive and that first day back, when he'd seen me in my window. I'd never expected this, to be the one hopping out of his car.

"You're burnt," he said, lightly touching my shoulder, which was, indeed, one of a matching red pair. In my urgency to finish all the pretzels, I must have forgotten to reapply sunblock.

"Oh, I am," I said, enjoying his fingers on my shoulder despite the slight sting.

"I know you'll probably say no, but I honestly have the best stuff for burns. Way better than normal aloe," Ryan said, turning in his seat toward me. "Do you want to come up? Or I could bring it down to you."

"I'll come up," I said, with no hesitation. Ryan had claimed the Landrys' carriage house when he was eighteen, and since then, I'd thought of his room as a mysterious Shangri-la of boyness. To finally have an invitation after all my years of wondering was too enticing to resist.

"Okay, then," he said.

His room was situated above the Landrys' garage, just like mine, but where my space was still obviously filled with my mom's things, Ryan's was all his. It smelled like fresh paint; Ryan must have been painting his room on that first day I'd seen him.

Remembering our picnic conversation, I giggled when I saw there was, in fact, a shelf full of trophies from various Harborville High sports: baseball, basketball, football.

"I thought you said those were backlit," I said, pointing.

"Oh, that's just for my really impressive trophies," Ryan said. "They're hidden behind that bookcase over there. If you pull the correct book, it spins around and you get to see all my glory."

"I'll have to find the right one," I teased, crossing to his bookcase. It was, I saw, brimming with books. He had autobiographies of Julia Child and Anthony Bourdain, some business books, and a half shelf of Stephen King and some thrillers. He also had all of Dave Eggers's books and older classics, ranging from Charles Dickens to J. D. Salinger. Toward the top was an entire shelf of cookbooks. I caught myself petting my favorites, and getting excited that Ryan was a reader.

I also took in the neat way he'd made his bed, and the writing desk with its Mac laptop and a notebook opened to a list of ingredients, along with notations about the farmers markets and which suppliers were the best. The top of his pen was chewed up, which I'd never have expected from calm, easygoing Ryan.

Ryan emerged from the bathroom with a tube of blue gel. "Here it is," he said. "My aunt got it on a cruise and now our whole family swears by it. I order it online."

He squeezed some onto his fingertips and started to reach for my shoulder but pulled back. "Sorry, can I?"

"Yes, please."

He gently touched my shoulder. The gel tingled and the coolness of it provided instant relief. The chilling sensation only served to contrast the heat spreading throughout the rest of my body as Ryan continued to make soft circles on my skin.

Take it slow, I reminded myself even as I felt my body relax. I leaned my head back against his shoulder, my back pressed fully against his chest.

Ryan began to work on my other shoulder, his touch even more featherlight. I inhaled and exhaled, thinking my breaths sounded impatient, and that I'd made a huge mistake putting rules around our physical contact.

So when Ryan dropped the gel onto his bed, I let out a sigh of relief. His right hand went to my waist as his left lifted the hair away from my face. He kissed me along the neck, lightly at first, then with more pressure.

"Is this okay?" he whispered.

"Yes," I said, my voice thick. I leaned my head further to the side, offering him more of me, wanting his lips to be both fixed on my neck and everywhere else all at once.

He turned me toward him, combing his fingers though my hair and down to the small of my back. I tilted my head back as he kissed me, then pulled back, looking at his face as I ran my hands over his chest. I studiously traced along the muscles over his ribs, and the indents of his abdominals, memorizing him by touch. He grabbed me tight, leaving no space for light between our bodies as we pressed into another kiss. For a moment, my legs wobbled beneath me and I thought we were still on the water.

Ryan sat on a faded green love seat under the window. He pulled me on top of him, my legs wrapped around his hips. He ran his palms up my thighs, squeezing my hips and bringing me in even closer. Every nerve ending in my body was shot through with electric imaginings of where this would lead.

My hands tugged at the bottom of his shirt, lifting it over his head. He pulled my tank top up and away from my skin, and then our upper halves were touching. The suction between us made it impossible to pull away, so we didn't, weaving together in an unending kiss. Finally, Ryan pulled back, or I did, not without an effort.

The left side of Ryan's mouth lifted in a smile. "I guess this isn't really taking it slow, huh?"

I laughed. "If it is, then we have our work cut out for us."

Stage Four: completely and utterly ignore all plans to take it slow.

CHAPTER TWELVE

THE BANGING AT the door to the studio came fast and loud. And at the worst possible time, since I was scrambling to get my bag together before heading over to Grace's. I'd barely been able to sleep after yesterday's date with Ryan. I was too distracted. I'd forced myself to get a few more paragraphs of my cartographer story written, and then allowed myself to zone out. Matt had sent me an e-mail with lists of fun things to do in the Bay Area as well as questions about how my summer was going, but I'd had no desire to write him back.

I opened the door to find Eliza standing there, her wedding binder sticking out of the top of her canvas tote bag. My throat filled with dread. There were few things worse than a type A with a binder, except for a type A older sister with a wedding binder.

"Morning, sunshine," Eliza said, looking past me into the studio and making a face at the clothing and books I had scattered around. I thought of Ryan's neat room and how I'd need to clean mine if I ever wanted him to see it.

"Morning," I replied.

"So, I wanted us all to go check out the Chatham Bars Inn for brunch today. Devin was saying we should just splurge on the rehearsal dinner. I think it's too much, but he keeps reminding me that we're saving money by having the wedding and reception right here on the beach. We only get to do this once, you know?" Her tone was excited but her eyes were anxious. "Can you go? In about an hour?"

It was pure Eliza. For all her planning, she often forgot that other people had plans.

I shook my head, spying the bathing suit I'd worn sailing with Ryan on the floor and feeling guilty and anxious even though it gave nothing away. "I would love to, but I have to go to Grace's today," I said. "I'm actually running late."

Eliza walked past me into the studio, running her fingers through a low vase filled with sea glass. "And you can't just tell her something came up and you'll come in late? That it's really important?"

I probably could have done that, given that Grace was so flighty. I'd be lucky if she remembered she'd asked me to come in today at all. But I didn't feel asking "how high" the second Eliza said "jump." Besides, it wasn't like we hadn't been to Chatham Bars Inn before. A few towns over, in the richer part of the Cape, the hotel was famous everywhere for being one of the grandest spots on the water. It would be completely pleasant for a rehearsal dinner, and we didn't need to pay it a visit to know so.

"She's a huge author. It's not like trading shifts at Dale's Dream Cone," I said, referring to Eliza's past summer job, feeling a little bitchy.

Eliza sighed but, like always, didn't crack or break her pleasant game face. Her words, though, were cutting. "Sometimes I wonder why you came to the beach house at all," she said. "I get it, you're not a kid anymore, but you're suddenly too busy for any of us. Doing such important things, I suppose." I could have sworn her eyes went to the bathing suit of guilt.

"I just could have used a few days' notice, is all," I said. "Next time, I'll make sure to go. For whatever."

"Fine," Eliza said, sauntering past me to the door. "Next time I'll make sure to call your assistant so you can pencil us in."

I was trying to translate what looked like a haiku but was clearly one of Grace's grocery lists—detergent apples/paper towels chicken breasts/milk wine mushrooms Chex—when she tapped me on the shoulder.

"Something's off," she said, pulling up a seat at her dining table and leaning in close to inspect my face. "Is this about writing? I told you, pain is part of the process. Weren't you going to bring me pages?"

"Oh yeah," I said, gathering the pages of my cartographer story from my canvas bag. Grace had promised to take a look at them, but the idea made me a little nervous. "It's only half-done."

"Nothing is ever done for a writer. Even after they publish it," Grace said. She folded the pages in half and put them in the pocket of her bathrobe. "But this isn't a writing thing. What's going on? Even your pores look upset."

The last thing Grace probably wanted was an assistant whose drama added to her chaos. "No, I'm okay," I said, waving the shopping list under her nose. "This is for the grocery store, right?"

She squinted at the paper. "Hope so. As a shopping list, it has some artistic merit but as a novel just no reader interest."

I put it in the pile with Grace's other non–book related notes. Even after I processed them, she wanted to save these scraps because people didn't send letters anymore. "At least the world will have my shopping lists," she told me as her reasoning. I'd also seen a letter from Smith College, Grace's alma mater, requesting some of Grace's writerly "artifacts" for the school's archives. When I'd tried to mention it, though, Grace had muttered something about archives being for writers everyone thought was dead, so I hadn't broached the topic again.

I moved on to the next scrap, the only word of which I could make out right away being "pronged."

Grace grabbed it from my hand. "Put that down and tell me what's going on," she said. "What's the point of having a young assistant if I can't live vicariously through you?"

Okay, so maybe she *did* want to add my drama to her chaos. What to tell her? I had plenty on my mind, between not knowing how to proceed with Ryan's and Eliza's annoying behavior this morning. Or, should I have brought up the fact that, though I'd really thought using my mom's studio would inspire me, everything I wrote felt like forced drivel? Well, she'd see that for herself when she read my story.

"It's my sister. She's getting married and dragged us all to the Cape to have her wedding here. We haven't been back since my mom died." The words were spilling out. "And she just seems to assume I'll drop whatever I have going on to make my life revolve around hers."

Grace wasn't looking at me, but at a note written on the label from a can of dog food. She didn't have a dog.

"This is a phone number. Daniel. He had a collie. Loved the dog, hated the guy." She flicked the paper into the useless pile.

"I never had a sister. Not even a sibling, really," Grace continued. "When my mother's brother died, his son came to live with us for a while, but he was older and morose and all my friends got crushes on him, probably because he seemed like someone who would emotionally destroy them." She looked at me now. She had an impish, young face, even though she was in her sixties. Her expression looked like Becca's when she was hiding a secret.

"Your sister might be the one who gets everything, or seems to, but going first is never easy. Oldest children, I think they sometimes do things out of obligation, more than really wanting to. She might want you along for the ride because you have what she doesn't. The freedom to just be."

Grace's words sounded good but, like she'd said, she'd never had siblings. And she didn't know Eliza. I loved my sister but she treated being firstborn like it was a ticket to the first and best of everything.

It had been Eliza who'd gotten the new car on her sweet sixteen, and who'd gone to every prom in a new dress, and who'd had our mom around at least until she got out of high school. I wore the hand-me-down dress, and drove my dad's old car, and had never gotten to excitedly tell my mom when Matt asked me to prom. I wore a blue gown of Eliza's that she'd worn when she got asked to prom as a freshman. Because it was too short, I had to have it hemmed to be a tea-length dress, and because it was too big in the bust, I had to have it taken in. I'd never been that into dresses, but even I knew that it hadn't been the dress of my dreams.

I couldn't quite see the areas where Eliza was being denied her "freedom to just be," as Grace had put it.

My stream of thoughts was interrupted by Grace tapping a pen on the table.

"Now, you're still my assistant, and I would love if Clark's Coffee could deliver us a banana-cream pie and a kale salad. And the next time you tell me a problem, throw in some sex. I like the sex ones."

CHAPTER THIRTEEN

I SPENT THE rest of the week ensconced in Grace's odd notes and talking to Ryan every night. On Wednesday morning, he'd caught me outside before my run and we'd jogged down the beach together. He'd had to go meet a supplier and had headed back to our houses before me, which was a relief, since Eliza was drinking coffee on the porch when I returned from my jog. "I just saw Ryan coming back. Did you bump into him?" she'd asked without any suspicion in her voice, and I just shook my head, relieved.

Thursday night, Ryan and I had snuck out for a short date. We mostly made out in the last row of a movie theater as it played a terrible old horror movie about a possessed pet shop. As we walked out, it started to pour, and we spent several hours at a diner near the theater, where we'd come up with all the bad sequel possibilities, a surprisingly easy and fun task given how little of the movie we'd seen. We weren't exactly taking it slow, but because Ryan worked so many nights and I spent days at Grace's, we were managing better than our time in Ryan's room would have led me to believe possible.

Friday night, with Ryan at work, I was ready to just crash. I'd just composed a text to Ryan to let him know I was going to bed early and to see if he wanted to join me for a run in the morning.

But, best-laid plans and all, I wasn't going to get my wish. Tea ambushed me just before I pushed send, as I was putting away dishes in the kitchen from dinner. "Hey, I was just talking to Pete," she said, gesturing to the Landry house. She and Becca had been floating between our two houses all summer, just like it had used to be. I knew part of the difference for Eliza and I was that we were older now, and not just that our mom was gone, but I was still glad that my younger sisters were still enjoying that particular perk of the beach house. "We're all going to the restaurant after closing. Eliza and Devin, too. Get ready. We're leaving in ten minutes."

I couldn't say no, and not only because my littlest sister was asking. For one, not going when I clearly had nothing to do would look weird. And joining in would finally get Eliza off my back about spending time with everyone. The side benefit, as I saw it, was that—as long as Ryan kept his promise to keep us under wraps—it would be a way to show Eliza and everyone else that there was nothing going on between us. While part of me wanted to tell the world that I'd been kissing Ryan Landry for the better part of the summer, part of me was scared of what might happen if everyone knew.

If Eliza was still mad about my not calling off work for her impromptu brunch, she wasn't letting on tonight. If anything, she was positively giddy. I'm sure she was grateful for a wedding-planning diversion, and for her and Devin to have a chance to spend a minute together where they weren't discussing flower arrangements. I'd heard them arguing about hydrangeas versus peonies earlier. Devin had left work early and flown down to be able to spend the weekend with Eliza, but even he wanted to enjoy himself, I was sure. "This will be so much fun, you guys. Tea and Becca, you were too young the last time we were here, but we always had the *best* parties at Landrys' after closing." It was funny, because I didn't remember them that way at all. Most of the Landry parties were awkward affairs where Jessica and I played tabletop Pac-Man while Eliza, Ryan, and the older kids drank. But this group sounded smaller, and at least I knew I wouldn't have to watch Eliza and Ryan make out. That didn't help the fact that *I* would want to make out with him, but still . . .

The CLOSED sign was illuminated on the door when we got there, but we could hear the music from outside. When we stepped through the door, the bus boys whooped loudly and gave Becca and Tea high fives. I guessed they were becoming ingratiated with the staff after all their weeks at work. Some of the younger staff was already dancing to the one Top 40 radio station in Harborville. Maybe not everyone was as awkward as Jessica and I had once been. As I spotted Jessica across the kitchen, I saw that we had a chance to prove that times had changed.

Jessica yelled, "Hey, Kate, wanna play some Pac-Man?" She and Morrison were hanging out near the machine, drinking brimming glasses of beer. Behind them at the bar was Ryan. He smiled nicely at me, sending a shiver up my spine, but he didn't betray anything. "What are you drinking, Kate?" he asked. "Beer, or you want to try one of my signature cocktails?"

Morrison rolled his eyes. "Harborville doesn't need a bunch of fruity, weird mixologists screwing up a good thing. This is a man's place."

"Yeah, and men drink liquor, too, you Miller Lite pansy," Ryan joked. He was already whipping something up, muddling a cucumber into clear liquid. "This is no big deal, just a gin and tonic with cucumber instead of lime." He handed me the glass. "But it's good."

Eliza dragged Devin to the bar. "Ooh, that sounds good. Two more, right, Dev?"

Her fiancé grinned. "Sure, why not? I don't have work tomorrow. For real this time."

"I know," Eliza said, nuzzling into him. "Lucky me. I even booked us a room for tomorrow night at the Chatham Bars Inn."

"Oh, really?" Devin said with a smirk at Eliza's suggestive tone. "How's the job going, Kate?" He turned to me, looking eager to change the subject in front of all these people.

"She's devoted," Eliza said. "She even ditched the best brunch on the Cape because she had to be at Grace's."

"Well, it is a pretty big deal to be working for a huge author," Devin said. "It's probably a good idea not to take it too lightly."

"The job is interesting," I said, giving Devin a grateful look. He and I would probably never have a lot in common, but I appreciated that he didn't immediately take Eliza's side on everything. She needed that. "Tell your colleagues' book club that she's more eccentric than they'd probably ever imagined."

"I will," Devin said. "I'll need details."

"For sure," I said, trying to imagine how I'd explain Grace's dining room table. "But another time."

Eliza rolled her eyes, and glanced across the kitchen toward our sisters. "We can't let Becca and Tea get wasted. I never let you get hammered when we were younger."

"Might be too late for Becca," I said, pointing to where she and Garrett were taking shots from an old-looking bottle of peach schnapps. "But Tea is too responsible. And we're walking." Tea was talking animatedly to some of the bus boys, all of whom obviously had crushes on her. Of course, Tea would never even guess.

"Let her enjoy her fan club."

"Eh, guess you're right." Eliza looked at Ryan. "Remember how I would always be worried about Kate getting hit on?"

Ryan's gaze landed meaningfully on my face. I'd never known they even talked about me when they were dating. "I do remember. It was no easy task intimidating the busboys so that they'd leave her alone." I felt myself blush.

Before I had a chance to say anything in reply, Devin—clearly not jealous of Eliza's history with Ryan—asked Ryan a question about his other cocktail ideas. Morrison sidled up next to me and tickled my waist. I yelped a little.

"Hey, Kate, what's shakin'?" He was already a little drunk. "So you're not at Smokey's anymore?"

I noticed that Ryan's eyes shifted our way, but he kept up his conversation with Devin. "No, I got a job assisting Grace Campbell, the writer. She lives here part of the year," I said, hoping not to have to go into detail. While I'd promised Devin some dirt, details about the job would spoil an otherwise positive-sounding experience. And I *did* like working for Grace, even if I wasn't sure it was making me a better writer.

"Wow, that's really impressive," Morrison said. "Writers amaze me. I mean, I did pretty well in high school English but to write a whole book? That's crazy. Is that what you'd study at Berkeley, writing?"

I smirked. "I thought I told you, beer pong and quarters."

Morrison slapped his forehead. "Oh, how could I forget?"

"What about you? What are you up to these days?"

"Sort of like Ryan, I'm doing some work on the family business," he said. The Davies family ran several bed-and-breakfasts on the Cape. "Like, I can't believe we don't even have a website or listings online."

"So it's all word of mouth?"

"Pretty much," Morrison said. "It's fine in the busy season but it's not enough to bring people here in the fall. Maybe once I get the website going, you could take a look, check my grammar. I'll buy you lunch."

It was a thinly veiled excuse for a date, and one I could have seen coming. I hated that my not being public with Ryan meant I had to awkwardly rebuff his best friend, but it was my own fault. "I'll be happy to review it. You don't even have to buy me lunch."

Morrison's smile drooped at the corners and I could tell he was about to come back with another offer for something else. I was saved, though, when Becca and Garrett ran up to him, pulling him away. "You have to settle a bet," Becca told him. "Garrett claims that he and his friends never played a game where they undid girls' string bikini tops on the beach, but I know for a fact he has."

I did, too, and actually remembered Mrs. Landry banning Garrett from a week of beach time for his stunts. But I kept my mouth shut as Becca dragged Morrison by the arm.

Morrison allowed himself to be pulled away just as Ryan emerged from behind the bar with another drink for me.

"Here, try this," he said. "It's a St-Germain martini with a touch of lavender liquor in it."

I raised my existing glass. "But I'm not done with this one. Are you trying to get me drunk?"

"Nah, you're plenty of fun sober. I just wanted to talk to you," he said, looking around stealthily like we were in a spy movie. "Jessica was telling someone that you'll never date Morrison because you're not over your ex. Is that . . . is that maybe the real reason you want to take things slow?"

His expression was so anxious that it was adorable. I thought of Matt and the fact that answering his texts had started to feel more obligatory than fun. It wasn't a vote against him so much as it was a vote for Ryan.

I shifted my gaze toward Eliza but she and Devin were wrapped up in a conversation that sounded like it was about a drink menu.

"No, that's been over a while," I told him, touching his arm just under the cuff of his shirt. I did it for only a split second so that no one could see. He smiled instantly, making me happy that I'd taken the chance. "I just didn't want to tell her the real reason I'm not interested in Morrison. I like this and I don't want to subject it to the world until we're ready."

"Yeah, you've said that already." Ryan flinched away from me ever so slightly. "I just wonder why I feel ready and you don't."

I wanted to tell Ryan about what Eliza had said, so he'd understand my reasons for wanting to keep us a secret. But wouldn't that sound so girly and weird to him? "It's not that I don't," I said, noticing with a skinning feeling how closed-off his expression had become. "It's just more complicated than I can really explain right now."

I tried to imagine what Eliza would do in this situation. Would she allow me to impose a rule like hers, or would she just do what she wanted? Probably the latter, but that didn't mean she would be any happier about me dating her ex.

"I'd better get back to the bar," Ryan said, turning away from me.

"Wait," I said, stopping myself from reaching for his arm. Now I was the one looking around like we were on the run. "I have a question for you."

He must have heard the longing in my voice, or he too forgiving, because he came back to my side, a little smile on his face. "Yeah?"

"I wanted to know . . ." I lingered over the next words, trying to choose them carefully. "Are Becca and Tea working tomorrow night?" On Saturdays the restaurant stayed open later because the bar business was so good.

"Do you want them to be?" Ryan raised one eyebrow, like he knew where I was going with this.

I nodded, feeling a sly smile tug my own lips upward.

"If they're not, I can schedule them. For doubles." His smile widened. "Why do you ask?"

"My dad's on a business trip, and Eliza and Devin are staying at the Chatham Bars Inn for the night." I paused, watching my full meaning as Ryan let it sink in. "Maybe you should come over."

Now he glanced around and furtively traced a line down my arm with the backs of his fingers. That I knew his touch wouldn't go any further tonight made me die a little inside.

"I'm all yours."

CHAPTER FOURTEEN

DEVIN WALKED OUT of the house with Eliza's neatly packed overnight bag slung over his shoulder. "Sure you're okay here alone tonight?"

Even though I was eighteen, I had to admit it was a little nice to have someone acting like my big brother. Devin's protectiveness and interest in my life sort of picked up where my dad had left off. It wasn't that my dad didn't care; he just wasn't always present, even when he was here. Devin was. I understood why Eliza wanted to marry someone so stable.

"Yeah, don't worry about me," I said. "Just going to enjoy having the house to myself. Watch some bad reality TV."

"Well, call us if you need anything," he said. "Becca and Tea should have the number, too. Though, I guess the Landrys are right next door."

His word choice nearly made me blush. There was one Landry I wanted. Wanted very, very much.

"Oh yeah, they're great neighbors," I said, feeling a little guilty I hadn't made time to see Mr. and Mrs. Landry yet. Eliza had told me I'd missed a drop-by from them, too. It had been a night I was out with Ryan. Now, talking about them effusively, I tried to look anywhere but in the direction of Ryan's carriage house. I stared at the wooden GONE TO THE BEACH sign that hung just beneath the Landrys' porch light and pointed in the direction of Pleasant Street Beach. "You don't have to worry about me."

Eliza finally emerged, carrying nothing but her small clutch and a beach tote, which she handed to Devin. She sighed like she'd just done hard work. "Do you really think Dad had a business trip?" I asked Eliza. It was seeing her in the doorway, looking so much like my mom, that made me ask.

"Why would he lie?" Eliza asked. "I think that he's had a lot to do since his firm bought that start-up."

I shrugged. "I don't know. He's just so quiet all the time," I said. Before my mom, my dad used to have a summer policy of no business trips. He said life was too short to spend his beach days working. Now he seemed to look forward to work as a way to escape the beach. "I thought maybe being back here was just too much for him."

Eliza put her arm around my shoulder. "It's hard for all of us," she said. "But don't let yourself get too worried. Everything will be fine. Be good tonight. No boys." She winked, and a thread of guilt wrapped around my chest.

It wasn't boys, plural, that were the problem, just one in particular.

Ryan showed up not long after I sent him my text. I had gone inside the house to straighten up a bit, but the doorbell rang before I even finished clearing off Becca's half-empty soda cans from the kitchen counter. She was a bigger slob than me.

I opened the door, surprised to see Ryan looking actually . . .
nervous. He had a teddy bear in one hand and looked at a loss for
what to do with his other hand.

"Hey," he said, handing me the bear. A crooked smile filled
his face as he watched me take the bear and turn it over in my
hands. It was a soft brown bear in a tiny yellow Cape Cod T-shirt.

"I know it's weird, but I was on the boardwalk at lunch looking at flowers and I had this urge to win you a bear," he said. "If
you think it's totally cheesy, I'll bury it in my backyard or something."

I looked down at the bear and had a memory of being at the
boardwalk with Ryan and Eliza. Eliza would beg Ryan to win her
things but she only wanted the biggest, best prizes. Ryan would
balk and say, "No one ever gets the giant bear. It's rigged. What
about the little one?" She'd turn up her nose at the lesser prize
and say something like, "If I'm not worth going for the best, then
why bother?" Ryan would usually shrug hopelessly at me and say
something like, "If everyone knew what they wanted the way
Eliza did, the world would be a simpler place." I'd laughed at how
perfectly this summed up my sister. And secretly thought that I'd
have loved to have a bear won in my honor, no matter the size.

I squeezed the bear. "I love it," I said. I really did. I imagined
Ryan thinking about me on his lunch break. Even if he'd brought
back a pair of the giant novelty light-up sunglasses you won as a
consolation prize, I would have felt special and flattered.

"You do?" Ryan's grin straightened out. "That's good. It took
me, like, twenty bucks to win at the milk jug toss. Not that I'm
counting, but I think the guy running the booth thought I was
crazy. Or that I really like teddy bears."

"Well, there's nothing wrong with a grown man liking teddy bears," I said, playing with the hem of my bear's T-shirt.

Ryan laughed appreciatively. "I know, it was hard for me to give that one up," he said. A beat of silence passed between us. He leaned in to give me a kiss, but his lips hit my face somewhere between my cheek and the corner of my mouth. "Sorry."

"It's okay." I grinned a little at his sudden fumbling. Ryan Landry, Mr. At-Ease Anywhere, seemed a little anxious. "Why don't you come in?"

The whole thing felt oddly formal at first, with Ryan and me standing in the doorway, like I was a Realtor showing him the house. "I remember this." He walked over to the sea-glass mosaic. "Your mom had us all looking for sea glass every time we went to the beach."

"I think I found the most," I said, without even thinking.

"Competitive much?" Ryan grinned.

I shrugged. I was. "Maybe."

"Your mom was always so much fun. I remember those big sleepovers we had in this room, when she'd clear out all the furniture so we had a lot of space," Ryan said, walking into the living area. "We'd bug my mom to do the same thing for our sleepovers and she'd always tell us that it wouldn't be special if anyone but Mrs. Sommers did it."

I laughed. "Well, my mom would go nuts when we'd complain she wasn't as good a cook as your mom."

"Yeah, but your dad made those killer chocolate-chip pancakes," Ryan said. "I wish I knew how to master those."

"I think you just need Bisquick and some Nestlé chocolate chips," I said, looking toward the kitchen as if we might see an old

version of my father there, happily flipping pancakes and singing a Beatles song. He no longer played his role of short-order
cook on the weekends. In fact, it was only just now that I realized
Becca's newfound love of being at the stove had probably come
from my dad.

"I'll have to try that," Ryan said. He looked around the empty
house, then back at me. "So, are we really all alone here?" A sly
grin lifted the corner of his mouth and made a dimple there.

I nodded. "It's just us until Becca and Tea get off work. Unless
one of them gets fired tonight," I said.

"I put in place a strict do-not-fire rule on them for the evening," Ryan said, drawing closer and putting his arms around
me. He leaned in and kissed me, the pressure starting soft and
deepening. He opened my lips with his tongue and soon we were
making our way to the couch, toppling onto the cushions. He
was over me, kissing my neck and down the V of my T-shirt. I
ran my hands up the back of his shirt, willing him to get closer.

His fingers ran down my sides and up and under my clothes.
He traced a line across the low waist of my shorts, and then put
his warm palm against my stomach, moving his hand slowly up
to my chest.

We were breathing deeply, and the pace of our breaths
matched. I started to imagine one of my sisters coming home
because she'd gotten sick at work or something, or Eliza having
forgotten some wedding-planning necessity and returning to
retrieve it. As Ryan kissed along the back of my neck, I desperately wanted more privacy.

"Let's go to my room," I said in his ear, kissing the skin just
below his earlobe. He groaned and pulled away.

"Are you sure?" I could tell from his tone that he understood what the invitation meant.

"Yes," I said, to all the meanings in his question.

He stood up and I took him by the hand. "I took over the studio," I said, to explain why we weren't going to my old room. "We'll be totally alone for the rest of the night."

Ryan pulled me to him for another deep kiss. "That'll be nice," he said, and entwined his fingers with mine. I led him outside.

The stairs up to my room felt interminable, like some force was adding more steps with each one we climbed. It wasn't that they were tiring; it was the fact that now that I'd invited Ryan to my room, I realized how desperate I was to have him there.

When we finally reached the top, we stood there in the door of the studio, the awkward Realtor feeling returning. I didn't know how to get us back to the heat we felt in the main house. Not that I wasn't still feeling a needy clanging in my entire body, but the change of venue had imposed an intermission on our make-out session. I didn't know if I should just jump right back in.

"So, this is where you write?" Ryan said, stepping into the room and looking at some of the bowls of shells and sea glass with more interest than he probably felt.

"Where I *try* to write," I corrected. The futon was such a prominent focal point in the room and I felt like its emptiness beckoned to us.

Ryan turned to face me. "It *is* nice and private. Finally, I get where you're going with that theme," he joked.

I didn't respond. Not with words, anyway. He was perfect,

from head to foot, and I wanted him. So, with the hem of his shirt, I pulled him to me, and put my lips on his.

The energy ricocheted between us, and our more tentative touches grew intense. Ryan slid his fingers inside my shirt, softly drawing along the curve of my waist upward. As he traced beneath the elastic of my bra, I reached back and undid the clasp for him. His palms grazed my sides as he ran his fingertips over my breasts, his touches so featherlight that I felt every nerve lighting up inside of me. I lifted his shirt, taking my time to touch every lean ridge of muscle and to kiss the planes of his chest. He pulled my shirt over my head, folding me into his arms.

He turned me around so that my back was to his chest. He pushed my hair to the side, kissing along my neck and shoulder. His fingertips dipped beneath the waistband of my shorts, running down the front of my thighs and back up. A tremor pulsed through my legs and I turned back toward Ryan, kissing along his neck and his chin as my chest pressed against his. I slowly ran my fingers down his chest and found the button to his shorts.

Stepping out of the last of our clothes, we made our way to the futon, falling onto it beside each other with total bare-skin contact. For some reason, Newton's laws of motion came into my head: *For every action, there is an equal and opposite reaction.* It applied right now. No touch went unnoticed or without a response. Things had been nice with Matt, but with Ryan, everything was an event.

Ryan trailed kisses across my collarbone, then down my chest. He entwined his fingers with mine and looked at me seriously, as moonlight filtered through the window.

"Kate, I'm falling for you."

What was the equal and opposite reaction to that? "I'm falling for you, too."

I pulled Ryan even closer to me and closed my eyes as I felt all of him for the first time.

CHAPTER FIFTEEN

RYAN LANDRY WAS in my bed. Ryan Landry, unclothed and sleeping with the faintest hint of a smile on his face, was in my bed, the morning after he'd told me he was falling for me.

I lay next to him, recalling the highlights of the night before. I remembered how one summer Jessica had told me she never went for perfect-looking guys, because they were never as good in bed as their looks. (This revelation was untested by Jessica because she was a virgin at the time, but it was a very Jessica thing to say.) And, maybe it was true in some cases, but it definitely did not apply to Ryan Landry. Not the first time, or the second time. He knew what he was doing. He really, really did.

Happily ensconced in the covers, and warm beneath Ryan's arm, I couldn't sleep. I knew I had to wake him soon, before the day really got going and my sisters woke up and discovered him. Fortunately, I was the earliest riser of us.

I heard a car pull into the driveway beneath us. Then, though muffled, I heard Eliza say to Devin, "I really think the ceremony should be simple, and the reception can be minimalist, too. We're planning this quickly and beach weddings should never be over-the-top. But the rehearsal dinner will be great at the Inn."

Devin mumbled an annoyed ascent. Poor guy. I'm sure he'd imagined he was heading for a romantic rendezvous, not a wedding-planning overnighter.

"Well, I'm doing all the work. I'm not trying to take over but we don't have much time, unless we want to wait for next summer, and who knows if we'll be at the house then?"

What were they doing back already? And why was Eliza worried about not being at the house? Just because I'd be at college didn't mean that I wouldn't come home for the summer. But I didn't have time to worry about that right now. I needed to get Ryan out of here.

"Um, Ryan . . ." I shook him gently, already hating what I was about to do.

"Hmm . . ." His sleep smile spread into a slow, wide grin across his face. "Good morning." He propped himself up on one arm and pulled me closer for a kiss. His fingers brushed my face.

"I don't want you to leave, but you have to leave," I said, loathing the abrupt clip of my words.

"What?" He sat up in the bed, looking like he'd just felt an earthquake.

"Eliza's back already. I heard her and Devin come in. When they go in the house, you have to sneak down the stairs and cut through the backyard to your house, okay?" I explained in my most this-is-just-the-fun-of-dating tone.

His grin immediately disappeared. "Are you for real?" The hurt and anger in his voice hit me right in the chest, but I was relieved that he pulled on his shirt and grabbed his pants from the floor.

I shrugged, and pulled my open hoodie tighter around me, suddenly self-conscious to be standing in front of Ryan in my underwear.

"We talked about this," I said, still listening for more signs that Eliza was outside. Or worse, might pay me a visit. "I just thought we were taking it slow, and waiting to tell people."

Ryan fumbled with his belt as he looked, it felt, right through me. "Oh, how dumb of me to assume that *sleeping together* meant we were no longer taking it slow."

He looked so hurt that I wanted to take it back. Still, Eliza's many possible and extreme reactions were seared into my brain. Out of all the ways for her to find out, seeing us emerge from the studio together was the worst. We couldn't just debut like some normal couple. And now that things had been going on for so long, I would need to prep my sister for the news, if I ever told her at all. Plus, I still didn't understand why our thing couldn't stay just ours for a little while longer.

"It's just, I'm not ready to tell people. I don't want this ruined. And then there's the wedding and college is coming and summer ends. . . ." I trailed off, not really knowing what I was getting at.

"So is that what you're really saying, that this is just a summer thing?" Ryan asked. He didn't sound angry, exactly, but more like he was articulating something he'd been thinking for a while.

"No, it's just, I don't know. I don't know what we are, exactly," I said. "I know I like you and I know I'm glad you like me."

"Yeah, I do," Ryan said, but it was more matter of fact than anything.

"And you are my sister's ex," I blurted, hoping this explained things.

Ryan shook his head. "We were kids. And your sister is getting married," he said. "If this thing between us really mattered to you, you'd just tell her and see what happens."

"It does matter to me," I said. "It's just—it's complicated."

Ryan turned away from me and looked out the window. "I don't see anyone down there. Now's probably a good time for me to sneak out," he said. "Should I move fast, or slow?"

"Ryan . . ." I trailed off guiltily.

"It's fine," he said, not sounding that way at all. He kissed me once, on the cheek, leaving me a little cold. "I'll call you."

He disappeared down the steps without making a sound. Like he'd never been here at all.

I spent the next hour polishing my cartographer story with all the willpower I had in me. I desperately needed a distraction. I hadn't gotten notes from Grace on the version I'd given her, but I figured some extra time with it now couldn't hurt. I'd given my cartographer an island to map but its borders kept shifting, making it hard for her to figure out how to chart it. Even though I'd begun the story thinking it was total fiction, I was starting to feel like I was writing something I knew.

I had no idea how to define the borders and boundaries of my life. When had the summer become so complicated? It wasn't supposed to be.

Sinking onto the futon, I lay facedown on the pillows. I could still smell Ryan on the sheets and I wished he was still here. I thought of his "I'll call you" and wondered if there was any way he actually would. Even though I couldn't imagine him just cutting things off, I also couldn't shake the chilliness of his exit.

I picked up the bear he'd given me, turning it over in my hands. Why didn't he understand what a big deal it was to tell the world? Even without the threat of Eliza's anger, there were still so many other intrusions we'd have to deal with. Our families had been friends forever and since Ryan and I already had history, I just imagined more weight being thrown onto our emerging relationship than maybe we needed. I was going across the country for school. The summer wasn't forever. Why did it matter if this was just ours?

But my excuses felt hollow, even to me. And outside of thinking I shouldn't be dating my sister's ex, I was running out of reasons that didn't sound empty. Why *couldn't* I tell Eliza? Was I afraid of her anger, or was I more afraid she'd convince me that I'd never mean as much to Ryan as she did?

It was yet more uncharted territory.

Feeling antsy, I made my way to the main house. The scent of bacon, pancakes, and eggs wafted from the kitchen and I realized how hungry I was. I'd barely eaten the night before because I'd been filled with so much anticipation.

Becca was at the stove, while Tea, Eliza, and Devin sat in mismatched bar stools along the counter. My mom and dad never argued about furniture at the beach house, choosing instead to just mix and match things they liked, so next to a linear modern stool with sunny yellow upholstery was an old-fashioned red Naugahyde one. Tea, twisting on a high-backed cherry wood stool with brown leather cushions, was flipping through some pictures on her iPad. Eliza had her wedding binder open on the silver mosaic countertop. A deep stress crease bisected the spot between her eyebrows. Devin was next to her, idly scrolling the news on his iPhone.

"Do you want me to make you a plate?" Becca asked, smiling as wide as Alonzo, the Blueberry Man, when she saw me. At least someone was glad to see me. And I didn't get the sense that she suspected anything about Ryan. No one seemed to. Ryan would probably have been annoyed at how relieved that made me. *I* was a little annoyed at how relieved it made me.

"Yes, please," I said, uttering a "good morning" to Tea, Eliza, and Devin. Tea returned a chipper greeting, but Eliza and Devin just mumbled theirs. Apparently, neither of them had had a great night away. And my night had been great, until they'd shown up early.

I poured myself some coffee into a souvenir mug from the Berry Bog, where we'd gone on a tour of a cranberry farm, and thought about Ryan's and my awkward conversation about the lack of cranberry farm tourists. What if I'd just made everything about *us* a memory? The front door clattered open and the familiar cadence of my father's footfalls carried into the kitchen.

"Dad?" Eliza stood up, tilting her head to one side. "Everything okay? What happened to the business trip?"

My father shrugged. "There were flight delays and I didn't want to be at an airport all weekend, so I rescheduled. I thought my girls might be around." His sudden reappearance brought back a sudden memory.

Sunday morning. I was fifteen. I wanted nothing more than to go biking into town with Jessica, but my dad was holding us hostage, insisting he cook breakfast for each of us. "My girls need to eat," he said, steering me to a chair. "I've got chocolate-chip pancakes for Eliza. French toast for Becca. Cheese omelet for Tea. What about you, Katie? Chocolate-chip pancakes, just like your big sister?" They were my favorite, always had been, even if I was trying not to do everything just like Eliza anymore. I shook my head. "Cereal's fine." My dad waved his spatula at me in a joking accusation. "Trying to get out of family breakfast so you can do teen things, huh?" I rolled my eyes at his cheesiness. "Mom's not here, either," I pointed out. My mom had been in her studio, working, since dawn. "She will be when she knows I'm making banana French toast for her." My sisters and I all lifted our hands in faux surrender. "I'm not going to get her," Eliza said. None of us wanted to. When Mom was really into her work, she could get crabby when something broke her spell. "Nope, I will," my dad said, handing the spatula to Becca. "Man the stove. And no one let Katie leave 'til she's eaten." He disappeared out the door and was gone several minutes.

"Mom is going to kill him," Tea said, wide-eyed.

"What do you mean? He's probably already dead," Becca replied.

But a minute later, the front door swung open, hitting the wall. My dad carried my mom into the kitchen, her tan legs draped over his arms. She was fighting him but not really. "Ted, I was painting!" As he set her down at the kitchen counter, she shot him a dirty look but it quickly unraveled into a huge grin. "I want extra bananas," she'd said.

It made my heart ache for those lost summer mornings, and I wondered if my sisters had the same memories. For as nonchalant as Eliza had been when I'd asked her about dad last night, and whether he was okay, she looked positively elated to see him now—and maybe a little relieved. She *had* been worried about him. Sometimes I didn't understand why she felt she had to absorb so much instead of just telling the rest of us.

"Becca, can you make Dad a plate, too, please?" she asked, leading him to the kitchen table. It was covered in a decoupage of old Cape Cod postcards. When my parents were first married, they'd found the table beneath at the curb and decided to salvage it by turning it into an art project. I'd never given it much thought before but, with my mom gone, I now regarded it as a precious heirloom.

My dad ran his fingers over a few of the postcards, tracing around their borders. There were old pictures of the Cape, and some with women and men in crazy modest old-fashioned bathing suits. But he wasn't really looking at any of them.

Tea stood up and clapped her hands together once. "So, since we're all here, I wanted to bring something up." She sounded like a miniature CEO, even if she was wearing pajamas with roller-skating cookies on them.

Eliza shut the wedding binder with what seemed like relief and Devin put down his phone. Even my dad looked up from the table. Tea really did know how to work the room.

Tea held up the iPad and scrolled through some of the photos. They were of Mom's paintings. "So, I was thinking how we have so much of Mom's artwork upstairs and even if we all take our favorites, there's so much more at home and in our rooms and everywhere," she began. "But . . . Landrys' has two big banquet rooms that really have no personality and Mom always liked to share her artwork. Mr. Landry said he'd love to outfit the rooms with Mom's pieces and he'll make a big donation to a charity in return. I thought something to help kids. Mom would like that."

"That's a great idea, sweetie," Eliza said, and for a split second, I caught her exchange a meaningful look with my dad.

"Yes, good thinking," he added. It was almost too easy. He didn't even flinch. And what did the look between him and Eliza mean?

I caught Becca's eye over the counter. She'd seen it, too, I could tell.

Tea hadn't, though. "Great, I'll start on it and run everything by you guys first."

She happily buzzed up the stairs, forgetting to eat her breakfast.

CHAPTER SIXTEEN

IT STARTED TO rain after breakfast. Not a light summer rain, either, but a massive downpour that felt symbolic, a signal that any shot I'd had with Ryan was washed out to sea. I knew that was some pretty lackluster symbolism. But with my mind so focused on how I'd killed my relationship, I wasn't coming up with high-quality anything. Wallowing was, it turned out, not a great creativity booster for me.

My sisters and Devin decided to go to the movies, but I begged off, saying I had some work to do. The truth was that it was the movie I'd already seen with Ryan. My dad turned down the offer, too, and flipped on a baseball game. "See, it's not raining everywhere," he said as the Orioles took the field. It was what he always used to mention on rainy days, and it was comforting to hear him say it again.

We enjoyed an easy silence, drinking iced tea and watching the game like it really mattered to us, even though we were Mets fans. If I let myself just listen to the announcer's voice and the rain behind it, I could almost believe things were back to the way they used to be. If I walked up to the studio, my mom would be painting with the frenzy that a good rainstorm stirred up in her. But then my glance would drift out our back door and toward the Landrys' backyard, and I remembered that we were long past those days.

After a few innings, Dad looked sideways at me and said, "Everything okay, Katie?"

The rain was beating out a thumping rhythm on the windows. I bit my lip and said, "No, not really."

"What is it?" It was the first time I could remember my dad asking what was going on with me.

"Well, I'm seeing someone. . . ." I started hesitantly. I'd never talked to my dad about guy issues before.

He smiled, one of soft acceptance. "You're eighteen. I know you date," my dad said, urging me to continue.

"Well, the big issue is, I wanted to keep the relationship just between us—there are reasons—but he wants to be more . . . official," I said. *And Eliza might hate me if that happens.* But I didn't say that, knowing that, beneath the surface, there were more reasons that had more to do with me than Eliza.

"You can't push things. You need to go at your own pace," he said. He reached out and patted my shoulder. "Not everyone follows the same timeline for these things."

He was talking to himself as much as to me, I knew. Over the last three years, he'd been urged, by family, friends, and neighbors "to get back out there," and he didn't want to. In fact, Ryan had told me that he'd overheard his parents offering to set up my father and he'd reacted poorly. Mrs. Landry was worried that my dad was mad at her, a fact that made me sad. It explained why my father was watching the game with me and not Mr. Landry.

"Thanks, Dad," I said. If it had been my mom, she would have probed until she knew all the details. Then she would have given me an answer that was either as layered as one of her oil paintings or as black and white as one of her charcoals. My dad's help was neither nuanced nor succinct, but it was nice that he was trying. It was progress. Ironically, I knew the person who would give the best advice was Eliza—when I'd asked, she'd guided me through some of the few arguments I'd had with Matt.

I spent the rest of that day and the next just hoping I could get Ryan to talk to me. He sent a few texts to say hello and ask how I was. I sent effusive, cheery replies hinting at getting together. In one, I even signed off with a series of *x*'s and *o*'s, feeling their paltriness even as I typed them. I couldn't bring myself to ask any bigger questions over text, and I figured that Grace was right—talking was better. But I watched and waited for Ryan's truck to be around, and it never showed up . . . not after Grace's on Monday, and not when I peeked out my window at midnight.

Tuesday morning, after a poor night's sleep, I woke up fuzzy. Embarrassingly, I was clutching my bear tightly to my chest, as if someone was going to steal it in the night. I didn't want it to become a souvenir of that one time I slept with Ryan Landry, but I didn't want to get rid of it, either. I wanted us to be real. If I hadn't already lost him, it was time to make things official. And that started with telling Eliza.

Standing in front of the narrow mirror that leaned against one wall, I thought about what I was going to say to my sister and what she would say to me. Surely, she'd start with the fact that sisters didn't date sisters' exes. "But don't you think," I started, rearranging pieces of my dark hair around my face in what I hoped looked sophisticated. "Don't you think this is a lot different than if I dated, say, Devin? You and Ryan happened years ago, and you were basically kids." I looked at my Coolidge High Cross Country T-shirt and cutoffs and decided that I also needed a more mature outfit if I was going to say Eliza was a kid at eighteen but I was not. And mascara.

I put on a white sleeveless blouse and a pair of gray-and-orange-striped shorts from J. Crew, rehearsing the whole time. "I know you had Ryan first but it's unfair to declare him off-limits because of that. We've been dating awhile and we're really good together," I said. A wave of sadness came over me, as I thought about how we *were* really good together. I didn't like thinking that in the past tense.

With all of my arguments and rationales stacked up in my mind, I headed down the stairs to find Eliza.

She was in the kitchen, sitting at the table with my dad. A scribbled-in notebook was in front of her, her wedding binder closed at her elbow.

They didn't see me come in, and I heard Eliza say, "I'll help you with it." She patted my dad's hand. "It will be hard, but it will be okay. Right now, just take care of yourself. Try to spend some time at the beach, or on the boat. Or why not with the Landrys?"

"I know all that's good for me. It's just, doing those things takes more energy than you'd think," he said, a sigh deflating him around the shoulders. His hair was still dark, but he looked so much older than I'd ever remembered him being.

"I know, Dad," Eliza said. She looked woefully at her wedding binder, then back at my father. I got mad at her sometimes, but when I was being honest with myself, I knew she was the one my dad leaned on the most. Sometimes, it meant she took him on so the rest of us didn't have to, and she never complained about it.

Eliza looked up and saw me standing in the doorway. "Kate," she said, surprised. "You look so nice. Those shorts are cute." Her tone was chipper and obviously a cue to my dad to perk up for my benefit.

"Katie, come sit with us," my dad offered, patting a chair. He smiled, but whatever he'd been upset about was still bothering him. I could tell by the tone of his voice. "Are you feeling better?"

Even by the way he offered the seat, I could tell he wanted to be alone for a while. Besides, my speech to Eliza was branded in my mind, and I wanted to have our talk as soon as we could. "I am," I said, "but I was hoping Eliza had a little time." My dad nodded his understanding, like he thought this was a good idea. "Do you want to go to Main Street for a pedicure?" I asked.

She scrunched her nose at me. "I thought you hated pedicures."

"People change," I said. It was true; I had hated pedicures for a long time. The idea of making someone touch my feet always seemed like cruel and unusual punishment. As a runner, I always had blisters and calluses galore. But, problems aside, the way Ryan looked at me made me feel pretty, and it made doing something feminine feel acceptable.

"Okay, let me get my purse," she said, brightening. "Dad, you'll be okay?"

"Sure," he said. "I think I'll take the boat out."

"Good idea," Eliza said. "Just be careful." We each gave him a kiss good-bye and headed down the front steps. Ryan's truck, I noticed, was still gone. The empty parking spot triggered a hollow ache in my chest.

We decided to walk. Eliza talked about wedding plans on the way to Main Street. It made sense why. She had less than two months before the whole thing took place and most people took a year to plan a wedding.

"Was everything okay with Dad?" I asked her.

"Yeah, just some wedding details. Relatives. You know," she said with a shrug, but I could tell she was still stressed. She'd lost weight, and not in a healthy wedding-diet kind of way. Her cheeks weren't as full; she looked older. And the tan that had started to appear this summer had already begun to fade from spending time indoors wedding planning.

But her energy was there. As we walked, Eliza was like a human to-do list, rattling off tasks and things she needed to buy. I felt a little bad for her because she should have been planning all of this stuff with our mom. Mom, who would have tempered some of Eliza's high-strung nervousness. Mom, who was the best at knowing when things were too little or inconsequential to worry about. She'd tell Eliza that no one would remember the flowers, or the favors, or even the food. I think, deep down, I knew this, too. I thought about telling Eliza myself. But I wasn't our mom and it didn't seem right.

There was nothing I could offer her. I realized that, even though she'd brought us all out here, she really hadn't asked for *that* much from us as her bridesmaids. Or at least not much beyond basic sisterly bonding. She was shouldering the more boring responsibilities. A guilty twinge shot through me as I thought about having given her a hard time.

We took the boardwalk path, passing all the haunts where we'd spent time as kids. Dale's Dream Cone, Shakey's Sandwich Shack, where Becca had once won free sandwiches for a whole summer when she almost guessed the correct number of seashells in a jar. The bathing suit shop where I'd begged my mom for a string bikini and had changed my mind as soon as I'd tried it on.

Nails and Sails had a wait. It was busy, probably because the Fourth of July was a few days away and everyone was getting ready for parties. As soon as we sat down in the small waiting area, I began to feel antsy. I didn't want to wait to tell Eliza until our feet were soaking. What if she got really angry and I wanted to leave? I couldn't exactly just jump out of the footbath and take off down the street.

"So, you know how you've been wondering what I've been up to?" I said to Eliza as we both watched a little girl choose a pink polish to show her mom.

"I haven't been nosy, have I? I know you're a writer, and you need your space."

"Well, there's some writing," I said, trying not to think about my unsatisfying short stories. "But actually, I've been spending time with someone, and I'm worried it's going to bother you when I say who."

Eliza gave me her funny squinty look again. I knew the look well. It was a look just for me that meant, "Just say it already." Because if the situation were reversed, Eliza would have already said her piece without all the buildup. It was a look that embodied both how different we were and how well we understood each other. "As long as he's not a married man or something, why would I mind? Is it Morrison? He's cute. Even if he's a rebound from Matt."

She was making this worse. Or maybe I was. "No, it's not Morrison. . . ." I trailed off. Sighing, I let go, forgetting all the bullet points I'd practiced. "It's Ryan. Ryan Landry. Your Ryan." Why had I said it like that? My whole point was going to be that he *wasn't* her Ryan any longer. But here I was, acting like I was borrowing him. Was that part of my issue with going public? That people would never think of Ryan as mine?

Eliza cocked her head to one side, studying me with an impassive look on her face. "*My* Ryan?" She laughed. "Since when?"

This was weirder than if she had yelled at me. "Since forever."

"No, I mean how long have you been seeing him?"

Oh no. Here was the part I'd hoped she wouldn't ask. "Since a couple of days after we got here," I said. My shoulders closed in toward my neck, like I was a tiny animal hiding from a predator.

"And you're just telling me now? What, have you guys been going out in disguise?" I couldn't tell from her face if she was angry or impressed.

"No, just keeping it low-key." I looked down at my toenails in my flip-flops.

"Oh, he must love that," Eliza said, shaking her head. "You're dating the king of Harborville and you don't want anyone to know. What reasons have you been giving him?"

"That I, uh . . . don't want the whole world to know yet."

"Seriously, Kate? He's going to think you're embarrassed to be with him or something. Believe it or not, Ryan can be insecure."

I thought of the way he'd left the other day and felt even

worse. I hated when Eliza was right. . . . I'd thought of Ryan as more than human, and that all the things that would injure a normal guy's ego wouldn't bother him.

"I was afraid you'd be mad," I said softly.

Eliza playfully swatted me on the arm. "That's why you should have just told me right away," she said. "Crisis averted." She sighed and turned toward me.

"Look, it's been three years since I've even talked to Ryan, and I'm engaged to Devin. We're grown-ups. *You're* a grown-up," she said, her tone implying that I was doing a subpar job. "It would be pretty cruel of me to call dibs on a summer fling." She reached out and gave me a hug across the chairs. "Don't worry so much. That's my job, little sis."

I hugged her back, letting the relief echo through me. This had been the most hassle-free, go-ahead-and-take-him boyfriend transaction in history.

Eliza pulled back from the hug and nodded wisely. "You and Ryan, huh? I can see it. Two dreamers. It's cute." She grinned at me. "And he's a great kisser, right?"

I blushed, more because she'd just said what a good match we were. What did she mean, dreamers? I hadn't even thought about what kind of couple we were. . . .

"You can breathe now, Kate," she said, alerting me to the fact I hadn't answered her. "Your bad big sister isn't going to put the kibosh on your hot summer boyfriend. And really, if I did, you'd be an idiot to listen to me."

"What about sisters before misters?"

Eliza laughed. "I don't think that applies when the sister dated the mister before the official onset of adulthood." She shook her head. "You and Ryan. Just remember, I taught him everything he knows."

"Eliza! Gross." She *would* take credit. I tried not to think about the extent of her lessons.

Now she turned to face me, her eyes serious. "Hey, can I ask you something?"

"Shoot," I said, prepared to do just about anything for her.

"I'm having trouble with my vows. For the wedding." She pursed her lips and set down her coral nail polish, picking up a bottle of red from a small table. It was unlike her to be so fidgety and indecisive. "This is better for the Fourth. . . ."

"Your vows?" I prompted.

She turned back toward me. "I'm so flighty today. Sorry. Anyway, you're such a good writer. And I'm having trouble getting it all down. Do you think you could help me come up with something? Just about how much I love Devin."

The idea that she wanted me to, literally, put words in her mouth was slightly scary. She handed me a folded-up piece of paper from her spiral notebook, and I gently took it from her hands. It was huge for Eliza to ask for help, and I was flattered that she had thought of me. I opened up the note carefully. The vows she had going weren't much more than a list of adjectives: "generous," "sweet," "respectful." She watched me reading them. "I know, they're pathetic. When it's facts, I can do it. When it's feelings, I suck."

"Your feelings can count as facts. I mean, if you really feel them," I tried to comfort her.

"Maybe, but I do common sense stuff, agreed-upon facts. When I have to say the big stuff, it comes out wrong. Or weird. I wish I could tap into that stuff the way you do."

"I'd be glad to help," I said. "Is there anything in particular you want to say?"

"No, that's why I'm asking you," she said. "All the love stuff, I guess. How much he means to me, blah blah blah."

I laughed. "Yup. 'Blah blah blah' is where Shakespeare always started, too."

CHAPTER SEVENTEEN

IT WAS WEIRD, what letting go of a secret could do for you. At Grace's house the next day, I felt lighter. As I typed up her cryptic notes, my fingers moved swiftly over the keyboard and I even caught myself humming. I'd made decent progress on her mailing list, too. I missed the beach vibe of Smokey's, but this job was a better fit for me.

Only two things still weighed on my mind—making up with Ryan and figuring out Eliza's vows, which I planned to ask Grace about. True, she was sixty and single, but I'd found more than a few phone numbers and male names among her many jottings. As a writer, she had a way of making the romance in her books feel real but still magical. I hoped she could help.

Grace was at her desk, but I could tell she wasn't working. So far, nothing I'd typed up had been quite the gem she was looking for. She'd sit down, ready to go, wearing what I'd since learned was her lucky blue bathrobe over her clothes. But within moments, I'd hear her grumble. I knew that if I peeked in, her browser would be open to her latest addiction, celebrity blogs.

She knew far more about the latest scandals than any sixty-year-old should.

I tapped lightly on the doorjamb and watched as Grace minimized an article on a TV star's messy divorce. For some reason, she acted as though I would scold her for procrastinating. Actually, maybe I was supposed to be doing that?

"Grace, can I ask you something?"

"If it's the secret to writing the great American novel, I can't help you. I think I'm all tapped out." She sighed.

"I'll save that one," I said, approaching her writing desk. She had a collection of chairs in the room, scattered along the wall with her bookcases. No two were alike. My beach house's mix-and-match vibe was the product of my parents' joint choices, but here the eclectic feel was all a product of Grace's bizarre mind. I bet my mom would have liked her. Some chairs had ornately carved backs, while others were more modern and straight. Each one was upholstered with a different fabric—swirling paisleys, rich brocades, even one stitched all over with women's silhouettes. I chose that one and pulled it closer to the desk, sitting down. "This is a life question."

"Sexy one this time?"

"Not exactly, but romance related," I said.

She rubbed her hands together eagerly.

"My sister Eliza is getting married, and she's asked me to write, or help her write, her vows. All she gave me is a list of adjectives about her fiancé, and I'm not sure where to go from there."

Grace sucked in air through her teeth. "Geez, sounds like you can start by drawing up the divorce papers for them instead. Adjectives are cheap."

That seemed a bit out of line, especially coming from someone who didn't even know Eliza and Devin. But before I could interrupt, she ranted on.

"When you're crazy about someone, when you love someone, you should know what you love about them. Maybe some of it is inexpressible, because it goes beyond words. But you don't have to be a poet to be able to tell someone that when you look at them, the world makes sense. Or that they bring laughter to your life, or make you want to be the best version of yourself. And some of that is just Hallmark card crap, but the reason they sell so many cards is that it rings true. If she wanted you to fluff up the vows she wrote with some pretty language, that's one thing. But to *write* them? That's trouble."

"Er, well, thanks. That was helpful."

She turned back to her computer, huffing angrily when she saw an open document with two or three half-written sentences typed on it. And beneath her computer, stained with coffee cup rings, were the pages of the short story I'd given her—their significance amounted to a coaster.

I didn't want to take the advice of someone who obviously didn't even care about anyone. I knew that Eliza loved Devin, and I'd probably be intimidated by the thought of telling someone how much I loved them, too. Hell, I was scared of just telling Ryan how much I *liked* him. But her line about looking at a person and having the world make sense—that was a keeper. I'd use that.

I shivered on my walk home, even though the night was a humid soup. My nerves were getting to me. I checked my phone again as I trudged up the stairs of the studio. Ryan hadn't been totally incommunicado, but there'd been nothing since his text this morning: "Just checking in. Hope you're well." I hated that it felt like a business e-mail. I'd replied and said I was thinking about him. He hadn't responded.

Telling him how wrong I'd been was not going to be fun. I thought about waiting until he got home from the restaurant later, but that idea felt stalkerish, and I knew that the longer I waited, the harder it would be.

I pulled my nicest sundress over my head, navy eyelet lace, and slipped on a pair of gold sandals that were uncomfortable, but did wonders for my tan. Thanks to the outing with Eliza, my hands and toes looked fresh in a shade of light pink. Then, annoying shoes and all, I hopped on my bike and pedaled to Landrys' Restaurant.

Of course, there was a line out the door. I spotted Tea manning the hostess station. She looked wise beyond her years as she politely, but firmly, told an irritated man that the wait was forty-five minutes.

"Kate," she said, noticing me. "What are you doing here? And why are you so dressed up?"

I grinned. "Because I'm an idiot. And it's a long story. You'll see."

"Hey, where is she going?" the man asked as I practically skipped inside the restaurant. Now that I was here, this was happening, dinner rush or not.

I was a girl on a mission as I wove past the crowded tables and waiters weighed down with fresh seafood. Customers looked up at me with mixtures of curiosity and concern.

Ryan was in the open kitchen, an apron tied over his white T-shirt. He lifted a spoon of sauce to his lips and frowned as he tasted it. He turned to his cooks, gave directions, and then hurried to the prep station to add garnishes to a line of dinner plates. His focus and authority made him completely irresistible.

It was bad timing, but I couldn't wait. I marched toward the kitchen. Becca was prepping a plate of fried clams and looked up at me quizzically. I smiled, probably like a maniac, and tapped Ryan on the shoulder. He spun around. "I told you, Danny, the sauce needs another bay leaf."

When he saw that it was not Danny but me, his expression shifted to puzzled.

"Kate?" He took in my dress and my guided-missile look. It seemed like he knew what was about to happen because his confused look grew into a bemused grin.

I didn't say anything. I just pulled him aside, away from the clattering of cookware and the scurrying of staff, to a corner near the pantry.

It wasn't private by any means, but I was so glad to see him again, that I didn't care if the hustle of the kitchen stopped behind us. And it did stop. We were the entertainment and our spot in the corner just meant I'd created a perfect vantage point for Ryan's entire staff to see us.

Cooks stood still over burners and at the stainless steel counters, some of them with their spatulas and spoons held aloft, like they'd been frozen. Waiters carrying trays had stopped in their tracks. Grabbing the strings of his apron, I pulled him into me for a short, quick kiss. "So am I your girlfriend, or what?"

The entire kitchen burst into applause and cheers. Ryan's

brothers, Pete and Garrett, let out loud whoops. I caught Becca shaking her head at me but she was smiling, too.

The feeling was contagious. I laughed, right before Ryan pulled me in for a second, longer kiss.

"Just to make it official," he said.

CHAPTER EIGHTEEN

WHAT HAPPENED AT Landrys' didn't stay at Landrys'. By the next morning, I had a congratulatory text from Jessica, and she assured me that his off-the-market status was big news among Harborville's single women. "I'll need to start calling you *Queen Ho-Bag*," she'd joked by text.

Ryan had come to my studio after getting off work, and slept over. Well, we didn't exactly sleep. In the morning, we joined my family for breakfast, but not before he rolled me over in bed and kissed me softly on the cheek and made sure I'd go with him to Smokey's Fourth of July party on the beach.

When she'd caught Ryan grabbing coffee in the kitchen, Eliza had teasingly joked, "God, Ryan, date enough Sommers sisters?"

Tea chimed in between bites of her avocado toast. "Yeah, I haven't gotten to talk to you since your big show last night," she said, smirking. "I can't believe you disrespected my hostess station like that. No one disrespects the hostess station."

"Your boss was okay with it," I said, reaching for Ryan's foot under the table.

"More than okay," Ryan chuckled, rubbing his foot up my leg.

Tea rolled her eyes. "Gross. Anyway, Mr. Landry is really excited about the paintings I picked out. I'll tell you more about it when you're not making out." She gave our legs a kick under the table. As she got up to clear her dish she gave me a quick hug, trying not to knock over my plate. Then she gave Ryan one, too. "I like this," she said, pointing between the two of us like a relationship authority. It was weird to think that someday she'd have a boyfriend, too, that she wasn't so much my little sister anymore, even if I'd always think of her that way.

Ryan laughed. "I think she's one fifteen-year-old whose approval really means something," he said.

"Fifteen going on fifty," I agreed, liking the feel of Ryan as an honorary member of our family.

Smokey's party was in full swing when we arrived at sunset. It spread out like a wonderland on the beach behind the shack, with mountains of food, barbecue pits, and colorful buckets with sweet and salty munchies strewn about. Tiki torches and twinkle lights extended down to the water, marking our territory. Rows of Adirondack chairs in red, white, and blue were set up for viewing the fireworks. My favorite thing about celebrating the Fourth on the Cape was the chance to see all the tiny fireworks spread out across the horizon as each little town put on their own show.

A tall, thin DJ, who didn't look much older than Tea, stood on a raised platform cranking out some classic Americana. People danced and swayed in the sand, holding their cups aloft. I caught sight of Pete kicking around a hacky sack with his friends. Tea and

Becca ran off to join them. Some of the Landrys' restaurant crew saw Ryan and me together and lifted their cups in salute.

Eliza had stayed at home with my dad. Of course he'd been invited, but chose to stay out of the fray. He and my mom had always sent my sisters and I off to the fireworks by ourselves, eager for some alone time. Maybe it was comforting for him to sit with those memories, but I still wished we'd succeeded in getting him to come out. Eliza had seemed pretty chill about the whole thing, considering that Devin was unable to make it to the Cape for the Fourth. He had some out-of-town guests in the city, but Eliza had begged off heading to New York, claiming she had too much wedding stuff to do. She'd promised me that they'd watch fireworks from the porch, and I let it go. I just hoped that, by the wedding, Dad would be more a part of things.

"I'm glad you came to your senses in time for this party," Ryan said with a sly grin, looping an arm around my waist, his fingers resting where my shirt lifted away from my shorts.

"Me, too," I replied, leaning my head on his shoulder. Why had I resisted this? It felt magnificent to show the world, or at least the Harborville universe, that we were together. Attached at the hip, as it were. For the first time in our relationship, I could be with him and that was it—just be. Nothing could kill my bliss, as Smokey would say.

Smokey was the first to approach us. "I knew it," he said. "And not just because I saw you guys kissing that day at the shack. That day you came for a job and your bike broke down, I thought, When some things fall apart, other things come together."

I laughed as Ryan quirked an eyebrow. I didn't even think Smokey had seen me that day.

"If you saw my beat-up bike, why didn't you help me?"

"I knew the fates were already working on it," he said, wiggling his fingers in the air like a two-bit magician. "Gimme some credit."

"We'll never doubt you again," Ryan said, and gave Smokey a fist pound. He waved us off toward the rest of the party.

We greeted more people as a couple. There were tons of guests that Ryan knew better than I did, and the age range was an eclectic one. Smokey was a popular guy.

There was a tiki hut serving tropical cocktails along with several different kegs. I finally broke down and asked Ryan how Smokey could afford such a crazy party. He looked at me like I two heads. "You didn't know that he's the heir to some insane fortune? Never had to work a day in his life. He just loves being at the beach."

I was so surprised, I laughed out loud. "No way. Am I the only person in Harborville that didn't know that?"

"Maybe, but you're even more adorable when you're so oblivious," Ryan said as he gave me a peck on my forehead and pulled me toward the drinks. We only got a few steps farther before he got pulled into a horseshoes game with some of the fishermen who supplied Landrys'. I wished him good luck and offered to get him a beer.

Jessica was talking to Aaron by one of the kegs. She held up a finger to him when I arrived. I knew from a text update that she'd called him out for allegedly flirting with a girl from New York, but it seemed like things were okay now. If feigning indifference was her strategy, it worked. Instead of looking annoyed, he seemed to be panting for Jessica's return. She was wearing a white fringe bra top that showed an expanse of her flat, tan stomach and short red shorts that sank low on her waist. "So, good for you," she told me, nodding in Ryan's direction. "Does this mean you're over your ex?"

I gave a guilty thought to the series of texts from Matt that I'd been ignoring. In one, he'd asked about the wedding, and if I knew what Eliza's colors were so his tie wouldn't clash. I'd have to tell him fairly soon that he was no longer my date.

"Yes, that's definitely over," I said, not wanting to go into detail.

"And how was Eliza with it? I see no scars from the catfight."

"Surprisingly cool." I nodded slowly. For all my worries, telling Eliza about Ryan had actually been really good for our relationship. At the nail salon, we'd talked, really talked, for what felt like the first time in ages.

"Well, bravo, girl. He's a big catch in these parts," Jessica said, sending a quick wink to Aaron.

"He's not a fish," I said, filling up two red cups. I was, however, somewhat smug. Was this how Eliza had felt, coming to all the Harborville parties on Ryan's arm, knowing that everyone was noticing you?

"Well, his ex thinks he's the only one in the sea," Jessica said conspiratorially, pulling me farther away from the keg. "Ashley Miner. Queen Bee of Harborville High. I think she expected Ryan and her to get married and start popping them out. They dated for two years, I think. She does hair at Ships and Clips. I don't see her here tonight, but maybe it's because she had a panic attack over him dating a summer person."

An ex? Ryan hadn't mentioned an ex. Not that I really had

talked that much about mine, either. The name didn't sound all that familiar, but she would have been older than me. Maybe Eliza knew her.

I pictured someone who looked like Eliza, but with Jessica's fashion sense. Someone more overtly sexy than me. With hair-styling skills. I couldn't get over Ryan dating someone for two years. Though I supposed it was crazier if he hadn't. What did I think, that as soon as summers ended, the Landrys and the rest of Harborville hibernated in boxes, waiting for the return of summer people?

"So, when did they break up?" I asked.

"Less than six months ago," Jessica said. She looked at me seriously. "I don't think you have anything to worry about. Morrison told me that, now that the secret's out, Ryan's told him that he's totally into you. I mean, he said that in the dude way."

Hearing that made my stomach jump. After our fight, I'd worried that Ryan had backslid with another girl, and I hoped it hadn't been with this Ashley chick. But if he was telling his guy friends about me, I was probably just projecting my own insecurities. It's not like I'd started texting with Matt when Ryan had been acting distant.

I nodded covertly at Aaron, who looked forlorn as he stood with a group of friends at the edge of the tiki hut, like he thought Jessica was ditching him. "Speaking of our boys, you'd better get back to yours."

"Duty calls, poor me," Jessica said with a grin, adding a swagger to her walk as she zeroed in on her date.

On my way back to Ryan, I noticed Becca and Garrett sitting in a pair of Adirondack chairs, their heads close together as they spoke intently.

I didn't know the middle Landry brother that well, beyond the fact that he was a bit of a goofball, like Becca. My sister seemed to like whatever he was saying at the moment, because she threw her head back and laughed. I thought of the surprised look she'd given me in the restaurant and wondered if she had a secret of her own. Or maybe Garrett wasn't really a secret at all, and I just hadn't been spending enough time with Becca this summer. I'd have to make point of some sisterly bonding soon. But right now, the sky was darkening, and I wanted to stake out a spot for the fireworks with Ryan.

He was looking for me, too, and his face broke into a wide grin as we made our way toward each other. *He's so into me*, I thought disbelievingly. And the thought didn't make me scared in the slightest.

"I can't believe this party," Ryan said, taking his beer from me. "Do you know that the caterers were on *Chopped*? I'm totally geeking out. Do you think the owner will talk to me?"

Hearing Ryan use the phrase "geeking out" was beyond adorable. And I loved how passionate he was. "I don't see why he wouldn't," I said. "But maybe after the fireworks?"

"Definitely," Ryan said, taking my hand and leading me to the back row of chairs. The view back here was more expansive and had the bonus of offering a little privacy for fireworks-inspired kissing.

"You know, my parents are around tomorrow. . . ." he said, waiting for me to sit down in my chair before settling into his. He draped his arm around my back and pulled in closer.

"That's not how a lot of guys start those sorts of questions," I said.

He laughed, "Well, it is if I want you to join us for dinner."

"You know I'd do anything for a home-cooked Landry meal," I said with a sly smile.

"Anything?" he said as he ran his hand up my thigh. I focused on the first silver fireworks igniting in the distance to calm my racing heart. I'd already met his parents—many times—but never as Ryan's girlfriend. As Grace would say, context was everything.

"*Almost* anything."

CHAPTER NINETEEN

I'D BEEN INVITED to the Landrys' house for dinner countless times. "Invited" wasn't even the right word: We'd just pop into their house and vice versa, like our kitchen tables were connected to each other.

Invites had been extended this summer but, with everyone getting older and having their own lives, we'd all been too busy. And I got the sense that the Landry boys rarely ate dinner together. Not because there was anything wrong, but because they were all on different schedules. It was part of growing up, I guess, but thinking of it made me strangely nostalgic.

I clutched a bottle of wine to my chest and rang the doorbell, laughing a little at Mrs. Landry's chipped green planter that burst with the marigolds and petunias she planted every year. She always claimed that she was not a gifted gardener and that it was her special green planter that kept the plants alive.

She came to the door. "Katie! I mean Kate. Ryan told me you go by Kate now. I need to get used to that." She flung open the screen and gave me a big hug. Her dark brown hair had a few threads of gray, and when she smiled, more creases appeared around her eyes. But she was the same Mrs. Landry, right down to her perfume. It gave me a small pang in my chest to realize that I'd never get to see my mom grow old. She'd always be stuck in time for me. "Why haven't you stopped by already?" Mrs. Landry drew me back to reality.

Before I could answer, she took the wine out of my hands. "What is this?" She shook her head. "Are you crazy? You don't bring a hostess gift. You're *family*." She practically dragged me into the living room.

Before I stepped inside, I couldn't remember exactly what the main house looked like—surely some things had changed over the years—but it all came rushing back to me. The little gust of air that tickled your ankles as the screen door whooshed shut behind you, the aromas of butter, garlic, and lemon from the kitchen, the sense of being lived in. There was a messy arsenal of sports equipment by the back door, and the aura of men as the majority, unlike our home. Mrs. Landry did her best to overcompensate, with pastel bowls of seashells and floral candles amid the video game controllers and beaten-up copies of *Sports Illustrated*. A painting of my mom's hung over the couch—two women chatting under a pink-and-yellow beach umbrella.

The reminder of my mom calmed the shifty, twisting bumps of my heart.

"Mike, Katie—Kate! I keep messing it up—is here," she said. "How are you, dear?"

I grinned despite myself. I was still nervous—after all, I'd seen their son naked and Mrs. Landry was no fool.

"I'm good, been keeping busy," I said. Since Mrs. Landry

seemed unwilling to take the wine bottle from me, I set it down on the dining table. It was set with the same floral dinner plates I remembered from three years ago.

"Katie!" Mr. Landry bellowed as he walked in from the kitchen, a can of beer in his hand. His belly had expanded a little, but he still had the same ruddy complexion and kind eyes.

"You must still be running," Mrs. Landry said. "Look at those legs, Mike. God, I'd kill for them. Keep it up."

"Well, no wonder Ryan likes her," Mr. Landry said. "This is an athletic household." He patted his stomach, then pulled me into a hug.

"You know," he said as he gave me a final pat on the back, "you didn't have to wait 'til you were dating Ryan to come over and see us," he said.

Mrs. Landry swatted him. "She knows that," she said. "Kate's a busy girl. She's working for Grace Campbell, the writer."

"That's right, very impressive." As Mr. Landry raised his beer to me, I realized that Ryan had filled in his parents. Was he as nervous about this dinner as I was?

"We're going to eat in just a few minutes. Peter might join us a bit later but Garrett's at work," Mrs. Landry said, confirming my theory that they didn't have their big dinners together as often as they used to.

"Ryan is in the kitchen, by the way," Mr. Landry said, pointing toward the kitchen door with his beer can. "Perfecting." His tone was affectionate but a touch sarcastic, the same as always.

"And where do you think he gets that from? Not his mother—" Mrs. Landry quipped.

"I was just starting to wonder," I interrupted with a smile. "I'll just go say hi."

It was only now, when I started to let myself breathe again, that I smelled the delicious aroma of roast chicken. Ryan's back was to me as he stood at the stove, vigorously stirring the contents of a small saucepan. I couldn't help but admire his butt beneath the ties of his apron. If his parents weren't ten feet away, I might have stepped up behind him and squeezed it.

"Smells amazing," I said by way of greeting.

Ryan looked over his shoulder at me. "Don't be mad, but I can't kiss you right now. I have to be all about this risotto. If I stop stirring, it dies."

I slid up next to him and planted one quick peck on his cheek. "I couldn't possibly disrupt a life-or-death moment," I said. "In exchange, I merely require a taste when it's ready."

"Deal," Ryan said. "So how'd this morning's writing session go?"

"I got a couple of things down on the page," I told him. The new timbre of our relationship had lifted some of my anxiety, and I'd been able to focus on my writing. The story about the society where kids were born with unbreakable bones was coming together, and I could even see it turning into something longer. If the delicious dinner Ryan had prepared was any indication, we were feeding one another's creative energies.

"Can't wait to hear more," he said, smiling even as he gave his risotto the evil eye. "Do you mind getting out a serving spoon for the mushrooms?"

I went, by instinct, to the drawer where the Landrys kept utensils. They were still in the same spot. I put the spoon in the casserole dish and plucked a single mushroom from it.

"Whoa," I said after the mushroom had practically melted in my mouth. "What was that?"

"Asiago-and-truffle-oil cremini mushrooms. Do you like them?"

"Um, yes, I'm marrying those mushrooms later."

"Pervert," Ryan joked. He began pouring the risotto into a serving bowl and I grabbed another spoon for him. Even though I could hear Mr. and Mrs. Landry talking about something in the next room, for a split second, I imagined Ryan and me in a kitchen of our own, getting ready for a dinner party with our friends. But what friends, exactly? Morrison and Jessica? Besides that, there wasn't much overlap. And what would happen when I went west, and Ryan stayed here?

How had one spoon in a serving dish led me into all these questions?

Mrs. Landry popped in the kitchen, breaking the spell. "Need help with anything, honey?" Her voice was light, but her posture was tense. I could tell she wanted to get back into her kitchen and start taking over. Even though Ryan and Mr. Landry both cooked at the restaurant, this place was Mrs. Landry's domain.

"Nope, I'm good," Ryan said.

"And everything's tasting good?" I didn't see how she could doubt the flavor of food in Ryan's hands.

"Yup, great." He sounded a little annoyed.

"Okay, then, I'll be in the dining room."

"You didn't have to go through all this trouble," I said as I helped Ryan carry dishes to the table.

"I wanted to," Ryan said, leaning down for a slightly longer kiss as he balanced the platter of chicken. "I like cooking for you. You appreciate it."

There was a catch in Ryan's voice and I wasn't quite sure why.

Once his plate was full, Mr. Landry pointed the remote at the TV and clicked on a baseball game.

"You still a Mets fan, Kate?" He directed the question to me but his eyes were on the TV.

I nodded. "Course," I said. "Born and bred."

"They look good this year, bastards."

Mrs. Landry slapped his forearm. "Mike, you shouldn't be calling people bastards."

"Why, it's what they are. Right, Ry?"

"Yup," Ryan nodded, watching as his dad gobbled the contents of his plate without even really looking at the food.

"What bastards are we speaking of this fine evening?" It was Pete, shouting as he let the screen door bang shut. He left a trail of his baseball equipment across the floor as he moseyed to the table.

He didn't sit down, just pulled a drumstick off the chicken and began to eat it like a bucket of KFC. "What's the fancy stuff?" he asked, pointing at the side dishes.

"Rice, mushrooms," Mr. Landry said, still looking at the game. "Ask your brother.'"

"It's very good, dear," Mrs. Landry said. "No rosemary on the chicken, though, hmm?"

"Not this time, Ma," Ryan said. "Fennel, thyme, garlic. A few other things."

"Ah, interesting," Mrs. Landry said. I wondered, with all of the amazing flavors, how she could possibly miss the rosemary.

I didn't know if I should try to talk about myself, or ask questions of the Landrys, or what. Because I knew them, and they knew plenty about me, the pretense of a family dinner all felt a little awkward.

We all let ourselves get absorbed into the game, and grew quiet. Throughout the meal, Pete hovered half in and half out of his chair, gulping the food like he was barely bothering to taste it. It took me a while to notice how sullen Ryan had become. He was still eating, but I could tell that something was off. He wasn't considering his food, how it tasted and if it could be improved. I wanted to think of the Landrys as blameless and perfect compared to my own family, but it was clear that they just didn't get this piece of Ryan. They considered him the sports star, not the gourmet chef.

"I think Ryan's cooking is pretty amazing," I said. "And like I told him, I don't use that word lightly. Can't go around calling everything amazing, you know?"

"You can call the Red Sox amazing." Mr. Landry pointed at the TV.

"Not today." I grinned, looking at the score. I could feel myself blushing, but this needed to be said. "Ryan's got real talent, and a dream, and I respect that. I wish I could cook like this. Or someone in my family could."

"This family's full of good cooks," Mr. Landry said. "Ryan's mother's outstanding."

"Oh, you guys are the best, but Ryan's doing something different. And I think that's special," I said.

"Good risotto, Ryan," Pete said, actually slowing down a bit to chew.

Mr. and Mrs. Landry nodded, looking from me to Ryan and back to me again. "Yes, very nice job, honey," Mrs. Landry said. Maybe they were irritated with me. But it didn't matter. I looked over at Ryan and took his hand under the table. He squeezed mine and smiled.

CHAPTER TWENTY

I WAS HALF-AWAKE in a state I was starting to refer to as beach sleep. It was an ideal state. I still felt gripped by the night, my limbs and body liquid and warm and painlessly melded with the mattress, while my mind felt just awake enough to register that the breeze coming through the window brought with it the smell and texture of the ocean. You didn't wake up from beach sleep. You rolled in to the day on a soft tide of gently returning consciousness. And beach sleep was that much better the mornings after I'd been with Ryan the night before.

My phone buzzed on the nightstand next to me. Ryan. "Run this a.m.?"

I smiled to myself and asked for a half hour. The one thing that could pull me from beach sleep was Ryan. Since having dinner with his parents, we had spent every spare second together. During our morning runs, I no longer felt like I was running *from* anything. We'd strolled down the boardwalk and Ryan had tried to win me another teddy bear—this time, I stopped him after he'd won the giant light-up sunglasses. We'd even taken a late-night dip in the Landrys' hot tub, after everyone was asleep, and watched the steam rise into the darkness.

And while sex didn't feel like the whole point of our time together, when we were alone—usually at the end of the day—it seemed impossible for one thing not to lead to another. We were, I thought as I tied my running shoes, both physical people.

Now we met in the space between our houses. I pulled Ryan toward me by his shirttail, giving him a kiss that wasn't long but felt like it needed to be continued. "That will be motivating," Ryan said. I knew exactly what he meant.

"Let's head south today," I said, already jogging toward Pleasant Street Beach. Normally, we headed in the direction of Morning Beach but I thought it would be nice to head through the neighborhood around our houses.

"Sure," Ryan said. We took off at a medium clip, easily falling into pace with one another.

"Sleep okay?" he asked, looking at me sideways. I could see his mouth upturned at the end with the sly grin that had grown so familiar to me these past few weeks.

"I did. You?" I circled around the spindly branch of a flowering dogwood tree, one of the perfect white dish-shaped flowers tickling my upper arm.

"Yeah, no idea why," he said. I reached out and playfully slapped his wrist.

We were a few blocks from our houses when I started to turn down Wilcox. Ryan reached out for my arm and gently pulled me back. "Let's not go that way," he said.

I stopped at the curb, bouncing on the balls of my feet. "Why not?"

Ryan halted, too, staying a few yards away and looking down Wilcox like he expected a monster to pop out of someone's hedges. He stared at the ground, kicking the dirt with the toe of his Nikes.

"It's just . . . you know. Well, my ex lives down Wilcox," he finally said.

"Ashley?" I blurted her name before I remembered that I wasn't supposed to know it.

He squinted at me. "How'd you know that?"

I shrugged. "Jessica Ambrose strikes again."

Ryan nodded knowingly and I was relieved that at least my gossiping wasn't going to be an issue. "I just, *I'm* over it and I think she is, too, but it seems like a jerky thing to do, to go running by her house with my new girlfriend," he said.

"We'd be running, not knocking on the door," I said, trying to tamp down the irritation in my voice. Really, we would have been past her house in five seconds. Was Ryan really worried about her feelings, or was he still just too hung up on her to see her front door?

Ryan shrugged. "You never know if she'd see us. Just, would you want to run by your ex's house?"

I thought about this and thought about all the texts from Matt I'd left unanswered. Surely, he had to have some clue that maybe I was dating someone but it wasn't like I'd reset my Facebook status to "In a Relationship" or posted pictures of us on Instagram. I supposed he had a point.

"I guess, well, maybe not," I said. "But it's not like he's here, either. Are you and Ashley . . . do you still talk?"

Ryan shook his head with a vehemence that wasn't

characteristic of him. "No. Not at all. She took the breakup pretty hard."

I felt a tiny glimmer of satisfaction knowing that Ryan had broken up with Ashley, and not the other way around. Now *I* looked down Wilcox, half fearing I'd see a girl running angrily toward us, wielding a scissors from her salon.

"What about you?" Ryan asked. He was walking a little ahead now and I started moving, too, down the sidewalk perpendicular to Wilcox. "Do you still talk to your ex?"

"Matt? Yeah, we're still friends," I said. Ryan nodded, making it hard to see his expression. "We're both headed west in the fall so, you know, it will be good to know someone out there."

Out there. West. The fall. With those words, I felt how easily the conversation could go from talking about our befores to our after. What would the end of the summer mean for us?

"Oh. Yeah. I can see how that would be . . ." Ryan trailed off and stopped walking, looking at me. "Does he . . . does your ex know about us?"

"We haven't really talked this summer," I said, not pointing out that there was no reason I couldn't have returned one of Matt's calls by now and worked Ryan into the conversation. "I mean, if we do . . . I will . . . He'll know."

Ryan reached out and squeezed my shoulder. I stood on my toes, brushing my lips against his. Wrapping his arm around me, Ryan kissed my forehead. "Well, now that that's out there, do we stop talking about our exes?"

"It *is* supposed to be in bad taste," I said. I did, honestly, want to know more about Ashley but the topic seemed fraught with potential for talking about the future. I wanted the end of summer to stay far away, like it had felt before this conversation.

"You're right," Ryan said. "Let's run."

We both threw ourselves into it now, eager to leave the topic behind, our feet lifting and falling fast.

As the day went on, I found myself wondering if Ashley was pretty, and what they'd done when they were together. Did she like Wes Anderson movies, too? Had Ryan cooked for her? I knew I was being crazy, but what was a relationship without a little insanity?

I needed to talk to someone about it. Jessica was out of the question. She was a good friend, but she loved drama and would have a field day with my jealousy. And her love of gossip might mean I'd learn more about Ashley Miner and Ryan than I ever wanted to know. But I wanted to know *something*.

After Ryan left one morning, I got a text from Grace saying that I had the next few days off. She'd been in a strange mood recently, which made me suspect she had a male visitor coming to stay with her. She'd gone to get her hair colored, and had been playing jazzy torch songs, singing along to the sad lyrics but in an upbeat way. It was very Grace.

I decided that if she wasn't writing, then I would take a crack at it. I'd kept working on the unbreakable bones story and started a totally new one, too, as the cartographer had rated no word from Grace. But between the stories and my false starts on Eliza's vows, my mind kept drifting to Ashley. I wondered how I'd never heard of her before. Maybe she hadn't lived here that long. I started to imagine her as a new girl at Harborville High, and

Ryan offering to show her around. Would they have walked the halls, Ryan giving her tips and tricks about surviving the school? Would she have looked up and laughed at his funny observations? Had they caught hold of one another's eyes and felt a mutual attraction? I had Ryan and Ashley's story more developed than anything I'd been working on today, and I didn't even write real romance stories.

I gave up on the writing and headed downstairs. Becca was sprawled out on the couch, half watching an atrocious yet addictive Katherine Heigl movie.

"Has she ever been in anything good?" Becca said, clicking the mute button on the remote. "And why am I watching this?"

I flopped down next to her. "I have no idea."

She sat up straight, like she'd had a burst of energy. "Do you wanna do something?"

I paused, considering. Should I let my little sister in on just how crazy I was feeling over a guy? Especially over a guy who'd done absolutely nothing to make me feel insecure?

"Do you want to spy on Ryan's ex-girlfriend with me?" And there it was. I hadn't even tried to stop the question from spilling from my lips.

But Becca didn't judge. She grabbed her laptop from the coffee table and immediately went to Facebook. "Have you looked her up?"

"I've been resisting," I said. Even though I could clear my history, I felt like Ryan would somehow know if I'd used my computer to look up his ex. But Becca's computer was another story. . . .

"Ashley Miner. Miner with an 'e,'" I instructed.

Becca typed the name into the search box and an Ashley Miner in Harborville was the first result. She had two mutual friends with Becca—Pete and Garrett Landry. So, Ryan's brothers must have liked her enough to add her. Of course, they were friends with me on Facebook, too, but I'd known them since we were kids.

Ashley's profile photo was of a flower and her cover photo was a shot of the empty beach at sunrise. "Um, can you say generic?" Becca asked. We clicked into her "About" section but Ashley's privacy settings had most of the information blocked. None of her other photos were visible, either.

I sighed in defeat, watching Katherine Heigl argue with her love interest on the TV. "Do a Google search," I said.

Becca typed her name into the search bar, and tons of results came up, but almost every click showed an Ashley Miner in Omaha, Nebraska, who owned a sugar-cookie bakery that had catered the Omaha mayor's inauguration.

"I know she works at Ships and Clips," I offered helplessly.

"I don't think getting your hair cut by your current boyfriend's ex is a good idea," Becca said. "In fact, that's probably the worst idea of all time."

She closed her laptop and gave me her most mischievous look. "But I have a better one. Come on."

We were in the kitchen of Landrys' Restaurant. I was red-faced and sweating—and not from proximity to the fryer.

"What if Ryan sees us?" I hissed.

"He won't," Becca said. "Thursday afternoons, he goes to the Provincetown Farmers Market to pick up supplies for the weekend. He's so into it. He never comes back until the evening."

It was cute, picturing Ryan choosing produce and talking to the farmers. I felt a twinge at being so sneaky while Ryan did something so completely harmless.

The kitchen was bustling. No one even noticed me standing there. I watched, impressed, as Becca navigated the thrumming space. "I have an order going out, people," she said. "It's urgent."

Garrett nodded a hello to me and squinted at Becca. "I didn't know you were here today," he said to her.

"My sister and I were grabbing an early dinner and I saw the rush. Just helping with one order and taking off." Becca grinned. "What can I say? I'm committed."

"You *should* be committed somewhere," Garrett answered, pinching Becca's waist teasingly. She laughed, and again I wondered if something was going on with them.

He walked off, but Becca's grin didn't dim even as she carefully boxed our skewers of grilled shrimp and rice pilaf.

"Okay, let's go," she told me. Becca's—completely idiotic or mind-blowingly genius—plan was to bring a fake delivery to Ashley's house.

"I know which street her house is on, but I don't know the exact address," I said.

"Oh, done a little stalking already, have we? Don't worry, she's in the system. I have her home address and her work address," Becca said. I checked my phone. It was five-thirty. Hair stylists didn't pull late hours, did they?

"Let's try her house first," I said. "And let's get out of here before Ryan gets back."

* * *

We raced our bikes toward Ashley's street. Becca held the plastic bag of food in one hand, where it kept banging against her handlebars.

"The food is going to be all messed up," I complained, straining to be heard over the noise of the boardwalk and our bikes' spinning tires.

"She didn't even order it," Becca said. "I'm not too worried that she'll complain about the quality."

We stopped one house over from the correct address. The plan was for me to wait on the sidewalk while Becca went to the door.

There was nothing for me to stand behind, so I felt totally naked, holding my bike and trying to act like I just hung out on this block all the time. But Becca was completely at ease. She strode to the door and knocked like the most competent of delivery girls.

An older woman, probably my dad's age, answered. Not Ashley. Or at least I hoped and assumed not. Probably Ashley's mom.

She gave Becca an awkward smile and turned into the house. I heard her call for Ashley. A few seconds later, a short, curvy girl with long dark hair came to the door. She was physically my opposite. Her head would have come up to my shoulder, and I was no match for her in the chest. I could tell from here that her nails were painted hot pink and probably not chipped. Her hair looked photo shoot–ready. I always let my hair air-dry and hoped for the best.

When Becca handed her the food, I could hear Ashley's voice go up several decibels. "I don't eat at Landrys' anymore," she said, pushing the bag back into my sister's hands. "I don't know who put you up to this, but it's not funny. I am not paying for that, and if you don't leave, I will report Landrys' and Ryan Landry to the Better Business Bureau." She was wagging a scolding finger at Becca, and then she looked right at me.

"What is going on here?"

My eyes locked with hers for a solid five seconds and then I was on my bike, literally backpedaling. This was a horrible idea. Ashley came down a few of her front steps and watched me. She must have been privy to Harborville gossip, too, because she shot me a look that said she knew who I was and didn't like my presence one bit.

Becca played it cool, walking back down to her bike. "I'm sorry, wrong house. This is for 4712, not 4217! I think our phone operator might be a little dyslexic."

"Becca, come on," I said, already down the block. Ashley clearly didn't believe Becca's cover-up.

My sister pedaled to catch up with me, looking back at Ashley, who was on her cell phone in her front lawn.

"Now I just have to hope she doesn't call the Better Business Bureau," I said over the sound of our spokes as we pedaled crazily along like our lives depended on it. "Or worse, Ryan."

"She won't," Becca said. "What if the operator really does have dyslexia? She'd look like such a jerk."

"And of all the numbers to mix up, he sent us to Ryan's ex's house?" I laughed.

"Ha, didn't think of that," Becca said. We reached our house and dropped our bikes to the ground, running inside like Ashley might be chasing us.

At the kitchen counter, we made sandwiches and devoured them, without even waiting for the bread to toast. Spying took a lot of energy apparently.

"Hey, you owe me one," Becca said, seeming perkier than I'd seen her all summer. "Can we take the boat out?"

"You got it," I promised. "But let's make sure to check the boat for holes first. Ashley seems like she has a taste for revenge."

CHAPTER TWENTY-ONE

IT TURNED OUT that the best thing about a beach wedding—or at least about Eliza's beach wedding—was that the bridesmaid dresses were not going to be the multitiered taffeta stuff of nightmares.

One of my mom's friends, Lucy Jennings, was a dress designer on the Cape, and her specialty was custom-made sundresses. She was tailoring Eliza's wedding dress and hand-making the bridesmaid dresses. Lucy had been ecstatic to do something for the daughters of Lanie Sommers.

Now we were at Lucy's small studio, in Provincetown, seeing sketches of the designs and getting measured so Lucy could get to work.

"This is what I was thinking for each of you, based on your heights and different looks." Lucy opened a huge sketchbook to a page where she'd drawn renderings of me, Becca, and Tea. "For Tea, I did an A-line party dress with a sweetheart neckline and some light seashell beading." She showed us a drawing of an aquamarine dress that would nip in at Tea's teensy waist.

"Becca, you have curves and should show them, so I put you in something strapless and a little more fitted." Becca's dress was turquoise, and would adhere to her hourglass frame to the hips, where it let out into ethereal wisps of fabric. Becca actually gasped when she saw it.

"And, Kate, you're so athletic, so you're in a halter to highlight your great shoulders and it's a little shorter, to show off those runner's legs." My dress was a not-quite navy, but darker than my sisters', with a tie-back halter on the top and a swirling skirt that hit several inches above my knees. Tiny shells were stitched into the halter straps. I loved it and couldn't help imagining what Ryan would say when he saw me in it.

"And I'll be working the lace from your mom's old dress into each one. Then the rest will go to making Eliza's wedding dress—she should have it on by now. Eliza, honey, do you need help with the rest of the buttons?" Lucy called to the back of the studio.

"No, I've got it," came Eliza's reply.

Eliza emerged from the dressing room in the corner. My sisters and I cheered. Not just because she looked beautiful—she did—but because she looked so much like our mom. From her tan skin and blond hair to her uncertain half smile, she was almost the spitting image of my mom from her own wedding photos. Lucy had taken a basic sheath dress for the bottom layer and then stitched a gauzy overlay out of soft white tulle and lace from my mom's old dress. As Eliza stood in front of a huge window, the sun shone in behind her and rays of light funneled through the dreamy fabric. Tea burst into tears.

"You look just how you're supposed to look," she said, blubbering as Lucy handed her some Kleenex. "You look just like Mom."

Eliza crossed to the standing mirror next to Lucy's large worktable. She looked herself over in one quick glance and said, "Yeah, it's great." Though she could be blasé and less than emotive, her nonresponse was strange even for Eliza. "Can someone unbutton me?"

Lucy went to help her. "Make sure it's what you want. We still have time to change things." I could tell she'd been expecting a bigger reaction, so I crossed to stand near the two of them.

"The detail is amazing," I told Lucy. Here and there, the overlay had little stitches with tiny, shimmery beads laid in. They weren't overpowering, though; instead, they gave the dress a subtle glow. I'd never been the kind of girl to imagine her own wedding day, but this dress almost made me. "I wish our mom could see it." Mom would have loved the art of the dress and that it wasn't a carbon copy of anything you'd see in a bridal magazine. "Eliza, don't you love it?"

Eliza smiled. "Of course I do, it's beautiful. Thank you for all your hard work, Lucy." I believed her words, but there was no emotion behind them. "Besides, there's no time to change things! I still have to put in the catering order, decide on cake, do the seating charts, make sure we have music. . . ."

Holding her unbuttoned dress tight around her chest, she stalked back toward the dressing room. The obvious stress was not like Eliza at all. She thrived in overwhelming situations. I exchanged a look with Tea and Becca. Maybe all the wedding stuff was too much for her. I'd been offering to help more, and so had my sisters, but Eliza hadn't taken us up on our offers. The only responsibility she'd given me was her vows.

Her vows. I thought about what Grace had said. I'd been so

dismissive of her pronouncement on Eliza's relationship, but what if she was right? Deep down, I knew Eliza could handle planning this wedding. My sister was someone who could have probably handled planning her own wedding *and* someone else's in a short time span, while still having time to work on her tan. This was definitely more than wedding stress. Maybe she wasn't being herself because she really wasn't sure about getting married?

"I'll talk to her," I said, heading toward the fitting room.

I pulled back the soft cream curtain and poked my head half-inside. "Hey, E, do you have a second?"

The wedding dress lay half-crumpled on the floor. Not my sister's all-hangers-should-face-the-same-way style at all. "Yeah, sure, what do you need?" Eliza was pulling on her T-shirt over her bra.

"Is everything okay? Are you stressed about the wedding? Or worried about something?" I tried to make eye contact, but Eliza turned away from me and checked her phone. "Eliza?"

She looked up like she'd just realized I was there. "It's all fine. Just wedding stuff," she said.

"Your dress is beautiful. You should be really happy with it." It seemed like a way in. Maybe she actually didn't like the dress, or maybe the dress was just one layer of a larger problem. She was only twenty-one; part of her had to be wondering if she was ready for such a huge step.

"Oh, I am, it's so nice," she said, as casually as if she were commenting an on-sale handbag. Then she perked up, as though an idea had just come to her. "Weren't you talking about bringing Matt to the wedding?" she asked.

"Yeah, though obviously there's a change of plans with that,"

I said. After my run with Ryan, I had told Matt not to worry about coming to the wedding, but I still hadn't told him that I was dating someone else. He'd joked that he could be my "in case of emergency" date, and I knew that he was still hoping to get a last-minute call asking him to drive up, and that he was keeping the date open.

"Oh, well, yeah, I suppose there would be. So, you're thinking of bringing Ryan?" She started playing with her phone again, as if she wasn't the least bit interested in the answer.

"I mean, if it's still okay to bring a date."

"Of course, sure," she said. "I just wasn't sure if you guys were that serious."

Was *she* serious? Ryan and I were spending all our spare time together and she knew it. She looked back down at her phone: another wedding checklist, no doubt. I tried another tactic. "The vows are going great, though. I've jotted down tons of ideas." That was true, even if I'd thrown them all away. I had nothing so far, besides the sentence Grace had given me.

"I'm so glad you have that covered," she said, her voice distant.

Really, I could have used more input from Eliza on why Devin was the one. As she fiddled with her touch screen, though, she was making it clear she wasn't in the mood for heart-to-hearts.

So I lied. "They'll be ready any day now."

I'd taken an extra day off of work for the fitting. But to keep up with Grace's Dining Room Table of Despair, I'd taken a bag of notes home with me to transcribe for the next day. After the dress store with Eliza, I'd put off working on them to take another try at Eliza's vows. But I couldn't get her behavior in the dressing room out of my mind, and I finally pulled out Grace's folder, and headed for the house. Becca and Tea were out with the bus staff, and Eliza had gone to bed early after today's wedding errands. My dad was home, but he'd decided to take a long walk after dinner. Ryan was with Morrison tonight. He'd subbed in for someone on Morrison's softball team earlier, and had gone for beers with the team. I'd wanted to go watch the game, but knew I needed an evening in.

Grace wasn't the hardest boss in the world, but I did want to get through the notes—with the hope of sparking an idea, and getting to help her with something more interesting. Fine, so I may have had a fantasy in which she put my name in the acknowledgments of her next bestseller, and then her agent asked who Kate Sommers was, and Grace said, "You know, she gave me some of her writing. . . ." Then she'd sort through the clutter on her desk and unearth the unpolished short story I'd given her. She'd hand the coffee-stained pages over to her agent, he'd read them and see my diamond-in-the-rough talent and sign me immediately.

Clearly, I could finish short stories when they were complete and utter fantasies.

Sitting at the kitchen table I surveyed the work ahead of me, holding a cup of peach tea in my hands. I unfolded a Chinese food menu scrawled with several different notes. One definitely said, "When Marilyn Monroe met Arthur Miller . . . sexpot plus intellectual equals *what?*" The rest were harder to read: one- or two-word affairs that were spaced at random around the margins of the menu.

I checked the clock. 11:27 already.

"You're up late." My dad trekked into the kitchen from his walk. As he grabbed some leftovers, the refrigerator light brightened his face. He'd always been handsome, but his once pranksterlike eyes were different now, more sad and restrained.

"Where'd you walk?" I asked.

"Just up and down the beach," he replied as picked up a chicken leg, and began eating it at the counter. It wasn't something he normally used to do, always being a man for manners, but I was just happy he was eating. "You're writing? Anything good?"

"Just doing some stuff for work," I said, watching as he cracked open a beer.

"Want one?" I wasn't drinking age, but my parents had always said that in their house, as long as driving wasn't on the horizon, the drinking age was eighteen. I shook my head and cheers'd him with my tea. "At the bike shop? Why would that be keeping you up so late?"

I sighed. I couldn't believe my dad still didn't know about my summer job. He used to know the names of all our teachers, all our friends, and even who our celebrity crushes were. Now, he didn't even know where I'd been spending my time for the last month. "I'm working for Grace Campbell, the writer? She needs me to transcribe all of these to see if there's something useful for her next book."

He came to the table with a bottle of beer and sat down next to me. "Wow, Grace Campbell. That's great," my dad said, picking up a half sheet of notebook paper littered with random words. He chuckled. "Your mom had the worst handwriting.

She'd always say I was a bad grocery shopper but the truth was, I was always guessing at what she'd written down. 'Milk' would look like 'nachos.'"

He stared out the window and we both listened to the water for a minute. I felt the first prickles of a tear behind my eyes but I held it back.

"Here," he said, taking the Chinese menu from my hands. "Marilyn Monroe . . ."

"I got that one," I told him.

"Well, this, next to the kung pao platter says, 'not spicy enough.' And the word 'smashing' is next to the sesame chicken. And 'got gas' alongside the moo shu pork."

I smirked. "So she's a food critic, too."

We went on like that, my dad helping me translate notes and us laughing about the weirdness of some of them. He didn't bring up my mom again, but he would stop and just look around, like he could see her in the room or something. I wondered if he could and, if so, why I couldn't.

I must have fallen asleep at the table, because I woke up the next morning to the sound of Becca making French toast. There was a blanket around my shoulders and a throw pillow under my cheek, but half my face was stuck to the table. Becca laughed as I pried my forehead off a "Wish You Were Here" postcard from the 1950s.

She brought over a paper towel. "Drool much?" Sure enough, there was a puddle of drool left behind next to my keyboard.

The document on my computer was much more filled-in than I'd remembered. But then, I didn't remember falling asleep, either.

Then I saw a note on the table, in my dad's easy-to-read block letters. "Finished these up for you. Tried to move you to the couch, but you weren't having it. My stubborn Katie. It was fun. Love you."

Now the tear I hadn't shed for my mom last night made its way out of my eye. I spent so much time thinking about how I missed her that I sometimes forgot I missed my dad, too.

CHAPTER TWENTY-TWO

"YOU'RE GOING TO a townie party?" Eliza raised an eyebrow. "Like, *pure* townie?"

"We're not just summer people, remember?" I imitated our mom's words.

Eliza was in my room, braiding my hair into a pretty fishtail side braid I'd seen in a magazine. I wasn't as skilled at hairstyles as she was, and I had a feeling that Ashley Miner might be at the party tonight. I wanted to look good.

"No, we're not, but townie parties can get weird," Eliza said. "It's fine when you're just hanging out with Harborville guys, but when you start dating one, watch out."

"You went to parties with townies," I said.

"At Ryan's," she reminded me. "No one bothered me on my boyfriend's turf. But they didn't exactly like me, either. Where's tonight's?"

"Aaron Gray's apartment. Somewhere farther from shore," I said.

"Oh God. The farther you get from shore, the less you should be there," Eliza said. She ably looped strands of my hair over one another and I marveled at how easy this was for her. How were some girls seemingly born with these skills?

I rolled my eyes. "Well, if the townies tie me to a stake, hopefully I'll be able to call you on speaker phone," I said.

The first thing I noticed about Ashley were her nails. The hot pink had been traded in for a beautiful shade of blue-green, and they were so neatly filed they each cast their own sharp shadow against the beige walls of the apartment. Mine were mostly unpainted, unless you counted the last hanging-on bit of pink polish that clung to my pinkie nail.

Thankfully, the party was crowded and cigarette smoke filled the rooms, making the whole apartment feel hazy. Ashley and her friends were standing in the TV nook, where I hoped she couldn't see me.

Aaron's apartment was perfectly nice, but felt distinctly suburban. It could have been anywhere. In fact, it reminded me of a complex in Jersey where I'd been to a party with Matt. His cousin, who managed a Foot Locker and went to night school, lived in a nondescript gray building with eight units. Aaron's was nearly the spitting image of that, except tan on the outside. His small balcony overlooked a Days Inn parking lot.

The tiny orange-and-cream kitchen was packed with people, and clusters of plastic liquor bottles lined the counters. Jessica, holding court as the unofficial lady of the house, poured shots for people. She'd informed me that the apartment wasn't technically Aaron's he was just subletting until he left for Syracuse.

Besides Jessica and Aaron, I was probably one of the youngest people here. Most of the crowd had come from work, and most of them worked at various tourist-centric places in Harborville.

"You okay?" Ryan said, his hand on my back. I looked up at him for some sign he'd seen Ashley or was looking for her, but mostly he just seemed focused on me. He ran his fingers up my spine and twisted the end of the braid around his fingers. A shudder went through me and I wished we had stayed home tonight.

"Yeah, totally," I said. Now I touched my braid, feeling like it would come loose at any moment just by virtue of being on my head. "I just don't really know that many people."

"You know Morrison," Ryan said, pointing a few feet away to where Morrison was talking to a pretty blond girl. Morrison tipped his beer bottle toward us and smiled a hello. "Though I guess we shouldn't get in the way of his game."

There wasn't much to do in the apartment, except stand around, talk, and drink. The TV was tuned to some extreme martial arts match and some guys clustered around it. Here and there people bobbed their heads to the Jay-Z song playing, but people weren't dancing. It was a typical house party that was just getting started.

Ryan said hi to a guy in a Patriots cap who introduced himself as Jeff. "This is my girlfriend, Kate," he added. A little thrill shimmied through me on the word "girlfriend."

"Good to see you, man," Jeff said, slapping Ryan a high five. I shook his hand. "Nice to meet you."

"You, too." I smiled. Jeff was nicely tall and broad. More of a barricade from Ashley.

"Cheers to the weekend, right?" Jeff said. "I had the worst day at work today. These sisters from Boston chartered one of my boats and wanted to go paddle boarding, and they all thought they were, like, princesses or something." In a singsongy voice, he mimicked them: "'How do we do this?' and 'Can we get an extra hour?' They wanted everything, even though they didn't reserve that much time in advance. You could tell they thought I'd bend over backward because they were cute. God, summer people, man." He shook his head in despair and looked at me. "Where do you work?"

"Oh, um, I was at Smokey's, but now I'm working for the writer, Grace Campbell."

"Don't know her. So that's your job year-round?"

"Kate's not from here," Ryan said, stepping in. "She's from New Jersey. She's going to Berkeley in the fall." He didn't seem as embarrassed as I felt. In fact, he seemed proud to announce this to Jeff.

Jeff held up his hands in surrender. "Ah, my bad," he said. "It's a compliment. You didn't seem like one of those summer-kid princesses."

"No worries," I said, not really knowing where to go with the conversation.

"Well, uh, catch you later, Landry," Jeff said, sauntering off.

"Sorry about him," Ryan said. "He can be a jerk. Look, I'm going to get a beer really quick. You okay or you want to come with?"

I hesitated. If I went with him to the kitchen, I might bump into Ashley, or put myself in her line of sight. If I stayed here, I could probably see who Ryan talked to, and if he made a point to talk to her. "I'm good. Can you just get me a Light?"

"Sure thing," he said, kissing me on the cheek.

I tried to look like I belonged, pulling closer to a group of girls who were talking about the bad behavior of some guy across the room. I was fiddling with the end of my braid when two fingernails lightly tapped my shoulder. I turned around, hoping to see Jessica. Instead, I came face-to-face with Ashley.

She was more made-up than I'd realized from across the room. I was surprised, again, by the idea that Ryan had gone out with someone who used so much foundation and eye shadow.

But she was pretty, with big doelike eyes and full lips.

"You're one of the girls who brought that food to my house." Her voice was soft and not mad so much as interested. I thought of how, at that first clambake, I'd hated the wide-open space of the beach and how everyone could look at you. But now I was missing the horizon that would have allowed me to put more space between me and my boyfriend's ex. What could I do now? Deny it?

"I'm sorry, that was . . . that was just wrong of me." It had been, and I was truly embarrassed.

She shrugged. She had some kind of lotion on that made her shoulders sparkle. I wondered if Ryan liked that kind of thing. "It's not a big deal. I've done weird stuff to learn about a guy's exes before."

She laughed then, and I appreciated it. I laughed a little, too.

"Yeah, but I should have just asked him," I said.

This, it turned out, was the wrong thing to reveal, or the wrong way to say it. "Ryan hasn't mentioned me yet?" Now her eyes narrowed.

I shook my head. "I mean, sort of, but . . ." I really didn't know how to make her feel better about it. And, really, was I required to? I noticed that, a few feet away, some of Ashley's friends were now watching us. Did they think I was going to turn this confrontation physical? Worse, were they?

"Well, whatever. We were together for two years. Two *years*," she emphasized, and even though she didn't say the words aloud, I could practically hear her add, *Summer Girl.* "What are you playing at?"

"Playing at?" Now I really wished I had a drink. "I'm not playing at anything. I've known Ryan since we were kids, and now we're together."

"But we're adults now, aren't we? So you'd better be serious. Are you serious?"

"Uh . . ." I had no idea what the right answer was. Was it worse if we were really together, or just a summer fling? And which one were we, anyway? "I really care about him," is what I decided on. "That's all."

She eyed me appraisingly. "Well, if you really cared about him or Harborville, you'd know better than to come in and take a souvenir," she said.

I blinked. "What do you mean, a souvenir?"

"Your little romance. Girls like you go off to college, and maybe you say you'll keep in touch with Ryan, or the guys like him, but you never do. And you give them these big ideas that they're better than this place."

"I love it here. I'm not . . ." I trailed off. She clearly had a piece to say and I wasn't going to stop her.

"Yeah, you love it because you don't have to live here all the time. And then you go off to your bigger, better life somewhere, and you can talk about that time you took home a little piece of Harborville, by stealing one of its boys' hearts. And then we . . ." Here, she gestured to the room of Harborville women with a game-show girl's wave of her arm. ". . . get stuck being compared to a summer person who had a big life and big dreams and stuck our boys' heads full of what-ifs."

"Ryan's his own person," I said. "I'm not filling his head with anything. We're having fun. And we're really good together."

"Well, go ahead and have fun. But don't think you can take him with you. He was made here and he belongs here." She was wagging her finger now, and even though she was looking me directly in the eye, I felt like she wasn't addressing me so much as giving a speech she'd given before, in her head or to her friends. "Take home your little jars of sand and your precious seashells, but just remember that some things will always belong to the beach, and you can't just come in and decide otherwise. He won't work in your world."

Then she waved, right in my face and, without giving me a chance to respond, rejoined her group of friends.

I just stood there, not even trying to pretend I was with any of these people anymore. Obviously, I wasn't, and they didn't want me.

I found myself wanting to call Eliza. So *this* was what she'd meant by a townie party. I looked around for Ryan and saw that he was talking to someone, beers in hand. He must have gotten pulled aside on his way back, and obviously hadn't seen anything. I didn't want to go running to him, so, instead, I snuck into the kitchen to talk to Jessica.

She was sitting on the kitchen counter, pouring lemon drops from a pitcher into shot glasses. "You want?" She gestured to her line of drinks.

"I'll take two," I said. I downed them quickly.

"Whoa, Sommers, what's up?"

I tried to explain Ashley's rant as best I could. "She basically said he doesn't belong in my world and vice versa and I can't just roll out of town with him as my souvenir."

Jessica grimaced and helped herself to a shot, flipping her long auburn hair back over one shoulder. "I wouldn't sweat it. She's not a threat, or anything," she said. "The souvenir thing's a little weird. But, she's not totally wrong. It's hard being around here all year, it's really slim pickings if you know what I mean, and you snagged one of the good ones. One of the best ones, really."

I nodded, surprised to hear it coming from Jessica. I couldn't deny the truth of what she was saying, but it also didn't mean I was about to give up Ryan. "Yeah, I guess you're right," I said, though I had no intention of saying as much to Ashley. "I'd better go find Ryan."

Ryan folded me instantly under his arm and kissed me, deep, right in the middle of the party. He held out the beer. "You want?"

"Not so much, anymore," I said. I'd downed the shots too fast.

He looked around. "Steal me away from here, why don't you?" he said. "It's the same old people every time. I'd rather just be with you."

It should have felt like a victory, but I wondered why he was in such a hurry to leave. Was it Ashley, or had Ryan thought better of mixing me in with Harborville?

It didn't really matter right now. I was ready to go.

I pulled him toward the door. "Let's get out of here."

CHAPTER TWENTY-THREE

OF ALL OF us, Becca was the biggest sailing nut. I'd always thought that if she could live out in the middle of the water, she would. She was positively giddy as we made our way to the marina and our boat. She'd waited for me to get back from Grace's house, and had packed food and drinks for dinner, plus a wireless speaker so we could listen to music from her iPhone.

"I'm so excited to finally take the boat out," she said. "I can't believe we haven't used it at all this summer."

With a pinch of guilt, I thought of taking Ryan out earlier in the season and decided not to mention it. Becca was crazy excited at the prospect of this outing, and even more excited that it was just the two of us. It was like we were getting away with something.

She steered the boat out on the water, choosing to go for the same somewhat remote stretch of water that I had gone to with Ryan. She liked to find less-crowded spots because she had a tendency to speed.

"So, are you feeling better about Ryan's ex?" she called from the steering wheel.

I laughed. "Well, she was a little scary at that party," I said. I'd told Becca about my face-to-face with Ashley. Since her souvenir metaphor, I couldn't walk down the boardwalk without getting an ominous feeling as I passed the shops selling knickknacks and seashells.

"But that's crazy," Becca said. "You know Ryan is a person, not a thing you just put in your pocket and take with you. Maybe you'll have to do long-distance, or whatever, or maybe it doesn't last forever, but it's not like you're ruining him for Harborville. She sounds like she has a giant chip on their shoulder."

I shrugged. I hadn't brought it up to Ryan, and he'd never mentioned that his ex had been at the party. I did half wonder if that was why he'd wanted to leave so hastily. I wished I could ask him, but after I'd almost screwed things up by wanting to keep our relationship a secret, I decided it was better to let this one go.

"I just wish she looked less like Mila Kunis with a chip on her shoulder, but I guess so. I mean, it seems like it's really over, you know?" That was the other thing: Even though Ashley was extremely pretty, it was harder to picture her with Ryan than it was to see myself with him. From the way she'd spoken to the extreme precision with which she put herself together, I envisioned her as the kind of woman who'd always keep him waiting as she got ready, or who wanted to know the day's plans before doing anything. Ryan seemed to appreciate my spontaneous side.

"I think he really likes you," Becca said, stopping the boat and sitting next to me on the low bench seat. "He talks about you at work sometimes, how you're a writer and going to Berkeley and how great you are. I mean, it's kind of sickening."

I swatted her. "Shut up," I told her. "Maybe I'm worth it."

"Whatever," she said. "But I'm glad you're happy."

She opened our cooler and pulled out a bottle of water. After taking a long drink, she turned toward me with a faintly sly smile. "Can I talk to you about something?"

Becca, I noticed, had gotten older. Obviously, that was the way things worked, but the person I saw before me was different from how I thought of her in my mind. When my mom died, she was only thirteen, and Tea was twelve. I'd always seen them as my two little sisters, like there was a big dividing line between the two of them and Eliza and me. I could still regard Tea as the baby, organizational chops aside, but it was clear to me that Becca wasn't a kid any longer.

"Of course," I said just as my phone vibrated in my pocket. "Just hold on a second."

The message was from Ryan. "Know it's last-minute, but can I see you tonight? It's important."

I texted back that I was on the boat with Becca. "Later tonight?"

"Was hoping before sundown. Like now. Sorry. I understand if you can't." I knew I was going to feel terrible for ditching, but suddenly the end of the summer glimmered on the horizon, and I felt a racing, urgent need to spend every second with Ryan possible. Becca and I could go boating later in the week, I decided. I texted that I'd meet him in the marina.

"Becs . . . don't hate me but, can we go back to shore?" I sheepishly peeked in the cooler, where Becca had packed food and my favorite strawberry icebox cake.

"Wait, really?" Her look made me feel like the worst sister in the world, but I knew there was no going back now.

"Ryan says it's important. . . ."

"Of course it's important." Becca turned away and started the boat. She didn't look away from the shoreline the whole way back in. I started to think about how I'd make it up to her and what I could say, but I knew that Becca was best when she had some space.

Ryan was waiting by our slip when we pulled in. Becca smiled pleasantly at him. "Hey, Ryan," she said, and I felt some relief. If she were really upset, wouldn't she have been angry with Ryan, too?

"Hey, Becca. So, I heard you were making a delivery the other day," he said. I suddenly felt both sick, and like I should dive in the water and swim far, far away. "That's weird. For a cook to make deliveries. On her day off."

Becca's eyes shot panicky darts in my direction, as if to say, *tell him.* "I'm going to go unload the boat."

I let her leave, then turned to Ryan with my best *Who, me?* puppy-dog look. He cut the tension by laughing, and raised an eyebrow. "So you wanted to know more about Ashley," he said.

"I know way too much about her now," I said, feeling a little sick to my stomach but relieved that this was at least out in the open now. "I met her at the party, you know. We had a weird conversation. Sorry for not bringing it up." I felt my face heat up. "Did you know all along?"

"Katie, Katie." He used my nickname in a chiding tone, but there was a lightness to it. "You can't make a delivery from my restaurant without me knowing. Especially when the receiver didn't make the order."

"I'm sorry," I said. "Did she come to the restaurant?"

"Yeah, but not 'til today. Typical Ashley, I had my hands full with two orders and she wanted me to literally drop everything." He shook his head and it wasn't one of those fond that's-just-like-Ashley shakes, but more an annoyed one. "Anyway, she told me she was just going to let it go, but then she met you at the party and I guess needed to inform me of my bad decisions. I think there was more, but I told her we had a date and she stormed off."

"I'm sure she was thrilled to have your conversation cut short so you could come meet me," I said, and then felt a little bad. I *had* started it after all.

He smirked. "She must be threatened by how gorgeous and smart you are." He leaned in to kiss me, and some of my worries slipped away.

"If you wanted to know about my ex, you could have asked," he said, whispering in my ear. "Though I kind of like that you were jealous."

Becca must have been eavesdropping because she'd been moving extra slowly to take things off the boat. Noticing that the storm had passed, she tugged on the cooler and hefted the boating supplies off the dock. She'd gone to a lot of trouble for such an abbreviated trip. I'd definitely make it up to her.

"Want some help?" Ryan asked.

Becca shook her head. "No big deal," she said. "I'll be fine on my own. Just ask Kate."

The comment stung, but I wasn't about to start this conversation with her when Ryan was standing right there. We would have to talk later.

"Thanks for sharing her," Ryan called after her.

Becca wheeled the cooler past us with a halfhearted wave as she threw everything into the car and sped off. Ryan and I were alone.

My face still warm, I asked: "So, was that what was important? The Ashley thing?"

"Nah," Ryan said. "I just like messing with you." He took my hand guided me toward his truck.

"We're driving somewhere?" I asked, surprised. I looked down at my cutoff shorts and T-shirt. "Am I dressed okay?"

"You're fine. We're not going to prom or anything. Just something I want to show you." He opened my door for me and I got inside, curious. The Ryan glide was missing a little, and he seemed somehow fidgety, tinkering with the rearview, constantly changing the song on his iPod.

We pulled onto Route 28, which was technically a highway that ran through the Cape, but was charmingly low-key. We drove past lines of houses and shops, shaded beneath a lush canopy of full green trees. I closed my eyes, letting the breeze coming in my window and wash over me. Ryan found a Black Keys song and let it play. We listened and drove, the cars in front and behind us filled with families heading back from the beach. In a few months, these streets would be mostly silent again, as vacation ended and fall reclaimed lives with new starts and responsibilities.

"You know about Castaway Lighthouse, right?"

"Yes, I went there once as a kid," I said. Castaway Lighthouse was a few towns up the Cape from Harborville. Ten years back, it had been badly damaged in a hurricane. Perched on the same cliff had been a famous restaurant inside an old mansion, which had also closed due to extreme damage.

If we were going to the lighthouse, I didn't quite understand why. It had been beautiful once, but it was still roped off. I remember lawn signs from a campaign a few years ago, when a Massachusetts congressman had rallied to get funds to restore it and reopen as a museum, but didn't have any luck.

Instead of taking the road that led toward the lighthouse, Ryan veered toward the old restaurant. Gravel crunched under the truck's tires. I looked down, wondering how stable the roads were here since the hurricane.

When we reached the summit, he pulled next to the mansion. Though it was faded and water-damaged, you could still see the shimmer of the sunset-orange paint beneath the dust and weathering. Since it had once been a home, massive picture windows stood on either side of the French doors. The glass had been blown out and you could see inside, to where the previous owners had opened the main rooms into one large dining area, with a viewable kitchen area off to one side. A huge verandah unfolded off the back of the home onto the cliff side, giving you a view of the water and the entire Cape as it stretched out on either side. It was truly breathtaking.

"They don't want as much for it as you'd think," Ryan said behind me.

I spun to face him. "Who doesn't?"

"A bank owns it now. After the insurance settlement, the previous owner just turned over the mortgage because he didn't have the energy to restore the place. And, there's actually some grant money to fix things up because it's a historic site."

I wasn't sure if I was following. "So . . . you want to buy it? And then do what with it?" The question came out sounding a little accusatory. I thought Ryan flinched a bit as my words reached him, but he rebounded with a smile.

"This would be my restaurant," he said. "And something totally different from the other places on the Cape. I think if the menu is special enough, we might get East Coasters year-round, like some of the best places in Nantucket."

I thought of him cooking for me, and at his parents. I had assumed that was just for fine-tuning the menu at Landrys' to get the younger crowd and bring in new business. I'd had no idea he wanted to be a real chef, let alone a restaurateur. Definitely not to the point that he saw himself running a restaurant this enormous, nor as high-profile as it would be if it became what he was talking about.

"I know what you're thinking," he said. "That I'm not a trained chef. But there are schools where I can finish in the off-season, while the renovations are under way. And I have ideas anyway. I could really start developing a menu tomorrow." He looked at me eagerly.

"So even if you go back to school, you'd want to open a restaurant here?" I said.

"Yeah, absolutely." He nodded. "Harborville boy for life."

I thought back to the conversation with Ashley. She'd been right about some things, but wrong about others. Ryan had his own dreams without me putting them in his head. He was talented and I felt as strongly about that as I did about him. But she was right about him belonging to Harborville, through and through. This was what he wanted, to be here, and to create a future here. He didn't really belong to my world, except as maybe a memory I'd store somewhere amid the pieces of the new life I'd build when I had to move on from the summer. When I looked at my life for the next few years, I saw Berkeley, and then nothing. Not "nothing" in a bad way—more like one of the blank pages in my writing notebook, a wide-open space for me to fill in. When Ryan looked at his, he was here. With all the details clear in his head.

"So, you're in it for the long haul?" I asked again, though I already knew the answer. I wasn't sure what my expression said, but I could tell Ryan was disappointed.

His maintained a semblance of a smile. "Isn't that the dream? Simple life, beautiful family, live on the beach year-round?"

I offered him a weak grin in return, not because it was my dream, but because I understood now that it was his.

"So, what do you think? Can you imagine yourself as a Harborville girl?"

I let my mind drift. I *could* picture getting serious with Ryan. I *could* picture his restaurant, and even him in it—running the kitchen the way he did at his family's restaurant, but this time, in a space filled with white tablecloths, the sun setting over the ocean in the background. But when I tried to get past the summer, my summer, I just saw myself at Berkeley. I saw my first trip down the hall of my dorm, my first moments inside my room, my first huge and anonymous lecture hall course. And I was alone. Just me, and a new start. My chance to figure out who I was, to not be the girl with the dead mother, to not just be Eliza's little sister, or one of the Sommers girls.

"You can't, can you?"

He wasn't looking at me, but was facing the boarded-up restaurant. His light green eyes were darkened by his thoughts, as they roved over the coast, past me, past everything. In that moment, he was farther away from me than he'd been when we'd argued about keeping us a secret.

I took his hand in mine and squeezed it, leaning against his shoulder. He pulled me close. I was relieved he wasn't angry, and that had to mean something about us, but I knew it didn't mean that I saw myself here forever.

"We always have the summer," I told him, dusk falling fast, as if to remind us that time wasn't really on our side. The summer had felt so infinite just weeks ago, but the days were getting shorter already.

Real life would rush in as swiftly as the night, and Ryan and I had different paths to take.

CHAPTER TWENTY-FOUR

THE NEXT MORNING, I woke up with intent. No matter what was going on with me and Ryan, I did need to start thinking about Berkeley and my classes. I cared for him, a lot, and I didn't want to hurt him, but I also didn't want to be so carried away by romance that I forgot to think about my future. Ryan's future was right here, but mine was a coast away. I had to be ready for it.

I took a few of my required reading books down to the main house, along with a few of the short stories I'd finally finished and wanted to review. I didn't have to work at Grace's today.

Becca was nursing her own cup of coffee and staring off into space from her seat at the kitchen counter.

"Hey, Becs," I said. "Sorry again about yesterday. Ryan just had something really important to talk to me about, and I couldn't make him wait. How was your night?"

She just swirled her mug of coffee and didn't look at me. "We're almost out of coffee creamer," she said, more to the room than to me. "I'll put it on the list."

I waved her off. "I'll do it," I said. "I can run by the store this afternoon."

"As long as nothing more important comes up," Becca said. Her normally raspy voice was flat and barely carried.

When we'd parted ways yesterday, I'd thought we were okay—or at least that we'd be able to talk about it if we weren't. And I'd been apologetic, hadn't I? Or did I not say sorry? I played back our abbreviated outing and realized my interest had been so piqued by Ryan's invitation that I'd asked her to steer me back without a second thought. Right after she'd wanted to tell me something.

"Becca, I realized how crappy I was yesterday with the Ryan thing. I completely blew you off, and you'd been about to tell me about something important." I approached her at the counter and put a hand on her shoulder blade. She didn't exactly brush me off, but her back tensed beneath my hand.

She nodded toward my Berkeley reading. "Don't you have some reading to do?" She turned toward me and I saw that her eyes were watery around the rims. "It will be so nice for you to get completely away from the rest of us. First stop, Mom's studio, next stop, California."

A ball of guilt formed in the pit of my stomach. Had I really been pulling away so much that I seemed eager to leave them behind? "Will you please just talk to me about what was important yesterday?"

"The big problem is, it was important yesterday and today it's already done," she said. "I already lost my virginity. I can't get it back to see if my big sister thought it was a good idea."

What? The information headed straight to my gut. As did the words "big sister." I sometimes was so busy being Eliza's little sister that I forgot Becca was mine.

"With who?"

"Why does it matter?" Becca asked, with narrowed eyes that said she didn't think I deserved to know.

"You know it matters," I told her. "And you know you want to tell someone. I had Eliza to talk to when it happened with Matt."

Becca pulled *Middlemarch* off of my pile of books and flipped through it. For half a second, I thought she was going to pluck a name off its pages to use as the identity of her deflowerer. Maybe "Tertius Lydgate" didn't sound like a Harborville name, because instead, she tossed the book back on the counter like it was another symbol of all the ways I'd failed her.

"Garrett Landry," she said. "There, you know now. You've fulfilled your sister-bonding time quota for the summer and can be on your way."

I nodded. I had had a feeling she was going to say Garrett. I may have been a little MIA for the summer, but I wasn't blind.

"I don't want to be on my way," I said, making my voice firm. "I know I've been distant this summer. I think with all the wedding stuff I was trying to finally stake out my own life away from Eliza. And then Ryan happened. So I got caught up in what everything meant for me."

"And you forgot that I need a big sister, too? Just like you need Eliza more than you think?"

I laughed. "You're like the double-whammy champion of guilt-inducing comments," I told her. She was right: As much as I was annoyed with Eliza, I also felt at times like I was losing her. Even going out with Ryan wasn't just about finally making something of Eliza's mine, but about declaring my separateness from her. It was a little lonely. I could only imagine what Becca had been going through. "But yeah. And right now, I don't matter. What about you? Are you okay? Did things go badly?"

Becca threw up her hands in an *I don't know* gesture. At least she was looking at me again. "No, I don't think so. I mean, he was so sweet. It was his first time, too," she said. "It was short. But then we did it again and it was longer. And nicer. His hands were freezing, though."

I laughed. It was surreal, talking to my little sister about this. Even though she was the one who'd taken a big step, it made me feel more grown-up, too. "He was probably nervous," I said. "Where did it happen?"

"We went to his friend's house. The family is out of town and Garrett's been getting their mail," she said. Color rose to her cheeks. "We used the parents' bed."

"Wow, was that weird?" I was happy at least to hear that Garrett had looked for a private place for them. It meant he must have respected Becca and cared for her.

"Not until after, when we decided to wash the sheets. Then we just sat there listening to the laundry machine and, like, talking about work. And that was the weirdest part," she said. "After."

A sense of sisterly protection warmed the blood in my veins. "He didn't blow you off, did he?"

Becca shook her head. "No, no, it was just while we waited for the washing machine. I think we felt like intruders, or like they might come home any second or something," she said, smiling. "After we put the clothes in the dryer, it was totally different. We put on a movie and cuddled on the couch. It was nice. I felt really close to him."

I nodded at her cell phone on the counter. "And has he called?"

"Geez, are you going to go kick his ass?"

"Maybe! I just want to make sure he's a gentleman."

"He called early this morning. And sent two texts today." She raised an eyebrow. "Is that good enough for you?"

"Yes," I laughed, relieved. "Just so he knows not to mess with my little sister."

"Oh, you think being all protective is going to make me like you again?" Becca grinned.

"No, I'll be protective even if you don't like me," I said. "But why, it is working?"

"Yes," she said with a smile. "In fact, it gives me an idea."

"Oh really?"

"Yes. A double date tomorrow. Dinner." Becca pulled up Yelp on her iPhone, starting to search. "Not Landrys', but somewhere kind of nice, with cloth napkins."

"What, you lost your virginity and now you think you get to be all fancy?"

"Hey, if there's ever a time to be fancy . . ."

We found a place with cloth napkins. It was two towns over, in Ribbon Cove, and situated on the end of the pier. The Sneaky Pelican was a lot like Landrys'—nice but still a place where you could dress fairly casual. Becca and I had on sundresses, and Ryan had worn a nice button-down over khaki shorts. Garrett, however, had worn pants and a tie. He looked stiff and nervous in the clothes. He couldn't have looked less comfortable than if he'd been forced to carry around a ventriloquist dummy. He kept blushing every time I looked in his direction. He was so red, I could detect the hue even beneath his close-cropped light blond hair.

It was a little cool outside that night, so we asked for a table in the main dining room. It was filled with families and older people finishing their early suppers. We'd beaten the rush, though, and were taken to our seats by a young hostess. Garrett helped my sister into her chair, but as he sat down, he knocked over his water glass, right into Becca's lap. She shrieked at the cold but waved it off, and started to laugh. Meanwhile, Garrett fetched napkins with the intensity of an EMT saving a life.

"I'm so sorry," he said, almost more to me than to her. Did he think I was going to beat him up for spilling water on my sister?

I looked at Ryan and smiled. He was grinning, too. It felt like an oddly mature smile exchange for us, like we both felt older and wiser than the two newbie daters across from us. It was a nice relief after the intensity of our conversation two days before. We were fine, but I kept replaying the entire conversation in my head, wondering if there was a different way it could have gone—if there was an alternate path our relationship could have taken. I was sure Ryan was, too.

"It's just water, little brother," Ryan said over the top of his menu. "Are you okay, Becca?"

My sister giggled. I could tell she was enjoying Garrett's sweet apologetic-ness. "Yeah, of course."

"Okay, Gar, she's fine. Look at your menu." Ryan gestured for him to sit. "Can't take you anywhere."

"Yes, you can," Garrett said defensively. The poor kid. I knew he had a sense of humor, but tonight he was so tightly wound he looked permanently hurt.

"It's an expression." Ryan laughed. He looked at Becca.

"Sorry, Becs. I think my little brother is trying to impress you and I'm probably making it harder for him."

"Yeah, you are," Garrett said with a half smile toward Becca.

Becca looked at him—was he her boyfriend? I supposed so—then and said, "This is a nice place, Garrett. Thanks for picking it."

"No problem." Once again, Garrett looked at me and Ryan. "Is everyone okay with it?"

"Yes, it's great," I said. I looked at my menu. "They have a macadamia-crusted sea bass. That might be good."

"It's no Landrys', but it'll do," Ryan teased. I squeezed his hand under the table, hoping to convey that he needed to ease up on his brother. I'd never seen a sixteen-year-old have a coronary and I didn't want tonight to be my first time.

The waiter came to take our orders.

"My date would like some more water, and an iced tea. Iced tea for me, too, please," Garrett asked, looking pleased with himself for ordering on Becca's behalf. My sister, I noted, seemed happy with the development, too. Ryan ordered a beer and I ordered a Diet Coke.

"And how about an order of clams for the table, and your crab cakes," Ryan asked. "Do you do anything special with your remoulade?" I grinned, now used to Ryan's many inquiries about how food was prepared.

"I think it's traditional," the waiter said.

"Okay, then, just some extra lemons with it," Ryan said.

Across the table, Garrett piped up. "And can you also bring us a shrimp cocktail?"

"As you like, sir." The waiter wrote everything down and left to place our order.

"Told what?" Ryan asked innocently.

Becca's eyes went wide now and I shook my head so she'd know it was just Ryan being a tease.

"Nothing," Garrett said. "Private stuff. I need some air."

As he got up and headed to the door, I saw Becca looked concerned. I didn't want her to worry, so I rose and followed Garrett as he left the table. I found him outside, leaning on the pier railing and taking deep gulps of the sea air. He looked panicked when he saw me.

"I really like your sister," he said before I could get a word out. "I mean, I think I love her. I don't want you to think . . ."

I patted Garrett's shoulder. "I don't," I said. "She just told me about you guys because she was happy." I didn't hint that she'd talked about his cold hands or their abbreviated first time. That was TMI and probably *would* be heart attack-inducing. "Don't let Ryan get to you. He's just messing around."

"Okay." Garrett breathed out.

"So why don't we go back inside?" I said. "And take off your tie, maybe, so you'll be more comfortable."

Garrett looked relieved. "I thought it would seem more professional, or something."

"Just keep being nice to my sister and we're fine," I said. Garrett smiled and undid the tie, shoving it in his pocket. As we neared our seats, I could see Becca smiling at the fact that me and her boyfriend were getting along.

"Oh, and if you really want to get back at your brother," I whispered out the corner of my mouth with a quick glimpse at Ryan, who was tasting the remoulade and squeezing in extra lemon, "just tell him how much you like the food here."

"Sir, wow," Ryan said. "It must be the tie."

"Come on, Ryan, so I want to look nice," Garrett said. Becca shot me a look across the table that indicated that though she was fine with Ryan's joshing, Garrett had maybe had enough.

"So, Garrett, how has your summer been?" I asked, to change the subject.

"Good, good," he said, nodding like a bobblehead. "I've been working a lot and, you know, getting ready for the school year, trying to do some summer reading."

"Oh, that's great," I said. "What are you reading?"

"Uh . . . what was that book you said Kate likes?" Garrett looked at Becca.

"*Cat's Cradle*?"

"Yeah, that one," he said. "*Cat's Cradle* was really cool."

"So you like Vonnegut, then?"

Garrett twisted his cloth napkin at the ends. "I mean, I didn't finish it yet, but I'm going to."

He was talking a mile a minute, until my sister put her hand over his. She leaned in close. "Garrett, it's okay. Kate knows," she said quietly, so quiet I could barely hear. "Like *knows* knows."

"You told?" But Garrett wasn't being quiet at all. He stood up from the table, this time rattling all the drinks on it.

"You *didn't*?"

I looked sideways at Ryan, whose brow was creased in a question. I wobbled my head from side to side in a not-universal-but-somehow-understood-by-Ryan gesture that meant, *your brother and my sister had sex.*

His eyes widened and his mouth formed an "oh" but then he grinned like the whole thing was comical, which it was, a little.

CHAPTER TWENTY-FIVE

A "REAL" DATE was what I'd been told to prepare for.

The double date with Becca and Garrett—which got progressively more comfortable once we'd eaten dinner and then actually became fun when we went out for ice cream afterward—didn't count, I was told, cloth napkins or not. Ever since our trip up the Cape to Ryan's future restaurant, he'd been saying we needed to go on a "real" date, even as I told him I was perfectly happy with our usual Harborville haunts. I *liked* playing Skee-Ball at Surf Arcade. I *liked* bonfires with Jessica and Aaron (her now boyfriend, or "summer boyfling" as she had taken to calling him, perhaps a little stung that he'd be leaving for Syracuse). I didn't say it, but in just a few weeks, I'd be leaving the boardwalk and beach behind, and I knew I would miss it.

Ryan was insistent, so a real date was what I put in my mind. Defining what a "real date" was, though, eluded me. The evening took shape in my mind like some lump of gray clay, formless and nondescript. I figured I couldn't go wrong by dressing up. I got my nails done again, for the first time since going with Eliza.

The manicurist had regarded my chipped polish with disdain. I bought a new dress—mint green and several inches above my knee, with a tied halter top. After our trip to Lucy's studio, I tried playing up my legs and shoulders more. My tan looked amazing against the light wash of color and, seeing myself in the mirror, I felt somehow older than when the summer began. Not in a bad way; I looked ready for whatever was next in my life.

Ryan told me he wanted to pick me up at the main house so he could say hi to my dad. Once I was dressed, I joined my family in the kitchen. Becca and Tea were working, and my dad was camped out in front of a ball game in the living room. Eliza was hunched over her iPad, inspecting photos on Pinterest as she picked at some food at the counter.

"I'm calling it," she said, without looking up. "We don't need favors. No one keeps them, no one wants them. If they don't remember a wedding, some chocolate-covered almonds are not going to help. And I am done doing last-minute stuff. Devin keeps saying weddings are an easy problem to throw money at, and I know he's being supportive and trying to de-stress me, but I think it's wasteful."

She was in Eliza monologue mode. It didn't matter if anyone was listening. Sometimes, Eliza just liked to unravel detail after detail to break things down to their necessary parts. It was her process, and I hoped it meant some of her tension was lifting.

"I think that's fair," I said. "But if you change your mind, there's still time to do something, if you want my help."

Eliza looked up. "Thanks, but let's pass . . . Wow. What are you doing tonight? Dad, look at Kate."

My father actually stood up and came into the kitchen. "You look really nice, Katiekins," he said, using a nickname I hadn't heard in years. "What are you doing tonight?"

As if to answer, a knock came at the door. Ryan. I got a sudden case of stage fright as I answered the door.

Ryan was wearing a light gray shirt, a few buttons beneath his neck unbuttoned, and dark gray dress pants. Besides my mom's funeral, when he'd looked stiff in his black suit, I'd never seen him so dressed up. It struck me that he was someone I could imagine on a red carpet or *People*'s Sexiest Man Alive issue. They were cheesy comparisons, but he really did make me feel like my skeleton was useless in holding up my body. That he liked me just added to the knees-into-jelly effect.

He had a jacket over his arm and a bouquet of dahlias in his hand. "These are for you," he said, looking right into my eyes. "Two-color hybrids. Science and magic." I smiled. He'd remembered my babbling from the first time we kissed.

"You look gorgeous," he said, and his eyes didn't leave me. They didn't go to Eliza, who I could feel watching us. She was in the spot I used to occupy: the person on the outside of the relationship, looking in. Granted, she wasn't looking in with a fifteen-year-old's admiring sense of longing, but there was an odd symmetry to the situation.

My dad came into the foyer. "Ryan, good to see you," he said, extending his hand to shake.

"Nice to see you, too, sir," Ryan said, a twinge of nerves in his voice. Now he knew how I felt at his parents'.

"Where are you two headed?" Eliza's voice broke through.

"Nantucket," Ryan said, his expression sheepish, like he had to get Eliza's permission. "But that's all I want to tell Kate for now. The rest is a surprise. Mostly because she'll try to argue against it."

"Me, argue? Never." I grinned.

"Just don't forget, we have our final dress fittings in the morning," Eliza called out behind me.

"Be careful, you two," my dad said as he turned back to the game. I smiled to myself. My dad had never really sent me off on a date before. With Matt, things had always been so casual.

"I won't keep her out too late," Ryan promised both of them as he took my hand and walked me to the car.

We took the ferry to Nantucket. The light spray of water on my face and the feeling of going somewhere totally new with Ryan built into excitement, and I pulled him toward me, kissing him as I ran my hands under his jacket and up his chest. He pulled me tight, his grip on my hips, but as our kissing grew intense, he let go and stepped back a bit. "I don't want to mess up your dress," he said. "You look so gorgeous."

"After, then?" I asked, feeling like I didn't want after to be too long from now.

"Yes," Ryan said with one last little kiss.

We leaned out over the railing, watching as the island expanded on the horizon, our fingers interlinked. Some dense-looking clouds built in the distance, and I could see Ryan studying them, a little furrow appearing between his eyebrows, as if he could make the possibility of rain go away.

"So, where are we going?" I asked. I had been to Nantucket restaurant few times as a kid, but not in years. Even though I loved doing simple things with Ryan, I felt a tiny thrill that we were headed somewhere special.

"If I tell you, you'll try to talk me into burgers and mini golf," Ryan replied. "So don't worry about it."

He took my hand to guide me off the ferry, and placed his palm on my back to guide me away from the pier into town. Little shops and restaurants were clustered along quaint cobblestone streets. Everything felt old, but not worn-out. More like, when you looked around, you could imagine yourself in a different era: It was the '20s, and I was dating a sailor about to cross the Atlantic. It was the late 1800s, and I wore a big dress and anxiously awaited the breezes off the water and the salt on my face. Harborville may have screamed "fun," but Nantucket whispered "romance."

I let myself lean into Ryan, partly to manage my high heels on the uneven paths and also because it was nice to feel coupled with him.

"The restaurant's not far," he said. "Are you okay walking or should I get us a taxi?"

"I like walking," I said, adding, "I prefer it, actually." I didn't want him feeling like he had to bend over backward for me. He seemed so nervous, like he only cared if I was having a good time. Meanwhile, I wanted *him* to enjoy the night out.

A drop of rain hit my shoulder, warm and soft. It rolled down my skin. I pretended I didn't feel it.

"Was that rain?" Ryan's voice wavered and he stared heavenward skeptically.

"No, I don't think so," I lied.

"Let's hurry," Ryan said as a plump raindrop fell onto his cheek. He looked up at the sky, like it was a new cook of dubious talents.

We'd only walked a few steps when the sky broke open. The resulting rain wasn't violent, but it was more than a drizzle. Ryan held his jacket over our heads as we ran toward our destination.

"Here, it's here," Ryan said, holding a door for me and urging me inside before I had a chance to protest. We were at Galley Beach, far and away the most well known of Nantucket's esteemed restaurants. Eliza had tried to come here a few weeks ago with Devin, but they hadn't been able to get a table. It was a favorite of celebrities and ultrarich Cape families, the kind of meal an average person didn't expect to ever have.

The entryway was so crisp and streamlined, white and clean like the sails of a boat that won every regatta. Nothing was overly ornate; the minimalism was what did it. It was the architectural equivalent of a perfect white blouse. This was a restaurant where any spill would show up and any embarrassment be magnified.

"Two tables for Landry. I mean, table for two, Landry," Ryan said, blushing as he fumbled the words. The hostess was a sleek blonde who looked like she'd come packaged as part of a Gourmet Restaurant play set.

She gave us a close-lipped smile. "For what time?" Her tone was interested, but not convinced. I smiled back. She looked down at her reservation list.

"Seven-thirty. We can sit at the bar if we're too early," Ryan said. He tapped his fingers nervously on the hostess stand, only stopping when the girl stared at his fingers.

"And it's Landry?" Hostess Barbie said.

"Yes, I have a buddy . . . a contact, I mean . . . who said he'd speak to the owner. I'm in the restaurant business, too," Ryan said. "My . . . contact is Russell, at Ocean Seafood?"

"We know Russell," the hostess said. "But I don't have anything here for you. I'm sorry."

"Are you sure?" Ryan asked. I could tell he didn't want to take no for an answer, but he didn't want to start an argument here, either. "I mean, I could call him. I just talked to him this morning. . . ."

He looked around, like Russell might appear from the back room and tell Ryan he'd been playing a prank and our table was fine. I could sense his panic that the evening would not shape up as he'd planned.

"Don't worry about it, Ryan," I said, squeezing his arm. "We'll just go somewhere else."

I pulled him toward the doorway. He resisted a little, looking once more toward the hostess, but she was already wrapped up in her reservation book again. The rain had mostly subsided now, leaving just little rivers of water in the cobblestones' crevices. Ryan was looking at his phone. "I called for a reservation. Russell called. I should have had him e-mail me." His voice was forlorn and defeated.

"Really, we can go somewhere else," I said. "I didn't like the Real Hostess of Nantucket anyway."

Ryan chuckled at my joke, and I felt a little better on his behalf. "Well, we're not going to be able to go anywhere nice without a reservation," he said. "But I have a buddy who works at the Red Lion Pub. We could at least eat if we go there."

"That's fine." I smiled. "I'm starving."

The Red Lion Pub was a place where I would not embarrass myself. Or probably wouldn't, at least. Ryan's friend Dave, a chubby guy with the air of a leprechaun, didn't check my ID and brought us two massive steins of beer. "You want burgers?" he asked.

Ryan looked at me nervously, then back to Dave. "You don't have like a steak dinner, or something? Not to be a snob, but we were supposed to go to Galley Beach."

"You totally sound like a snob, dude," Dave said jovially. "The cooks can do steak, but honestly, our burgers are the best. Better than a steak at Galley Beach, I think."

"A burger would be amazing." I looked at Ryan. "Really, this is perfect. And then mini golfing, right?"

Ryan shook his head with a grin. "You probably planned this," he said.

Dave was right: The burgers were good. And the fries. And the beer. Dave started up a round of bar trivia. "We've got an all-fish theme tonight, folks," he announced to the smattering of patrons that had signed up to play. It was me and Ryan versus a booth of guys who'd been drinking when we'd come in.

"What famous director was also a voice in the movie *Shark Tale*?"

Our competition started shouting over one another.

"Spielberg!"

"Nah, the guy who made Star Wars!"

"What are you talking about? It's not George Lucas!"

Ryan looked at me. "It's Scorsese, right?" I nodded. He gave the answer.

"Point for the gentleman and his lady friend," Dave said.

Ryan and I high-fived.

"Beginner's luck," called one of the guys, a small balding guy with a huge nose.

"This film inspired a sequel whose tagline was, 'Just when you thought it was safe to go back in the water.'" Dave read the question into the mic.

"*Titanic!*" One of the booth guys shouted.

"Dummy, that didn't have a sequel. Uh, *Deep Blue Sea!*" Our bald friend called out hopefully.

I looked at Ryan. "*Jaws?*"

"Yes, I can't believe they don't know that one."

This time, I gave the answer and we were awarded another point. Ryan kissed me. "My genius."

"Whatever," I said. "This is like stealing candy from babies."

After a few more questions, most of which we got, one of the guys shouted across the bar, "We're gonna buy you some beers."

"Yeah," the bald guy added. "Maybe if we get you drunk enough, you won't know everything!" We laughed, and when Dave arrived with the giant mugs, we saluted our competitors. By then, we'd racked up four more right answers.

"I think we need to send you sympathy shots," I shouted back after a long swig of beer. "Get those guys some tequila," I told Dave. I pulled the money out of my purse to pay for it, insistent even when Ryan wanted to put it on his tab.

"It was my idea," I told him.

"I know. Because you're amazing," Ryan said, pulling me into him and planting a kiss on my forehead.

The night rolled on and I didn't give a second thought to the original plans. Every so often, Ryan would say something like, "This was supposed to be so much nicer. You deserve a real date."

Every time, I kissed him on the lips and said, "This is the perfect real date. I'm having the best time."

I was, and even with some of his worries, it seemed like Ryan was, too.

When our losing competitors left, Ryan looked at his watch. "Oh my God, we're going to miss the last ferry. Your sister will kill me." He threw some cash down, thanked Dave, and we barreled out of the restaurant. Now rain was coming down in sheets. The music had been so loud in the Red Lion that I hadn't heard a thing. Ryan's jacket was no match for the downpour.

"Don't worry about the rain. Let's run," I said. I took off my shoes and we ran in the direction of the dock. But we were still a few blocks away when we heard the distinct bellow of the ferry's departure horn.

"I can't believe it," Ryan said as we ducked under an awning for cover. "This whole night has been ruined. It was supposed to be different."

"This whole night has been awesome, except that you're worried about everything being perfect," I told him, soaked by the warm rain. I was tipsy and the running had me out of breath. Even as a runner, the panicked sprint in bare feet and a date dress after several drinks was new for me.

"You're sure you're not mad?"

I stepped from under the awning and turned my face up to the sky, enjoying the fat, friendly raindrops. "Do I look mad? This was wonderful. I had no idea Nantucket could be so much fun."

Ryan joined me in the rain. His wet shirt clung to his chest, and I let him pull me against him. He kissed me slow and long as his hands ran down my sides. I trembled, and clutched his waist. "Yeah, I guess this isn't so bad," he said, looking down me. Water dripped off his lashes onto my face. "It was kind of fun, kicking those guys' asses at trivia. And being with you."

The rain was slowing, but it clearly wasn't going to be stopping anytime soon.

"There's an inn attached to the Red Lion," Ryan said. "I'm sure Dave can swing us a room, if you're okay staying overnight."

"I'd much rather do that than swim back," I said, already excited at the prospect of having utter privacy with Ryan.

By the time we were in our small but cozy hotel room, my dress clung to me. My hair was drenched and stuck to my back. Ryan's shirt was so wet, I could see the outline of every muscle, like he was the human embodiment of one of those cheap souvenir T-shirts they sold on the boardwalk, with a fit man's torso printed on the front.

I couldn't help it, I started laughing.

Ryan joined in, pulling me to him, laughing so deeply I could feel his body's vibrations against mine. And then he was kissing me. Our sodden clothes glued us together but Ryan drew me in even tighter, his arms folding into my back and drawing me into him. His eyes traced the planes of my face, and I felt myself shudder with pleasure. The way he looked at me felt almost as good as his touch.

He gently pulled one strap of my dress down my shoulder, then the other, easing me out of it. I slowly undid his buttons, peeling his wet shirt away from him, running my fingertips over his skin.

Ryan brought me down onto the bed, kissing my jaw, my chin, and my chest before working his way back up to my face.

He pushed my hair out of my eyes and hovered over me. He wrapped a strand of my hair around his fingertip.

"I love you," he said.

He loved me? "You're crazy," I said.

"Are you serious? I do. And the fact that you think I'm crazy is sort of just another thing to love about you," he said. "You have no idea how amazing you are."

His skin was touching mine, and even though I was naked, I felt warm and protected beneath him.

"But you loved Eliza, too, didn't you?" Why I brought up Eliza right now, I wasn't sure.

"That was a summer fling."

"You could say that about us."

Ryan leaned back, thinking. "No, with Eliza, she was this girl I put on a pedestal. Like she only came around once a year, so she was some kind of comet or something. But you can't really hold on to a comet. You don't even want to try," Ryan said, still holding me as he explained. "You just stand back and admire. So even though we were together, we were never really together in the way that matters. With you, I feel something real. You're real."

"What do you mean?" I knew I was pushing too hard, but I didn't want him to stop. Every new revelation sent a shiver of pleasure down my spine.

"You don't expect things to be handed to you, or to be everyone's favorite," he said, and I couldn't help but make the comparison to Eliza in my mind. "You know exactly how to be you—this girl, no, this woman, who makes me want to see my dreams through. You're inspiring. You inspire me. Like I said, this is real.

Unreal, too. Because I've never felt this way about anyone before. So, I'll say it again: I love you."

I'd heard "I love you" before, but never like this. With Matt, it was sweet, but perfunctory. Even though I'd lost my virginity to him, I half knew at the time that it wasn't true love as much as it was a truly solid relationship.

But Ryan Landry loved me. And, somehow, that pushed me to finally let go of everything else I attached to him—Eliza, our childhood—and just let us be us, in the moment. Whatever happened next, one thing was true right now.

"I love you, too."

CHAPTER TWENTY-SIX

AFTER A RAINSTORM, a blue sky on the Cape was like no blue sky anywhere. My mom had always said it was impossible to paint—no mix of colors could capture the fresh, rich hue of such a true azure.

Even the air wafting in through the gauzy white curtains had a newness to it, though whether that was from the rain or from the events of the night before, I wasn't sure.

I rolled toward Ryan on the pillow, planting slow, languid kisses along his neck and shoulder. He murmured in pleasure and I continued to his chest, feeling my body give way to his. I curled one bare leg over his as he pulled me on top of him. He fumbled for protection on the nightstand and eased into me. We went slow, kissing and touching with our eyes wide open. We'd always been together at night, and everything right now felt fresh, almost innocent. We were seeing each other, and feeling each other, in the light.

He traced up the side of my body with his fingertip. He was looking at me almost reverently. "You're so beautiful," he said.

I bent down to him, pressing my bareness against his. "No, you are," I told him.

We moved together, quietly, but with a sureness of each other's bodies that we'd been developing since that first time. We fit together in so many ways, and together we felt complete.

After, enjoying the liquid sense in my limbs and through my body, I could have lain in bed with Ryan all day, pretending the sky was just ours, and replaying every word he'd said last night. But then I remembered Eliza's words before I'd left.

"I have a dress fitting! My final one. Oh God. She'd going to kill me." I sprang out of bed, looking around the room for my clothes.

"She's going to kill me more." Ryan was already upright and halfway into his pants. "Okay, we'll hit the first ferry and I'll drive you straight there. Garrett can go to the restaurant to sign for orders if he has to."

"Oh no, I'm a mess," I said. I may have been beaming on the inside, but my exterior was a different story. My hair hung in knotty clumps and my eyes were rimmed with runny mascara. I splashed water on my face and ran a nubby washcloth over my skin, lathering my body quickly with the small bar of soap.

Last night's clothes were a catastrophe. My dress was still soaked and sat in a wrinkled pile. I had nothing else to wear, so it was going to have to do. It wouldn't be pretty, but I was sure I wasn't the first bridesmaid to show up for her final fitting looking worse for wear.

Ryan had paid the bill by the time I was able to make myself at least partially presentable. We hightailed it to the ferry, and fortunately were able to board a boat that was already docked.

My phone was buzzing, but I avoided looking at it. I didn't even want to know what frantic state my sisters were in. Once we were back in Ryan's truck, though, I checked the messages. Three calls from Eliza and several texts from Becca and Tea.

"WHERE R U? ELIZA PISSED," Becca's latest read.

"On way," I texted back, then put my phone in Ryan's center console to charge. There was nothing I could do now but get there.

Ryan was on his headset, walking Garrett through what orders to expect from which suppliers. He was calm under pressure, going just a little over the speed limit and talking in a professional, measured tone. He was nothing like some of the restaurateurs I'd seen on TV, all bluster and anger.

We pulled up to Lucy's, parking behind the building. Ryan asked Garrett to hold on, then pulled me in for a kiss. "You're okay if I head to the restaurant?" he asked.

"I think so," I said. "I don't think they'll abandon me here. And if they do, it's not *that* far a walk."

"If you're sure," he said, then grinned at me. "Thanks for the best date of my life."

Even though I was anxious to get inside, thoughts of last night, and this morning, made me smile instantly. "Thank you."

He mouthed the words "I love you" and I mouthed them back. Though I was headed to my doom, I practically skipped around the corner of the building to the front entrance.

Where I ran smack into Eliza.

She looked me up and down, my ratty dress and hair a dead

giveaway that I hadn't been home. "You've got to be kidding me," she said. She had bags under her eyes and her lips were pressed thin.

"I'm sorry," I said. "We missed the last ferry back last night and had to go to an inn and we fell asleep and I didn't think to set an alarm. . . ." Excuses tumbled from my mouth, but Eliza's expression didn't change.

"Of course you didn't think," she said. "No, check that. You think, but only of yourself. I brought us here so we'd have memories, *together*. And you've basically locked yourself away from the rest of us. No, you *have* locked yourself away from the rest of us. Even the thing that comes so naturally for you, writing, you can't do. Forget that you're the maid of honor in my wedding. What kind of *sister* are you? Or are you a solo act now? Because this whole summer has been the Kate Show. Kate's big job, Kate's fun summer fling with Ryan Landry . . . Does he know that you're only with him so that you can feel like the star?"

I'd been prepared, happy even, to apologize to Eliza. I had been planning to serve myself up on a platter as her utterly devoted servant from now until the wedding. But her treating Ryan and I like some kind of nothing was way below the belt. We were not just a throwaway summer romance.

"Look, I get that you're mad. But what right do you have to call me and Ryan a summer fling? You don't know anything about it."

Eliza blew out a sharp, sarcastic breath and rolled her eyes. "I know that you want whatever's mine, and I had Ryan first."

My blood was boiling now. "Name one thing?"

"God, these sandals." Eliza pointed down at her feet, at my mom's mermaid sandals. *My* mermaid sandals.

"I'm getting married. I wanted something of Mom's. But when I picked these up, you acted like I'd just taken your first-born."

"I didn't say anything," I protested.

"You didn't have to. It's the look of horror you give whenever I get something," Eliza said.

"Those were mine! Don't you even remember? The art fair, when you got the pressed-heart pendant? Mom bought those for me and her. You didn't even like them!" I yelled.

"Well, you should have said something," she said. She paused, looking down at the shoes. "I do remember, now. But instead of taking everything as me doing something to you, why don't you take responsibility for yourself and speak up when you're upset?"

"Because I always think you'll still just take whatever you want. You think everything belongs to Eliza. Well, guess what? Lots of things you think are yours just aren't." My voice was loud. If any windows were open in Lucy's studio, my younger sisters would surely hear me.

"What is that supposed to mean?"

"Oh, I don't know. Maybe that you're just jealous because Ryan actually loves me, and he never loved you. Not even once in all those summers. He told me so," I said.

"Are you delusional? Ryan and I were a summer thing. I've been with Devin for two years. And, maybe you haven't noticed, but we're getting *married*."

"You don't even love Devin." I was in Eliza's face now, and the words were flowing freely. "Everyone can see it but you. Those vows you gave me, they might as well be a pizza order. I've had deeper feelings for mushrooms."

"Oh God. I don't have time for this. If you're trying to ruin my wedding, keep up the great work." Eliza spun away from me and huffed into the store.

I was left feeling more dressed-down than when I'd arrived. I knew I had to go inside, put on a good face, and be the maid of honor, but first I had to get myself together. I leaned against the side of the building to close my eyes and take a few deep breaths. *One . . . two . . . thre—*

"You left this in the car."

I opened my eyes to see Ryan holding my cell phone out to me. Seeing his face was such a relief.

"I just had the worst fight with Eliza," I said. I didn't want to tell him the gist of it. I didn't even want to comment on the ridiculous point Eliza had made about us being nothing more than a summer fling.

"I know. I heard." His tone was flat. He couldn't even look me in the eye.

I panicked, trying to replay the argument in my head. What had he heard?

"I know I said some ugly things, but . . . I was enraged after Eliza called us a summer fling," I explained. I hated that he'd overheard us airing all our dirty laundry, but he had to know that I'd wanted to stick up for him—for us.

"That didn't bother me so much. It's her opinion," he said. "But I told you I loved you, and you immediately turned it around to use against your sister."

Oh God. I sucked in a breath as the truth of his words hit me.

I had done just that, hadn't I? I'd taken a gift from Ryan and used it as a blunt object to hurt my sister.

"I . . . I was so mad. I just. It was stupid. It was wrong." I scoured my brain for the right words, but they didn't come.

"You know, maybe Eliza is right. Maybe I am just some summer fling. Or some kind of trophy in a contest you think you're having with your sister."

My eyes filled with tears, but I didn't let them spill over. I had no idea what to say.

"Here's your phone." He handed it to me, still looking away. "I didn't mean to look at it, but you had a message. From Matt."

I looked down at the screen. Sure enough, there was a text from Matt, whom I hadn't talked to in weeks. It read, "Hey K, Keeping the weekend open. Give me a shout if you still need me to come be your date."

I felt sick. If only Ryan and I had stayed in bed this morning, like I'd wanted to, maybe none of this would have happened.

"Isn't that your ex?" Ryan said. "The Stanford guy? Would you rather go with him?"

I shook my head, looking at Ryan. "You're my date," I said. "I had told him earlier in the summer I might want him to come with me, but that was months ago—before anything happened with us."

"But you kept him waiting in the wings, just in case you decided to end your summer fling early?" Ryan looked at me sadly. "I mean, you still have time to change your mind."

"No, and you know you're who I want to be with." This was so screwed up. And it was all my fault. Why hadn't I just told Matt the truth about my relationship with Ryan? Why was I determined to mess things up? "Look, can we not do this right now?" I rubbed the back of my hand against my eyelids. "I screwed up. I know I did. But you're my date, if you'll go with me. So can we talk later?"

Ryan nodded slowly, turning away from me without a second glance. "Sure, later."

I hoped he meant it.

CHAPTER TWENTY-SEVEN

THE NEXT DAY brought the rehearsal dinner and my complete and utter contrition. I wanted to apologize to everyone. To Ryan, for leveling his "I love you" at my sister. For not making it clear to Matt sooner that our wedding plans were off. To Eliza, for what I'd said about her and Devin. I'd taken two of the most important people in my life for granted, in different ways, and now I felt like I'd lost both of them at once.

In hopes of that, I'd spent all of last night trying to come up with brilliant vows for Eliza. I had a start, though they weren't perfect. My plan was to get her alone at the dinner and try to work through them together, which I hoped would also help us work out our issues.

For now, though, I slugged some white wine and chatted up out-of-town relatives. I was trying to be a buffer for my dad, who could only take so many concerned stares and lowered-voice intonations of the question, "How have you been?" It was always asked in a way that implied the last three words, "*without your wife.*"

"Where's the groom?" My aunt Betty, a flirt even in her seventies, scanned the room.

I gestured for Becca. "Know where Devin is?" I said. The reception room at the Chatham Bars Inn was packed with people who'd flown in for the weekend.

"I saw him with his sister a minute ago." Becca had brought Garrett and was proudly introducing them to our relatives. Though I'd brought Ryan, things were still icy between us. We hadn't had a chance to talk as I was too caught up trying to be as maid-of-honor-y as possible.

Ryan had excused himself from my side to hang out with Morrison, who would be running the sound system during the beach ceremony. I knew I had to get Ryan alone at some point, to properly apologize, but I hoped in the meantime that some unwinding with his friend would put him in a better mood.

"Can you ask Eliza?" I was doing my best to be patient with Becca, who had seemed to make Garrett's comfort her priority for the evening. It was sweet, but I needed her on sister duty.

"She won't know," piped up Tea, behind me. "She's been bonding with family at the bar all night." The hint of concern beneath her chipper tone was probably only apparent to me.

Sure enough, Eliza was with our cousins from California, all of them toasting something with shots. Eliza tipped hers back like a pro and I could tell she was drunk by her sway when she slammed her shot glass down on the bar.

"Ugh, probably because she's still mad at me," I muttered under my breath.

"For what?" Tea asked. She fussed with the top of her sundress, even though it fit her perfectly.

"Nothing, never mind." I had to give Eliza credit. She hadn't ratted me out to our little sisters or so much as twitched half a dirty look at me during the fitting.

Instead, I found Devin on my own. He was a good sport, playing along even when my aunt Betty commented on the cuteness of his butt and went in for a squeeze.

"So do you work out, or is naturally round?" Aunt Betty giggled as Devin leaned toward me, his face a little desperate.

"Hey, if you get a chance, can you tell Eliza I'd really like her to meet my uncle Seamus? He's in from Ireland and he can't wait to be introduced." Devin sighed, looking toward the bar, where Eliza was laughing loudly at something our cousin Joey had said. "I think I've been stressing her out, but maybe if you say something."

Fat chance, I thought, but I knew Devin's request was a good excuse to at least talk to Eliza. "Absolutely," I said. "I just need to ask the photographer for a few shots that were on Eliza's list, and then I'll pass on the message."

"Okay, in the meantime, I'll watch my ass," Devin said. "Literally. Your aunt Betty's a trip."

"Yeah, don't let her get you alone," I teased.

Eliza seemed to have forgotten that she'd wanted some rehearsal dinner photos in the hotel's amazing gardens. She thought it would give the photographer more time to snap candids at the wedding if all the posed pictures of out-of-town guests were out of the way.

Since she didn't seem like she was going to ensure it happened, I thought I'd remember for her. It would be one more way to show her that I did care about her wedding and had been paying attention all summer.

I made my way around the room, stopping to hug and greet family I hadn't seen in forever. The last time I'd been around most of these people had probably been my mom's funeral. She was an only child and her closest relatives were cousins she'd grown up with on the West Coast, so they didn't exactly make the trip east often. It wasn't as bad as I'd thought it would be. Everyone seemed to know to keep the talk about the wedding; they didn't need to mention my mom because they knew we were thinking of her. How could we not have been? She should have been here.

At the bar, Ryan and Morrison had joined Eliza and my cousins. I tried to catch his eye, but he shifted so that his back was toward me. Ugh, I would have to deal with him later. Later. Later. Later. I had a lot to do later.

Finally, I spotted the photographer talking to my uncle Roger, my dad's brother. Uncle Roger was the kind of person who, as soon as he spotted some article of technology, would ask its owner dozens of questions about it even if he didn't know what he was saying.

"And do you think the pixel quality is adequate?" He was pointing at the camera's display as the photographer tried to politely consider the question.

"I'm not sure what you mean," she said. "I mean, I always download the raw files and then work with them from there. For the best quality."

As I approached, the photographer beamed. "Hi there, do you need something?" Her eyes seemed to say, *I'll do anything as long as I can get back to work.*

"Hi, Uncle Roger," I said. "I just need to borrow Sarah now to get some shots Eliza wanted." Uncle Roger gave me a chagrined look as I pulled the photographer aside. I'd just sent her off with instructions when Devin resurfaced.

"Hey, I'm sorry to bug you, but did you have a chance to talk to Eliza?" he asked. "I think we're all going to sit down and eat soon and my guess is Uncle Seamus will be too tired from the flight to stick around much later. He's no Aunt Betty."

"So sorry, but I haven't gotten a chance yet," I said. "But I will right now, I promise."

"You're a star, Kate. Thanks and sorry to be so pushy. It's just that at the wedding tomorrow I doubt they'll be able to really talk."

"You know I'm happy to," I said. Beneath Devin's polite inquiries was a touch of sadness. I didn't think the night was going the way he'd hoped. I really wanted it to, for both his and Eliza's sakes. Yes, the rehearsal dinner was partly about Eliza and him getting to spend time with people they hadn't seen in a long time, but wasn't it also about them doing it together? I wanted to tell him things would be fine at, or at least after, the wedding tomorrow, but it didn't seem like my place. I wasn't exactly the love expert lately, either.

I headed into the main reception room, my heart thudding nervously. Knowing that I'd have to approach Ryan and Eliza at the same time was a less-than-ideal scenario. I hoped that after I ripped off the first Band-Aid, it would be easier to do the next. I'd find Eliza, apologize, take her to meet Uncle Seamus, and ask for some time tonight to go over her vows. Then I'd go back for Ryan.

But the bar was emptied out when I got there, save for Morrison, who was chatting with my cousin Kira.

"Kate," he said. "Great party. And your family's nice, too." His wide grin took up most of his narrow face.

"Aren't they?" I smiled at Kira, who also had a happy flush, and seemed to be enjoying Morrison's company. "Hey, have you seen Eliza?"

He nodded. "She and Ryan were here and I think they took off, looking for you, maybe? Or something about checking on the food? I don't know."

Eliza and Ryan had been looking for me together? That was definitely strange, but maybe boded well for my apology plans. It was nice to know that Ryan still cared enough to help make sure dinner was perfect. I left the reception room and headed toward the hotel kitchens.

"Remember how it used to be?" came a voice that sounded like Eliza's. As I walked down the hall, I peered left, where the small ladies' lounge was partially open.

"Eliza?" I called.

"Don't you miss it?" Eliza was slurring. Who was she talking to?

I pried the door open the rest of the way. The lights were off and the room was dim, but there was no mistaking Ryan's silhouette. I could see his shadow, his back resting against the wall, and the light from the hall spilled onto my sister, who leaned against him, her arms looped possessively around his shoulders. She leaned in toward him—toward his lips.

"Kate—" Ryan straightened when he saw me, prying himself out of her arms.

"Kate?" Eliza said, scrambling away from him.

But I was dumb little Katie again, and I was leaving. I ran back down the hall, cursing that the only exit was through the reception room. I clipped past Devin and an old man who had to be his uncle.

"What happened?" Devin asked as I ran past. "Did you find Eliza?"

I couldn't look at him. "Go see for yourself," I shouted back, not stopping. In ten breaths, I was out of the hotel and into the night before anyone could stop me.

CHAPTER TWENTY-EIGHT

THE SUN WAS coming up, and I didn't care. I wanted to go to California right now, where people watched the sun set, instead of watching it rise. I was done with summer.

Carrier's Bluff, just a little ways up the beach from where Ryan and I had had our first picnic, had been my mom's favorite spot to paint. Even though I knew time had changed the coastline, both in ways natural and man-made, I felt like I'd stepped inside one of my mom's paintings. You could sense my mom in them, could feel her joy in each stroke, could imagine her heart filling as the light flickered over the water. She was gone, though.

Her joy and her love were, of course, always with us—I knew that was what I was supposed to think. But the people who said those things had never lost anyone. The truth was, when someone was gone, they were gone. Coming to their favorite places, you could have moments where you thought they might suddenly appear, like they'd be waiting for you. But they never did. They weren't. The things you wanted their help sorting out were all yours to bear.

The only person I wanted to talk to was my mom. I wasn't looking for her to make it all better, or to fix it. I knew what she'd say: that life was hard and full of hurts and even the people who were supposed to be on our side sometimes weren't. She was realistic that way.

It struck me that, maybe, in a way, she *was* here. I knew what she'd say, and I knew that somehow, eventually, no matter what had passed between us, I'd come out the other side with Eliza.

Not anytime soon, of course, but we would. I couldn't imagine my life without my sister in it. Maybe we'd never fully recover, but we'd be in each other's lives.

Ryan was a different story. It seemed like he'd gone out of his way to hurt me, driving a knife into my heart and then twisting it so that there was no way I could yank it out. I wasn't as sure what my mom would say about that. I had a feeling her advice would be to give it time, and eventually my heart would heal itself.

I knew I should start the walk back soon, before the beaches were brimming with people and the whole world saw a messed-up ex-maid-of-honor dragging herself home. My feet were dirty from running and the dress I'd worn to the rehearsal dinner was ruined. I had my useless clutch, containing just a lipstick and the folded vows—my phone wouldn't fit. It wasn't like I wanted to call anyone to come get me, but I had to get back eventually, even if the wedding was off. I had a feeling it would be. I didn't see how Eliza could have worked her way out of what had happened last night, if she even wanted to.

I took one last, long look at the ocean. The sun was up overhead and I felt especially warm beneath it. "I miss you, Mom," I said over the bluff. Even though no one said anything back to me, for the shortest of seconds, I could feel her next to me.

When I turned around, my eyes still squinting away the morning sun, I saw a figure in front of me that looked just like my mother. I knew, of course, that it wasn't. I knew instantly that it was Eliza.

Before I could walk past her, before I could surface the angry words I wanted to, I heard myself saying, "How did you find me?" Down the road, I could see the car idling, my father, Becca, and Tea inside.

"It was Mom's favorite spot," she said, like it was the most obvious thing in the world that I'd choose it. "We were looking for you all night but in the back of my head, I knew you'd come here. Everyone said that I was crazy, since you didn't take the car. You ran, didn't you?" She took in my wrecked dress and bedraggled appearance and sighed, like she wanted to take all the blame for it.

I shrugged. "It's only six miles. I've done more."

Eliza looked past me, toward the water. Her eyes were red and puffy. Her engagement ring was gone. For as disheveled as I was, she looked like she felt worse. She looked tired and small.

I let myself be a little less mad at her.

Eliza sat down in the sand, folding her legs up to her chest with her chin on her knees. "Stay with me," she said. "Please."

I'd been there all night, so what was a little longer? I crouched back down into the sand, and this time, I noticed how tired and sore I was. It hadn't registered before. The anger had kept my body coiled and unyielding and now exhaustion set in.

We were next to each other, but not looking at each other. The several inches of space I'd left between us felt like a particularly treacherous obstacle course.

But Eliza's voice was soft when she spoke. "I'm not the best at this. I'm good at the part where I'm holding back. But I don't know what else to do, so I'll just say it." She ran a hand through the sand, her fingers leaving four little curved trails behind. "I'm still completely and utterly fucked up over Mom."

"I know," I said, playing with the hem of my dress, which had ripped at some point. "I've always known. I never thought you were okay. I just never knew why you couldn't trust the rest of us to let us know."

She faced me, and grimaced. "Because you all have your own problems and had to go through plenty yourselves. And Dad was a mess and he needed me, so I thought I could just be the one you all needed."

Eliza moved closer to me on the sand. I didn't move away.

"Dad's selling the house. The beach house." She hurled the words into the air for me to catch.

"What? When did he decide this?" Moments ago, I had sworn I'd never come back here and now I felt like everything I loved was being taken away. How could we sell the house? We'd just learned how to be in it again. It was supposed to be ours forever. No one else could live in it the way we did.

"Ages ago. I knew it at the start of the summer. I knew it a year ago, really. It sort of prompted my whole idea to get married. Devin was ready, so we got engaged right after I told him about the house, and how I wanted to have the wedding here. Like it would be a healing event, or something. . . ." she said, trailing off. "Ha. Healing. He was so supportive, too. I really screwed up."

Eliza looked pale beneath her tan. She slumped into her knees, defeated. A great sense of guilt settled on my chest as I thought of all she had gone through to try to bring us together again as a family, to try to give us one last summer as a family. I resisted the urge to hug her; I didn't know if we were ready for that yet. Instead I asked, "Did you really want to get married? Did you want all this for yourself, at all?"

"I don't know. I thought I did. I thought Devin and I made sense, and we'd been together for a while and why wait? And I guess I've felt like a grown-up for so long that I just thought marriage was the next step." She had tears in her eyes. "It was easy to get caught up in it."

Seeing her like this, I regretted all the times I wished things wouldn't go her way. I dug my foot in the sand and lifted it out, letting the grains funnel through my toes. "Isn't getting married in a big rush kind of the not grown-up thing to do?"

Eliza laughed. "Yeah, well, I've always been able to get so wrapped up in a plan that the plan itself becomes more important than anything else." She sighed, long and loud. "I made such a mess. I knew, deep down, it wasn't right. Not me and Devin so much. I think we are right. Or, we were. But we could have moved into a place in the city together and eased into our lives, instead of hurtling ourselves into marriage."

She looked up at me. "Deep down, I was scared. And then I saw you and Ryan, and I remembered how much fun things used to be, for me, before Mom, and suddenly I realized I'm not a grown-up and I don't want to be yet."

I sniffed the air: the telltale smell of a hard night was coming off Eliza in waves. "You don't smell like one. Except for maybe Grandpa George." I'd made the joke to avoid asking her about the powder room, and about Ryan. I didn't want to hear that Ryan had lied, that he didn't love me. I didn't want to know that it just took Eliza being available again for him to change his mind.

"Ha-ha," Eliza said. "But I should explain. Explain last night, I mean. I was drunk, and I told Ryan I needed to talk to him about something important—he probably thought it was you— and I threw myself at him. He didn't even kiss me back. He really loves you, Katie. He wanted to come with us, and I think he's been looking for you all night, too. It's just I know this spot and he doesn't."

I shrugged. I felt a little better, though I wasn't sure I believed her. Ryan was Ryan; he'd look for a missing me, just like he'd fixed my bike when we were kids. It was his nature. Another aspect of our situation had become clear last night, after I'd left the rehearsal dinner. "Even if he does, it doesn't matter anyway. Not really. We leave in a few days. I love him, too, but it's not like we're going to be a Cape Cod–California long-distance romance. He's not a souvenir."

"What does that even mean? A souvenir?" Eliza said. "Look, you never know what's going to happen. I didn't think I was going to screw up my own wedding," she said, looking out to sea. "So, aren't you glad you didn't waste time writing my vows?"

I clicked open my clutch and pulled out the folded sheets. "Actually, I was going to show you these last night."

I handed her the papers. The truth was, when I'd sat down to write, most of what I'd come up with wasn't quite about Eliza and

Devin together. "I've only just started to get to know Devin, and he's a great guy, so I was going to show you these at dinner and then revise them with you," I said, giving her the notebook paper. "When I wrote these, I kept thinking of you and all you do for this family. I think a lot of these are really about you."

Eliza scanned the paper and started to read some of my sentences aloud, her voice catching.

"I vow to be strong for us, and strong for you, because when you become my family, you become my dearest treasure and I will protect you for life.

"What matters is family, and having the spirit and the will to keep it together no matter what.

"I vow to celebrate the great times with you and to make the hard times easier.

"When I look at you, the world makes sense."

I pointed to Grace's line. "That one, Grace helped with," I said, quietly. "And she said it in terms of a romantic relationship but, in all honesty, even though I never show it, I don't think I really make sense without you."

Eliza was letting tears pour down her face, giving in in a way I'd never seen her cry before. It was as though the years of holding back had finally converged into one endless stream of weeping. "You wrote all this about me and then I tried to kiss your boyfriend?" She coughed out the words through a fresh sob. "And I took your mermaid shoes?"

"I guess." By now, I was crying, too. For my mom, my dad, Ryan, the summer's end, and the way that it meant I'd be leaving my old life behind. For all the ways I'd been looking forward to it, deep down I was scared, too.

"Kate, I'm so sorry. I don't know if you can ever forgive me."

I looked out over the bluff and wondered if my mom was out there, if she could see us. I took Eliza's hand. It was nice to hold her hand in mine, just like I'd held my mom's before.

"That's a good start."

CHAPTER TWENTY-NINE

THE TEXT MESSAGES from Ryan had stopped yesterday. Now, he was on to phone calls and voice mails. He'd sent enough to fill my whole mailbox.

I wasn't mad at him anymore. Eliza had made it clear that he hadn't cheated and kept encouraging me to call him back. I believed her about him. Things still weren't perfect between my older sister and me, but I'd meant what I'd written in the vows. She'd protect me no matter what and I knew she wouldn't push me toward someone she thought would hurt me.

Ryan's nonstop texts, e-mails, and calls didn't seem to come from a place of guilt, so much as hope. He was a good guy and I knew it.

Still, what would be the point of calling him back? I was leaving soon. All we'd have would be a few awkward moments where we tried to fix us, only to say good-bye again. It'd be more confusing than if we just cut things off now. I wasn't coming back. Or if I did, it wouldn't be for years—without the house, and without Ryan as my neighbor, much less my boyfriend.

As much as I felt like I was losing everything, I tried to tell myself that maybe I needed to lose it all so the slate was clean for the next stage of my life.

Now, I put all my focus toward the last of Grace's notes. I liked spending my last days in our house, working at the kitchen table, trying to remember every last detail. The leftover smells of breakfast floated in from the kitchen, where Becca had made pancakes before taking off for a beach day with Garrett. The familiarity of the house and the hope that we could go away for three years—maybe even longer—and it would still be the same place. That Harborville wouldn't change enough to make it foreign. That time moved more slowly here, and your memories all seemed to coexist with the present. Couldn't I have a clean slate for a new life, and still feel connected to my old one?

My dad emerged from the master bedroom, a lumpy duffel bag in his hand. He came over and glanced at my notes spread out across the table.

"Some wedding, huh?" I said.

"Katie," he chided. "There are worse things." Dad had given Eliza a lot of money for the wedding, but it didn't seem to bother him. One thing about losing someone you love is that it tended to make perspective easier to gain on the things that really were smaller. Money was one of them.

"I know," I said, gesturing to an empty chair. "Do you have a minute?"

"Sure," he said, sitting down and looking at my computer. "Finishing your work for Grace?"

I looked at the Excel document, riddled as it was with nonsense. I didn't know what Grace could possibly do with it.

I felt like I'd failed because, while there were funny lines and odd little nuggets, none of these ideas seemed right for a new novel.

"Yup. It was definitely an experience. I'm delivering these in a bit," I said. I shut the laptop. "I just wanted to say, I did a lot of thinking after the . . . well, whatever that was. I know I'm going west and I know I haven't really been part of everything this summer . . . but this place is *still* our summer."

My dad must have known what I was getting at, because he shifted away from me in his chair, waiting for whatever I would say next.

"Eliza told me you want to sell the house," I said, getting right to it. "But I don't think that's a good idea."

"The Realtor is already at work on the listing. She's coming to take pictures once we leave," my dad said, resigned but firm. He looked around the kitchen and the living room, as if sizing up what the Realtor would see.

"I don't think Mom would want that," I said. I felt bad for invoking my mom, but I knew that it was the truth—she'd never want to sell this place. "Eliza said to let you do what you need to do, but I don't think she's right in this case. Mom is."

My dad sighed and put his hand over mine, squeezing my palm in his. His eyes welled up and he gave me a sad smile, like he couldn't let himself agree with me.

"Kate, your mom will always be part of me. She's more than part of me," he began. "This summer, I tried to just enjoy the memories we made here, but it's too much. Anywhere else, I can pretend to be a normal guy: house, job, kids. But here, I just feel like I'm walking around with a huge hole in my chest. I don't think living in the past is good for me, or for any of you girls. I just want us all to get a fresh start."

I knew he hadn't been happy this summer, but hearing him say all this out loud made me hurt for him.

"But don't you think it will hurt just as badly to leave behind all those memories? And to give this place up before we can make lots of new ones? Someday, we'll all have families, and you'll be a grandfather and this will be where we come. If we sell it, we're not just losing a house. We're losing our summers," I said, my eyes welling now as I imagined some blurry future full of my sisters and husbands and nieces and nephews and my own kids. I'd always imagined that it would be here.

"Maybe someday we'll find another place on the Cape, or another way to spend our summers," my dad said, looking at me like he expected this to appease me. "It's just this place is so much your mother that I come here and I feel like a ghost. And you say that now about you and your sisters, but you're all growing up and headed off to new things. This house was empty so much of the summer because you have your own lives. It's not the way it used to be."

I thought of how checked-out he'd been all summer, how much he was even less himself than he could be at home in New Jersey. And I knew, in a way, he was right about all of us being busier and off to our own lives. I still thought we should have a place to come back to, a place that felt like home, but better. I didn't agree with his decision, but I understood.

"So that's it?" I said softly. "We just move on?"

He nodded. "We just move on."

* * *

I could say one thing for my summer job: Grace's plants, at least, looked better than when I'd started working for her. I'd weeded out the truly dead and resuscitated the partially dead. Even in late August, the flowers were vibrant and the leaves shiny and healthy. It wouldn't be going on my resume, but I was proud.

Grace didn't answer when I knocked, but by now I was used to just walking inside. She would either be in the kitchen, making tea she left in half-drunk cups around the house, or she'd be seated at her desk, scowling at TMZ.

I'd printed the Excel doc containing all her notes. It was in a not-too-small font (her pet peeve) with the entries ordered by theme (things about love, things about family, things about work) and by type (dialogue, character, plot). I'd highlighted the rows that contained the possibly more interesting pieces.

"Grace?" I called.

She was not in the kitchen. She was not at her desk. "Grace?" I hoped she remembered I was coming. I was leaving the next day and I wanted to say good-bye. I also worried that if I left the document containing my summer's work anywhere in her house, she'd fail to see it, and next year, some other would-be intern would have to come redo all the work I'd just finished.

"Grace?" There was a still-warm teapot on the stove, so I knew she must have been here at some point.

"I'm up here," she said. She was calling from the second story of the house. I'd never been up there. Tentatively, I climbed the stairs, looking at the scattered artwork over the banister. Grace was nothing if not eclectic. Psychedelic-looking posters from long-ago concerts shared space with various nudes and modern, abstract pieces that were just lines of colors. None of the pieces were much bigger than a sheet of paper, and they were all placed close together so the effect was of traveling alongside a bizarre collage of Grace's thoughts.

Her bedroom was at the top of the stairs and took up the whole floor. Her king-sized bed was dead center against a huge floor-to-ceiling window that looked out over the water. "Wow," I said. I had had no idea the house was this impressive. Against the vast backdrop of the ocean, though, Grace looked smaller and older than I'd ever seen her.

She had a deep purple duvet pulled up to her chin and her curly hair was wilder than usual. She looked tired.

"Welcome to me at the end of summer," she said. "A whole season and I've got nothing."

I approached the side of the bed. This was an oddly intimate way to spend my last day of work. It wasn't like I was expecting a formal review, but Grace seemed to be having some kind of breakdown.

"Well, not nothing," I said, handing her the ream of papers.

She peered down at the neat rows containing her translated words. "This is scary. What is this?"

I could have been mad. She was basically questioning my whole summer's worth of work. Now that I knew Grace, though, I'd been expecting this reaction. I thought I might have even been hoping for it, mostly because I had something to tell her. Something I thought would help.

"This is a document of all your notes," I said. "And I think you should put it in a drawer and ignore it forever."

She flipped through the pages, chuckling to herself at some of the lines. "And why would I do that?"

"Because I think you needed this, to see that those piles of randomness came to something. But the truth is, if those things had been really great, you would have used them already. And now the table is wide open and you can start fresh." I gave it some more thought. "In fact, maybe you should write at that table, just for a change of pace. The old is gone to make way for the new."

"Look at your metaphors!" Grace cried, sitting up in her bed. "This is the student-becomes-the-teacher moment in our saga; that's what you're thinking, isn't it?"

I shrugged. "Not really. I just want you to write a new book," I said.

"Well, open that drawer." She gestured to her bedside table. I pulled open a drawer that was cluttered with notebooks and pens. I panicked for a second, thinking she was going to add these to my workload before I could be done. But then I saw the tattered pages of my cartographer story, with Grace's notes scattered in the margins.

I pulled it out, feeling excitement when I saw happy exclamation points and circles with bubbles proclaiming, "more of this!" "You read it," I said.

"Of course I read it," she said. "You're good. You need to get better, but we all do. If you remember that half of writing is self-loathing, you'll be just fine. And I like your cartographer. She reminds me of you, accepting that sometimes what doesn't make sense makes the most sense of all."

I laughed, though I wasn't quite sure what she meant. It sounded like a Smokey-ism. "Thank you."

"Get the notebook, too," she said, pointing to a spiral-bound notebook at the top of the drawer. "I'm not letting you teach me without teaching you."

I opened the notebook, which was filled top to bottom with Grace's handwriting. A slightly neater version of Grace's handwriting.

"I started writing that when I couldn't write anything else. It's my rules for writing, or tips on the writing life, or something like that. Really, it's a lot of self-indulgent memoir kind of crap but there might be something useful in there. Or at least something to remember me by," she said. "It's yours."

I started to read the pages, laughing at how Grace-like the words were. "But, you could publish this," I protested. A book about Grace's path as an author would be a big deal. I'd buy it, of course, because the way she wrote, the book wasn't just about writing. It was about life.

She rolled her eyes. "What, another old coot with nothing new to say writing about her glory days? Things I've learned? Nah. Nobody knows anything." She pulled the duvet away from herself. She was fully dressed with no bathrobe in sight.

"You're dressed. What were you doing in bed?" I asked.

"Read the notebook. I'm dramatic," she laughed. "You probably are a little, too, if you're a writer."

I thought of my six-mile barefoot run to Carrier's Bluff after the rehearsal dinner. I supposed I could be a touch dramatic.

"How did the vows go by the way?"

"The wedding was called off," I said. "They're still talking, though." Eliza had reached out to Devin and they were trying to work things through. Eliza was not in a fix-it mode, for a change, and had gone to Devin completely apologetic and open for anything—to going back to just being boyfriend and girlfriend, to living separately, if it came to that. Anything to keep him in her life. She wasn't worried about saving face, or pushing forward. She just wanted to be with Devin, I knew.

"Oh really?" Grace didn't want to seem overinterested, but I could tell she was.

"I think part of it is that my sister's only twenty-one. She just wasn't ready."

"Oh God, you never told me that," Grace said. "Of course she couldn't write her vows. It should be illegal to write vows when you're that young. You remember that, too. Maybe add it to my notebook."

Now, she put her arms around me in a tight hug. I was caught off guard for a second. For her eccentric bohemian vibe, she was not a touchy-feely kind of person. But I hugged her back, and it felt good.

"Before you go, you're going to help me set up my computer at the dining room table," she said, leading me to the stairs. "And you're going to give me your e-mail. I want all the sexy stories from Berkeley. No leaving the good parts out."

CHAPTER THIRTY

THE BEACH HOUSE was spotless. The fridge was empty. Any woebegone container of leftovers from Becca's and Tea's shifts at Landrys' had been eaten or discarded. I'd cleaned the studio of my things. Eliza had gotten a start packing some of Mom's old clothes from the attic.

Once the house sold, we'd be back to claim the more personal items, but the Realtor told Dad to leave the furnishings and art so the place gave off that "Cape vibe."

I was in my old room, the one where I'd seen Ryan on our first day back. I was going to take down the charcoal drawing of me that my mom had done. I wanted to bring it home now, so I could take it to school with me. We'd already packed up our favorites of Mom's work to bring with us to New Jersey, and Tea had done a walkthrough of the restaurant with Mr. Landry to figure out where to hang the ones that he had bought. She'd already given the money from the sale to the charity she'd selected, and made the donation in our mother's name. I was proud of her.

Becca slouched into my room. She'd also already grabbed a few of her favorite shells and tchotchkes from around the house. "I can't believe this is our last day here," she said, flopping onto my neatly made bed. "The years that we didn't come, I still knew we'd be back. But now we won't."

I flopped down next to her. "I know. Did you tell Garrett?"

She nodded. "Yeah, and he's upset, but we're going to try to see each other off season, too. It's not that far a drive. He might come to homecoming with me."

I smirked. "Well, at least one of us landed our Landry brother."

"Whatever," she said, poking my side. "You should talk to Ryan before we leave."

We didn't have time to get into it, because Eliza ducked her head into my room. "I think I convinced Dad to stop at Laurel's Diner on the way home to do breakfast for dinner. But we have to get a move on."

"*You* convinced him?" Tea's voice floated in from the hall. "That was me." She handed me an envelope. A thick envelope. "From Smokey. He said he'd told you there'd be bonuses and he never gave you yours."

I looked skeptically at the envelope. "It's not illegal, is it?"

"I got five hundred dollars," she bragged. "And, yes, totally legal. I'm almost positive."

There was two hundred and fifty dollars in my envelope. "What?" I said, stunned. "I only worked there for two weeks."

Tea grinned. "Believe me, he can afford it. I helped him with his books," she said, adding, "And he said that was for *your* books."

"Okay, guys, let's go," Eliza said. "Kate has to be in California by the end of the week, and you both start school tomorrow, so chop-chop."

I didn't want to go. It was nice, having all my sisters crammed into my tiny room with me. But I knew Eliza was right. Fall and real life awaited.

My dad knocked on the door, even though it was open. "Can I come in?"

"Can you fit?" Becca asked.

Tea piled in on the twin bed with us, and Eliza came farther into the room so my dad had space.

My dad took a deep breath as he began. "I know this summer has been a hard one," he said, looking first at Becca and Tea, then at me and finally at Eliza. "And I handled it by checking out and giving up."

We all murmured soft protests, but my dad held up his hand so he could go on. "No, I did," he said, looking at me. "But Kate made me realize that this place isn't just our past. It's our future. I can't run away from the memories with your mom because I won't get new ones with her. I just need to make a different kind of new ones."

Eliza was staring at him. "Wait . . . Does this mean you're not going to sell the house?"

"I just called the Realtor and canceled everything," he said, a slow smile spreading over his face. "We'll still rent it over the winter, like always, and we'll be back next summer."

Tea shrieked and Becca clapped. Eliza grabbed me off the bed and hugged me. It was the first hug we'd shared in a while.

A few hours later, we stood on the porch. The porch where

we'd return next summer, and the summer after, and many more
to come. Maybe not all of us, every year. Maybe in different stages
of our lives, with different concerns and issues and dreams. But
the house was ours, and would be. It would always be here for the
summer, whenever we needed it.

No one was going to do it, so I did. I gave the door three soft
knocks. My sisters and my father looked at me in surprise but
then they said the words, without my prompting. "Thank you
house. 'Til next time."

We'd loaded up the car. Becca had gone to the Landrys' to
say good-bye to Garrett earlier in the day. Tea was already complaining about being hungry and asking if we thought Laurel's
Diner would have soy milk. Eliza was checking the battery life
on her iPad. She'd turned down the offer from the PR firm in
the city, and had instead begun researching countries where she
could teach English. She and Devin were going to keep talking,
but they were taking some space.

I was just about to get in the car when Eliza blocked my
door. "If you don't talk to him, we're not going home," she said.
"You can just skip college." She pointed over my shoulder. On
the street, right where I'd first seen him this summer, was Ryan,
leaning against his blue pickup.

I was wearing cutoffs and a torn T-shirt from one of my cross-
country meets. My hair was in a sloppy bun. I no doubt smelled
after packing and cleaning. Ryan looked crisp and clean in dark
jeans and a gray T-shirt. This was not fair. But he was looking at
me so hopefully, and Eliza was clearly not backing down, so I
made my way to his car.

"Hi," I said, registering him instantly. Whatever we had or

didn't have, were or weren't, when we were together, I felt like we were electrons in a particle accelerator, eager to collide.

"Hi," he said, lifting a hand like he was going to touch me and then dropping it to his side.

"We're leaving," I said, dumbly, as though the loaded-up car wasn't incontrovertible evidence of our departure.

"I know." He turned his body toward mine, eclipsing me so our conversation instantly felt more private. "Just something's been bugging me. I lied to you."

"Oh yeah?" I thought immediately of the night he'd told me he'd loved me, and how I was real, and Eliza just an abstraction. That was the lie. Why had I even come over here? *Thanks a lot, Eliza*, I thought.

"Yeah." He grinned. I couldn't believe he was smiling. "You know how I told you I started planning our picnic the day you and I walked home from Smokey's?"

I nodded, looking at the car, wondering how long this would take, and how bad I would feel when it was over.

"Well, remember when I saw you in your window, that first day you guys got here?"

"Yes," I said, flushed to remember how I'd stared at him. How just the sight of him had made my body quake. He still had that effect and yet, this summer, my feelings had grown into so much more than an innocent childhood crush.

"Good. Because that was the day," he said. "That was the day it all started for me. I saw you and everything told me that I needed to ask you out. I'd ask you out again right now. That's the effect you have on me." He grinned his half grin and I smiled back. I didn't know what to say, but I was glad he hadn't taken back his "I love you." Whatever happened, I wanted that night, and that moment, to keep as my own.

"I didn't kiss your sister, you know," he said in my silence.

"I know," I said, and I did. Any residual doubt I had faded just by the way he was looking at me. "But it's still awfully complicated."

"Maybe." Ryan shrugged, coming closer to me. I felt his warmth surround me even with a good foot and a half between us. "I mean, I know you only liked me in the beginning because of your sister."

I rolled my eyes. "I've had a crush on you since I was a kid," I said.

"Yeah, but part of that was because I was with your big sister and you looked up to her."

I knew he was right. I spent so much time thinking about how Eliza got everything that I didn't ever register that I really did admire her. And so often she played into my own insecurities. She took things over and laid claim to things she wanted, whereas I didn't always know what I wanted or how to get my way. Some of my anger wasn't toward Eliza for being the way she was, but toward myself for not being more like her. When Ryan and I had started dating, I'd fought so hard to believe that I was just protecting our relationship by keeping it secret. But I'd also been treating him like he was some bad habit of mine to get over. The bad habit wasn't him, but my tendency to hold my life up against Eliza's, and feel like I was coming up short.

"You're probably right," I said by way of admittance. "And maybe this summer started out like that. Like, somehow I thought I could finally step out from under Eliza's shadow if I just could see what it felt like to be her. And then I'd get past all my hang-ups and move on."

"So, we *were* just a summer fling to you, then?" Ryan looked right at me, his eyes serious. He didn't want a lie, even if it was to make him feel better.

Fortunately, I didn't have to tell one. "No," I said. "Maybe my motivations were wrong, and maybe I didn't give you the fairest chance, but this summer and us, they're the realest things I've ever known."

I looked at our house and the car, where Eliza sat in the front seat, tapping away on her touchscreen. She was human, I realized. She was different than me, but she didn't have it all figured out any more than I did. I didn't know if I was comforted by the thought, but I felt closer to her. "I just let the past affect me too much."

"Well, you don't need to forget the past to move forward," Ryan said. Finally, he touched me, pulling me in by the waist and kissing me. Kissing me exactly the way I needed to be kissed to guarantee I'd need to be kissed like this again. He pulled his mouth away and whispered into my hair, "So, we weren't a fling, but you're leaving in five minutes."

"Pretty much," I said, going in for another long kiss, not even caring that my sisters and my father might have been watching. "But I've heard some people keep in touch, even across long distances."

"They do, do they?" Ryan said with a grin. "I've heard there are these things called planes, and you can use them to travel to people you love, wherever they are. . . ."

I stood on my tiptoes, pressing my forehead to his, kissing his lips for the last time that summer but not, I thought, for the last time. He wasn't a souvenir, like Ashley had said. Souvenirs were things you put on a shelf and forgot. He'd been my summer. And summers were part of you forever.

"It's true," I said, smiling and wishing I could stretch the minutes out just a little longer. "And you know, we'll always have the summer. . . ."

ACKNOWLEDGMENTS

IF YOU'RE A lucky person, you realize that you could use half your given words in a day saying thank you. I'm beyond lucky. I can and should bestow more thank-yous than I can possibly utter while still keeping this brief enough that someone might read it.

So why not start there? Thank you for reading. Books are an addictive delight, I know, and if you're even three percent like me, there are more to read than you can possibly get to, so I'm grateful you chose one of mine.

Thank you to everyone at Alloy Entertainment. Sara Shandler, Josh Bank, and Les Morgenstein have always, always been a joy to work with; every author should be so lucky. And a special thanks is due to Joelle Hobeika and Hayley Wagreich, editors extraordinaire. Talking through this book with these two was a fabulous experience. Really, talking about anything with them is fabulous because they're just great fun. And, readers, note, it is thanks to Joelle and Hayley that the sexy parts are sexier than I may have originally written them. (Ever wonder how much fun it is to have notes in the margin of your manuscript demanding "More Sexy!"? A lot of fun, I tell you.)

Thank you to Courtney Miller at Amazon Publishing for her excellent notes and speedy turnaround of these pages. She's been an ardent supporter of this book from day one and I'm so grateful.

Thank you to Paul Almond for always looking out for me, and to my agent, Fonda Snyder, who proves that sweet and fierce are not mutually exclusive traits.

Thank you to Shannon Peavey and Chris Petriello, East Coast–transplant friends who provided me beachy details and Cape Cod wisdom, plus are just fun people to have around.

Thank you to my father, Bill Palmer, who reminds me with frequency that he always has my back. He's always believed in trying to do something you really love and, yes, he's right. He also would do anything for his family. It's a serious stroke of luck to win the parent lottery like I have.

Thank you to my son, Clark Stanis, who never lets a day go by without amusing or delighting me in some way, whether by modeling how anything in life can be turned into a hat, pointing out when the moon looks most like a cookie, or preparing an impromptu plastic-food picnic and insisting I take five to dine with him. He may only be three but he is a font of support, going so far as to wake with me at the crack of dawn and set up his "desk" next to mine. I couldn't ask for a better, or cuter, collaborator.

Thank you to my husband, Steve Stanis, who sees me at my very worst—and, let me tell you, it is not pretty, not at all. Puffy-eyed, dusty wretches at the low point of a period piece have nothing on me when I'm truly down for the count. That sometimes he has to use the same techniques on me that he uses on our son ("Deep breath." "Count to 10." "Do you want a red Popsicle?") is maybe something for me to think about. Thank you for always knowing how to fix things and making me laugh while you do so.

Finally, I tend to, yes, be a touch flippant in all things. It's not for lack of feeling that I jest; if anything, it's often for too much feeling. I never thought I'd write something in which a character was dealing with a loved one's death. I also never thought I'd lose my mom when I did. My mom, Debra Palmer, bravely battled a fairly rare autoimmune disease, scleroderma, for two years. (Treatment is difficult, and a cure nonexistent; find out more at scleroderma.org.) She was always, always one of my most passionate supporters, so much so that I can still feel it now. I wish she were here to read this, and anything after. (Flippant aside, she'd probably make a "More Sexy!" demand herself.)

I wish I had thanked her more. So often we look at hopes as something for the future, so isn't it odd that the strongest-felt wishes seem to be a chance to go back and say or do things that we didn't?

DESPITE BEING BORN on the first day of summer long before too much sun was considered bad for you, Iva-Marie Palmer possesses no capacity to achieve a decent tan (or its cousin, the sun-kissed glow). Still, she relocated from her native Chicago to sunny southern California nearly ten years ago and only regrets the choice on the rare occasions when she forgets to apply sunscreen. A former journalist who oversubscribes to periodicals, she loves books, running, cooking and eating elaborate meals, classic screwball comedies, food sold off carts and trucks, old movie palaces, word games and crossword puzzles, adventures large and small, indulging her curiosity and overextending herself. She lives with her husband, son and a seeming inability to take her sunglasses off her head when indoors. You can find her online on Facebook, Twitter (follow @ivamarie), and at www.ivamariepalmer.com.